MAR   2015   P9-CAO-968

3 3488 00266 6996

THE MELODY
OF LIGHT

MAR 2015

By the Author

Who I Am

Pride and Joy

The Melody of Light

Visit us at www.boldstrokesbooks.com

THE MELODY OF LIGHT

by

M.L. Rice

A Division of Bold Strokes Books

2014

THE MELODY OF LIGHT

© 2014 By M.L. Rice. All Rights Reserved.

ISBN 13: 978-1-62639-219-9

This Trade Paperback Original Is Published By
Bold Strokes Books, Inc.
P.O. Box 249
Valley Falls, NY 12185

First Edition: November 2014

THIS IS A WORK OF FICTION. NAMES, CHARACTERS, PLACES, AND INCIDENTS ARE THE PRODUCT OF THE AUTHOR'S IMAGINATION OR ARE USED FICTITIOUSLY. ANY RESEMBLANCE TO ACTUAL PERSONS, LIVING OR DEAD, BUSINESS ESTABLISHMENTS, EVENTS, OR LOCALES IS ENTIRELY COINCIDENTAL.

THIS BOOK, OR PARTS THEREOF, MAY NOT BE REPRODUCED IN ANY FORM WITHOUT PERMISSION.

CREDITS
Editors: Lynda Sandoval and Cindy Cresap
Production Design: Stacia Seaman
Cover Design by Gabrielle Pendergrast

Acknowledgments

I would like to thank Radclyffe and the rest of the Bold Strokes Books community for welcoming me into their ranks and offering encouragement and support. Thanks, as always, go to the greatest editor a fellow cat-lover could hope to have, Lynda Sandoval. Thanks also go to Cindy Cresap and everyone else involved in the publication of this book.

I would also like to thank my friend Joel for helping me with questions regarding the Marine Corps, Emily for being my orange-blooded Longhorn Band sister for life, everyone who encourages and supports music and arts programs, the University of Texas, Austin—the greatest city in the United States of America, and Amy, who helps me in my life's goal to never grow up and believes in me even when I don't believe in myself. Hook 'em!

To the men and women of our nation's military.

CHAPTER ONE

It didn't look that far. Maybe it was because the darkness of the night obscured most of her view of the frigid water below. Still, she wondered if it would hurt much. Would it be over quickly, her body immediately succumbing to the bone-crushing force, or would she simply be painfully bent and twisted, only to sink slowly beneath the gentle waves, her body spasming violently as water replaced the life-giving oxygen in her lungs?

She shook her head to clear her thoughts. None of this was helping. What was the use in dwelling on it? She should just let go and be done with it. The more she thought about it, the more she hesitated, and hesitation wasn't high on the list of things she wanted right now. She had gone over the events that had led her here over and over again in her head. How much more torture could she stand?

No. This world was too hard. Every day as she was growing up she had tried to hold on to the belief that things would change for the better, that she would be rescued from the hell that was her life. After all, surely it was impossible to be kept so low forever. Even the most tragic lives had some rays of sunshine, right? Some glimmer of light in the darkness?

That was what she had thought, but the rays of light in the life of Riley Gordon had been few and far between. And now that the unthinkable had happened, she just couldn't bear the pain. It needed to end, once and for all. She was useless and she refused to drag the one person in the world who cared down with her. So what was the point in continuing?

The well-known cloud of despair descended upon her the more she thought about it. She was making the only decision that made sense to her anguished mind, yet she was still afraid. This had all made so much sense as she walked to the bridge, alone and shivering in the biting wind, in the middle of the vast expanse of Texas Hill Country. But now that she was here, standing on the outer ledge of the deserted Bluebonnet Highway Bridge at three o'clock in the morning, she was having doubts.

She took a deep breath, possibly her last, and leaned forward slowly, the wind stinging her numbed face, and willed herself to gather the courage to loosen her grip on the railing. She could barely hear the fast-moving river below, but she knew that it was there, waiting for her, ready to welcome her into its eternal embrace.

Now was the time.

The headlights approaching from down the road didn't even enter her consciousness.

As she slowly relaxed her fingers, the memories poured forth once again in a flood of abuse, sadness, and fire. Now, with the river rushing beneath her, she felt that it was finally time to put that fire out.

Eleven Years Ago

Flames licked out of the windows of the tiny house, and smoke that burned her lungs filled the air, but the multitudes of reflective yellow jackets and the forceful water from powerful hoses seemed to be making progress in fighting the fire that had taken over her home...if it could really be called a home.

"Hi, there. What's your name, sweetheart?"

Riley hid shyly behind the leg of a firefighter.

"Don't worry, little one. I'm here to help you." The woman with the short graying hair looked and sounded kind, but Riley wasn't used to adults being nice to her. Riley eyed her movement warily as the stranger bent to kneel in front of her. "My name is Detective Hutchinson. I'm here to find out what happened to your parents and your house and I could sure use your help. Can you tell me your name?"

Riley looked up doubtfully at the enormous dark-skinned man in the rough yellow pants who had pulled her from the house.

"It's all right. You can talk to her. She's a friend of mine." His voice was deep and soothing, and when he smiled, his white teeth brightened his face even though his skin was stained even darker with the smudges of soot that covered his cheeks.

Riley continued to look at him and asked with a tremor in her voice, "Aidan?"

The fireman's face fell, but it was the detective who asked, "Who's Aidan, sweetie?"

Riley turned to look at the woman, but before she could say anything else, a shout came from the burning house.

"We've got another one!" someone near the ambulance yelled as another firefighter ran out of the house with a large blanketed bundle in her arms.

"Aidan!" Riley screamed and started to run toward what was now a mass of firefighters and paramedics by the large red ambulance. Before she could take three steps, her towering protector swept her off her feet and held her close as she thrashed and called out over and over again for her older brother, the only friend, the only family she had left in the world.

"Whoa there, kid. He's gonna be okay. My friends will take good care of him. I promise."

Riley looked at the firefighter through the tears in her eyes as her lip trembled.

"Is Aidan your brother?" the detective asked kindly.

Riley nodded as she looked back toward the bustling activity around the ambulance. She wondered at the strange mask they were putting over her brother's mouth and worried that he too would leave her forever, just as their parents had.

"Where are they taking him?" she asked, anger and fear causing her voice to shake.

Detective Hutchinson answered. "They're taking him to the hospital, sweetie. They'll make him all better."

Riley didn't miss the worried look the woman shot at her firefighter.

"As soon as I find out what happened here, I'll take you to see him. Would that be all right?" The detective smiled reassuringly, and Riley paused, brow furrowed, but finally nodded as the tall man set her back on the ground. "I'll need to know your name so that we can find him at the hospital." She waited for a reply.

"Riley."

"That's really pretty. What's your last name?"

Riley hesitated. She wasn't supposed to give such personal information to strangers.

"It's okay, Riley." The firefighter ruffled her hair. "Detective Hutchinson is a police officer and she's here to help you."

Riley took a deep breath. "Gordon."

"Thank you, sweetie. This house is owned by"—she glanced at her smartphone—"a couple named Joan and Ted Stuart. Is that right?"

She nodded again, still holding on to the man's rough yellow pants.

"Were they your parents?"

Even though she was young, Riley had a sharp and active mind and she wondered at the use of past tense. "No. Aunt and uncle. Mom's brother."

"I see. Were they…did something happen to your parents?"

Riley's eyes welled with tears and she nodded.

"Okay. No more questions. You've been very helpful, Riley Gordon. I need to go work with the firefighters now to find out more about why the fire started, so I want you to go with Anthony here so that we can make sure you're okay." She gestured to the tall firefighter, who smiled down at her comfortingly.

Riley nodded again and walked with him across the yard to the other waiting ambulance. He stayed by her side while the paramedics checked her and put salve on the burns she had gotten before the fire had even started, and he held her hand for the rest of the night as they waited for the detective to finish her work.

❖

The hospital smelled similar to the bathrooms at her school. Clean, but too much like chemicals that were trying desperately to cover up more unpleasant odors. The walls were too white. The floor was too smooth. Riley didn't like it one bit.

She was glad that the detective with the short graying hair was with her, holding her hand and leading her through hallways that seemed to go on forever in a never-ending maze of people dressed in blue scrubs, worried adults wringing their hands in waiting areas, wilting flowers, and the nose-burning odor of antiseptic. Finally, they reached a ward decorated with painted murals of teddy bears and balloons. Riley could tell that they were in an area just for children.

Detective Hutchinson stopped to speak with the nurse at the desk. They had a brief conversation, but Riley wasn't listening. She could see into the room of a child whose leg was lifted in a sling and she was transfixed. It wasn't her brother, but her heart sank thinking about him being hurt like that. The light in the room flickered from the changing images on the TV screen.

Soon the detective was pulling her along, down to a room in the middle of one of the branching hallways, and Riley's heart leapt as she entered the room and saw her brother sitting up in the bed, eating ice cream.

"Aidan!"

Her brother's face brightened and he held up the bowl he was holding. "Look what they gave me!"

Riley ran over to his bed and stopped short as she saw that his leg was sitting on top of the blankets with copious amounts of gauze wrapped around his calf.

"What happened?" Riley asked, worry causing a painful ache in her chest.

Aidan dismissed the injury with a wave of his hand. "Oh, it's nothing. Just got a little burn. That's all. Nothing major." His voice was unnaturally scratchy.

"Does it hurt?"

"Yeah, but it's not any worse than"—he stopped short—"hey! I get ice cream!"

Riley looked back to his face and stamped her foot angrily. "I thought you were right behind me when that fireman took me out of the house. Where did you go?"

Aidan gestured to the singed shoebox on his nightstand and Riley understood. He had gone back into their room to rescue the only mementoes the kids had of their parents. Inside the box was a trucker hat their father had worn on his days off when he liked to take them to the lake to fish, both pairs of their first baby shoes, their mother's plastic-rimmed glasses, her favorite mix CD of classical music, and an album of family pictures Mom and Dad had started when Aidan was born. Riley was glad he had thought to go back for it, but couldn't help but be angry at him for putting himself in danger. He could have died in that fire.

The woman took the opportunity to approach Aidan in his bed. "Hi, Aidan, my name is Detective Hutchinson, and I've been assigned to your case. The fire, I mean. Do you mind answering some questions for me?"

Aidan looked at Riley, who nodded. They rarely did anything without the consent of the other. It was one of the only ways they had been able to make it through everything they had.

"Okay."

"Thank you. How old are you, Aidan?"

"Ten."

"And how old is your sister?"

"Seven."

"Oh, you're the big brother, I see. I bet you do a good job of protecting her." Her eyes twinkled and Aidan beamed. "Now, I'm really sorry to have to bring this up, but I did some research tonight and found out that your parents passed away in that big petroleum refinery explosion near Houston three years ago. Is that right?"

Aidan's smile fell, and he looked off into space sadly.

The detective had her answer, and she nodded solemnly. "That was a terrible accident and so many innocent people suffered because of it. I'm sorry for your loss."

Aidan shrugged.

"And you were put into the custody of your aunt and uncle?"

He nodded again.

"Were they nice to you? Your aunt and uncle?"

Aidan shot a glance at Riley, and they both looked away from the detective.

The detective's lips pursed. "Aidan. Riley. Were they nice to you? I'm here to help. You can tell me."

She looked between them, but it was Riley who answered. "No. Especially not Aunt Joan."

"What did she do?"

Riley looked with pleading eyes to Aidan, so he sighed deeply and answered for her. "She hit us. *They* hit us. They…burned us."

The detective pulled up a chair and sat down next to the bed, looking sympathetic. "I'm so sorry to hear that. Can you tell me more?"

Aidan leaned back into his pillow. "Uncle Ted usually just watched TV and drank beer. He didn't stop her when she hurt us, though. He just laughed or was already passed out on the couch. Sometimes, though, he would act really funny and hit us even harder than Aunt Joan did. One beating by him was way worse than a lot by her. They worked on some kind of chemistry set in the basement sometimes too. Scary people would come over and buy something from them. When that happened, they were even meaner. Like, something was wrong with the way they acted." Aidan quieted his voice to a suspicious whisper. "I think they may have been making drugs."

Detective Hutchinson typed something in to the iPad she was carrying. She then took in the deep purple bruises and round burn marks on Riley's arms and legs. She gestured to them and asked, "Did your aunt and uncle give you those?"

Riley nodded.

Detective Hutchinson leaned in closer to Riley and asked softly, "Did your aunt and uncle ever, uh, do anything that you didn't want them to do?"

Riley looked at her as if she had gone crazy. "Well, I never wanted them to do this to me!" She held out her damaged arms.

Detective Hutchinson looked uncomfortable. "What I mean is, did either of them ever touch you in an inappropriate way?"

Riley looked confused.

The detective shifted slightly. "Did they ever touch you...in your private areas?"

Riley shook her head vehemently.

"Well, I'm glad to hear that at least." The detective leaned back in her chair as if a weight had been pulled from her shoulders.

"Ma'am?" Aidan asked.

"Yes?"

"Did they make it out of the house? We were in bed when the fire alarm went off, but they're usually in the basement at night. They lock us in our room after seven o'clock. We can't even get out to go to the bathroom."

Detective Hutchinson paused as if trying to measure her words. "I'm sorry, kids, but you do need to know." She sat up straighter and had a determined, but pained look on her face. "Your aunt and uncle had a lab in the basement that they used to make a very bad drug and because of the way they make this drug there was an explosion that caused the fire. I'm sorry to have to tell you that they weren't able to make it out. They both died."

Riley looked at Aidan, who was deep in thought.

"Detective Hutchinson?"

"Yes, Aidan?"

"Is it bad that I don't feel sorry for them? I mean, I was so sad when our parents died, but...now I just keeping thinking of how Aunt Joan and Uncle Ted will never be able to hurt Riley again."

Detective Hutchinson smiled, but had sadness in her eyes. "No. That's not a bad thing at all. I can see how much you love your sister, and I know how poorly they treated you both. I'm sorry that you will have to face yet another change in your lives, but I know that we'll be able to find a much better home for both of you."

"Just make sure that we stay together, okay?" Aidan reached out and took Riley's hand.

"You're a wise and brave young man, you know that?" Detective Hutchinson smiled and stood to leave. "A social worker and counselor will be visiting you shortly, and I will personally make sure that you guys get placed in a foster home together. We won't separate you. Promise. Riley?"

Riley looked up at her with a small smile.

"You stay with your brother tonight, okay? I'll have the nurses make a bed for you."

Riley nodded and scooted closer to her brother's side.

CHAPTER TWO

The social worker assigned to them was a distracted woman in her late forties who had tried her best to get both Aidan and Riley paired with a nice foster family, but the only families willing to take in more children could only support one at a time. When Riley had screamed and thrown a very wild tantrum on the floor of the hospital at the mere suggestion that she and Aidan go to different homes, the decision was made to keep them together at an available group facility in a small, brushy, wooded area just outside the San Antonio suburb of Whitehill.

As they pulled up to the gate, Aidan placed his arm around Riley's nervous shoulders. He was always so good at reading her mood.

"Don't be scared, Nugget."

Riley relaxed a bit at his use of the pet name their parents had given her.

"This is supposed to be a good place. And you know that I'll never let anything bad happen to you again. At least we're together, right?"

He looked down at her and she nodded with wide eyes, still staring past the dashboard at the country house they were slowly approaching. Children were swinging on a rusted, but working, swing set, playing with toy trucks in a large sandbox, and a few girls were sitting on the porch, braiding each other's hair. It looked pleasant enough, but Riley had never been very social, and the thought of having to get to know all of these new and very different kinds of people made her nervous. What if they hated her? What if they bullied her like some of the kids at her previous school had? She looked up at Aidan, who smiled back reassuringly. As long as he was with her, she would be okay.

After being introduced to Ms. Suzanne, the head of the house, as well as rest of the children, Riley and Aidan were led to a room with three bunk beds lining the walls. Riley noticed that only girls were in the room.

"Where will Aidan sleep?" she asked Ms. Suzanne.

The woman smiled kindly. "The boys sleep in the rooms on the other side of the house. He won't be far."

Riley's pulse quickened and her breathing became shallow and hurried. She felt sweat bead up on her forehead and the room started to spin. Ms. Suzanne noticed and bent down quickly in front of her. "Riley? Look at me." Her voice was calm, but insistent.

Riley's eyes were wide with panic. She could barely focus on the woman in front of her. A jumble of terrified thoughts tumbled through her head. What would she do without her brother there to protect her from the people who wanted to hurt her? Who would comfort her when she had the awful nightmares? Who would know how to pull her back from what her brother had taken to calling "brain storms"? No one else knew the kind of fear and anxiety that leveled her on those occasions. They could come out of nowhere. They happened when she was getting abused. They even happened when she found herself alone.

She snapped. "No!" She screamed and flailed and tried to pull herself free from the woman's grasp.

"Calm down!" she said, trying to hold on to Riley so she wouldn't hurt herself.

Riley just continued to scream.

"Hey. Nugget." Aidan spoke forcefully and stood in front of her now.

She quieted, but fear continued to claw at her heart.

"No one is going to hurt you here. Aunt Joan and Uncle Ted are dead. They can't do anything to us anymore. We're safe now. Isn't that right?" He turned to the kind woman.

"Absolutely right." She smiled and moved to put a comforting hand on Riley's cheek. Riley flinched, seeing only a hand that meant to strike.

Ms. Suzanne instead held her open hand in front of her. "If you'll come with me, I'll show you exactly where Aidan will be staying. It's not far. You'll see."

Riley attempted to get her breathing under control. She hated losing her temper like this, especially in front of new kids. She glanced into the room and found five girls staring at her with a mixture of interest and fear. She shakily put her hand into Aidan's and was led to the far side of the house where the boys' rooms were located. It was true that it wasn't far, but after sharing a room with her brother her whole life, the thought of sleeping in a room with strangers without the security of his presence scared her to death.

Aidan seemed to know what she was thinking. "I need you to be strong now, Riley."

She looked at him with teary eyes and nodded. If he asked it of her, she would do it. She branded his words into her memory. She wanted to make him proud. This was going to be a scary new experience for her, and she wanted to have his voice and his support there when she needed it most.

I need you to be strong now, Riley.

She could be strong. No. She *would* be strong.

At least some of the time...

Riley and Aidan were briefly separated so that they could get to know their new roommates. Aidan was left in his room with two older boys who looked to be about fifteen, and Riley was taken back to her room where two snotty-looking girls her age glared at her from one of the top bunks. Luckily, the other three girls introduced themselves and invited her into their circle where they were play-acting at putting makeup on each other while talking about the cutest boys at the Home.

Unfortunately, it didn't take long for one of the girls, the one who seemed to be the leader, to notice the scars.

"What happened to you?" the girl asked, pointing at the small, ugly, and unnatural red circles that dotted the freckled skin of Riley's forearms.

Riley quickly rolled down the sleeves of her hand-me-down shirt. She didn't care that it was a hot summer day. "Nothing."

The girls glanced at each other uncertainly and whispered to each other, right there in front of her. Some of them laughed. A couple looked disgusted.

Riley fumed. Was it always going to be like this? Would she never just get to be a normal kid with a normal life? Why did bad things have to happen to her?

❖

That first night in the Home brought one of the worst nightmares Riley had ever experienced.

Someone slapping her. Fire. A monster with smoke hiding his face. Fire surrounding her bed. Fire erupting from the lit end of the cigarette that he crushes down on her arms. Pain. The smell of burning flesh and hair. Riley. *A hand grabbing her neck and squeezing tightly. Too tightly.* Riley! *She can't breathe. She wants to scream, but the strong hands are a vice on her throat.*

"Riley!"

The voice startled her out of her terrors. It took a moment for her eyes to adjust, but through her tears she saw the face of Ms. Suzanne. The woman was gently shaking Riley's shoulders to wake her up.

"Riley, you're having a bad dream. You're safe."

Riley shook and felt the cold sweat that had drenched her as she slept.

"Where's Aidan?" she managed to whisper.

"I can get him for you if you'd like."

Riley sniffed and nodded.

"Okay. Come on. Let's get you something to drink."

She picked Riley up out of her bed and carried her to the kitchen where she set her down at the table. A large glass of milk was placed in front of her, and Ms. Suzanne left the room to get Aidan.

Only a minute passed before Aidan shuffled into the room wiping sleep from his eyes. "You okay, Nugget?"

Riley didn't know how to answer, so she just took a drink of the milk and then held her arms out to him. He walked over and gave her his protective brotherly hug.

Riley buried her face on his shoulder. "They're still going to get me."

"No. No, they're not. They're gone."

"But in my dream—"

"They can't even get you there. They may try to scare you, but they can never hurt you again. Okay?"

Riley hesitated, but nodded and lifted her head. She saw Ms. Suzanne leaning against the counter on the other side of the kitchen. A tear ran down her face.

"Feel better?" Ms. Suzanne asked.

Riley nodded again.

"Ready for bed?"

The images from her nightmare reappeared in her memory, and the all-too-real cigarette burns on her arms started stinging and itching again. She nodded anyway. She was so very tired.

"Okay. Say good night, Aidan."

He hugged her again and said, "See ya in the morning. Then you'll see; things are going to be different now."

"'Night," she said quietly and followed Ms. Suzanne back to her room. She heard the hurried *shhh* of whispers as they opened the door. Of course the other girls had heard her struggling with her nightmare. She had been loud enough to wake up Ms. Suzanne in the room down the hall. A squirming sickness swirled around in her stomach. It was her first night in the Home and already she had embarrassed herself and drawn unwanted attention to her problems.

How was this ever going to get better?

I need you to be strong now, Riley.

She swallowed hard and let Ms. Suzanne tuck her back into her bed.

Maybe tomorrow. Tomorrow she would try to be strong. Tonight she needed to curl up in a little ball and cry the fear away.

❖

Despite the rough start, Riley soon realized that being at the Home with other orphaned or in-need kids was better than being used as a punching bag or ashtray almost every day. Still, she didn't make many new friends. Aidan was her protector, her best friend, and her confidant. He was big for his age, so the bullies of the Home left them both alone for the most part. Most of the other kids were nice enough, but some had come from situations even worse than theirs, and a few were just juvenile delinquents ready to age up into full-blown criminals. Those were the ones who scared her and kept her pinned to her brother's side at all times.

In total, the facility housed about fifteen kids, give or take, as some were taken into individual foster homes, sent back to their families, or aged out when they turned eighteen, but most were about the same age as her and Aidan. Ms. Suzanne and the other people who ran the Home were nice, but too busy to give much individual attention to each child. The elementary school children were taught on-site, all their meals were served in a large converted barn next to the main building, and there were always plenty of books to read and toys to play with. Still, the care felt impersonal and rushed most of the time.

"Aidan?" Riley asked one day after they had finished playing "War" with a few of the other children.

"Yeah?" he responded, sitting on the front porch with her, slightly out of breath after chasing down a laughing girl who was playing as one of the bad guys.

"Do you like it here?"

He turned the stick he had been using as his M-16 over in his hands. "Yeah, I kinda do. Why?"

"Just wondering."

"Do *you* like it here?"

She shrugged. "It's better than Aunt Joan's and Uncle Ted's."

Aidan put his arm around Riley, who was using her own gun stick to draw cat faces in the dirt. "I'm sorry I couldn't protect you better there."

Riley hugged him back. "You *did* protect me. They hit me less when you were around. I didn't want them to hit you instead, though." Riley always felt guilty about that.

"Well, they're dead now, and I won't let anyone hurt you ever again. That's what big brothers are for." He paused, thinking. "Is someone being mean to you here?"

Riley shrugged again. "Not really. Just stupid stuff. They make fun of my hair and my burns. They call me an ugly ginger."

"They're just jealous because your hair is different and awesome-looking."

Riley snorted. "I wish."

"Your hair is really cool. Boys like girls with red hair. Just wait. You'll see. And anyway, try not to think about it, and if they do anything serious, you let me know."

"I will. They're really okay for the most part, though. A couple of them scare me a little, but they usually just ignore me."

"They're stupid. Just ignore them back."

Riley smiled at him and then jumped up and ran after a squealing younger boy who had just tried to shoot them with a bazooka tree branch that was taller than he was.

As Riley and Aidan settled in permanently to their new home, she started to notice that whenever her brother was off with the other boys, some of the girls, despite their initial friendliness, had decided that they had a crush on Aidan and were becoming jealous of his devotion to Riley. She knew it was stupid, but slowly Riley became more and more ostracized from the other kids. She would find malicious cartoon drawings of herself taped to her bunk bed, her flaming red hair exploding in snake-like tendrils—nothing like the wavy shoulder-length hair she actually had—around a bucktoothed and freckled face. Unfortunately, that part was kind of true. Her weekly allowance would go missing mysteriously even as she changed the hiding place daily. At night, when she was trying to go to sleep, she was constantly bombarded with statements like "Your brother is totally cute. What happened to you?" or they would say offhandedly, "Aidan must have gotten out of the house first since you got all of the burns."

She regretted having told anyone about the fire.

The treatment by her so-called "friends" was ridiculous, and even at her young age, Riley could see how illogical it was for girls who wanted to go out with her brother to mistreat his sister. It didn't matter, though. She knew her brother would never give any of the girls a second glance. He was too into watching war movies and playing sports. Girls weren't on his radar yet. That, and none of the girls in the Home were worth his time. A few of the older ones were already smoking and drinking when the staff wasn't watching, and Riley had already been threatened with severe bodily harm should she ever rat them out. Most of the kids were decent and wanted nothing more than a family to call their own, but the few that ran things really could make life horrible for those that they decided weren't cool enough.

Riley wasn't cool enough.

She put on a brave face around her brother, knowing that heads would roll if he ever found out about the bullying, but she knew that he could tell when things were going badly. The problem was that Riley wouldn't tattle on the other girls for fear of their reprisal later, and those same girls who treated her like crap were the ones who were sugary sweet to her when Aidan was around. She felt herself getting more and more angry with them and her situation as time passed. She often took out her frustration on the person she loved most, and that only made her even angrier.

Two-faced jerks. Riley would fume as the girls batted their eyes at Aidan on the playground and pretended to be funny and witty. They failed miserably.

Aidan never fell for it, of course. He was a good judge of character and would simply roll his eyes and smile exhaustedly at Riley. This didn't help her standing with the girls either, but still, she was proud of her brother and knew that he would never be taken in by such dumb behavior.

It was always a struggle for Riley to be happy. She was still scared a lot of the time, but she couldn't really tell why. She got angry so easily too. She was getting better at hiding it, though; only Aidan could see through the act she put on. But the problem was that she didn't know why she got so upset so easily. She just felt…scattered. Like part of her was still back with her parents near Houston, another was still the cowering girl at her aunt and uncle's house, and the third part was either the blatantly invisible freak or the one who stuck out like a sore thumb at the Home. Nothing seemed able to keep her safely in one piece. Aidan was her only tie to the stability of the ground. Without him, she felt like she would disintegrate into a million minuscule shards that would be blown away to nothingness at the whim of the formidable Texas winds. During these times of fear, during these "brain storms," she could only focus on the words, *I need you to be strong now, Riley.*

Even after months of trying so hard she felt she would turn to stone, she had yet to live up to that request. Luckily, not all hope of good things to come had been lost.

❖

"Tell me the story again," Riley whimpered as Aidan consoled her after yet another particularly terrifying nightmare.

"You know it by heart," he said, tucking her back into her new bed. A large closet had been converted to house a single bed for her. It wasn't fair to the other girls in the Home to get woken up so often by her almost nightly screams and crying.

"Don't care. I wanna hear you tell it." She snuggled under her blankets, ready to hear the story their mother would tell when they got scared of the dark. Her mother had told it to her, and her grandmother to her mother before that. Aidan could recite it almost perfectly by now, word for word, just like their mother had. They had listened to it that many times with their mother playing soft classical music in the background. Now, Riley often asked Aidan to tell it because it made her feel close to her parents again.

Aidan took a deep breath. "Okay. Fine. Once upon a time there was a family of mockingbirds who lived in a tall tree on the edge of a beautiful valley."

"Meadow."

"Do you want me to tell it or not?" he asked irritably.

Riley nodded sheepishly, so he continued.

"Once upon a time there was a family of mockingbirds who lived in a tall tree on the edge of a beautiful *meadow*." He waited for an interruption, and when he didn't get one, he continued. "The mother and father mockingbird first had a little boy mockingbird, and when he burst from the egg he knew how to fly right away, without his parents having to teach him a thing. They were so proud. Soon, the mother laid another egg and out hatched the most beautiful little girl mockingbird they had ever seen. Once again, they were the proudest mockingbirds in the meadow. *But*," he said with emphasis, "they soon found out that the little girl mockingbird was never going to be able to fly like her brother."

"Why not?" Riley asked, already knowing the answer.

"Because the little girl mockingbird was blind, and if she tried to fly she would fly crash straight into the ground or into another tree and that would be the end of her! The mom and dad mockingbirds were desperate and searched the meadow for an answer. They asked the rabbit if he knew of a way to help the girl fly because she would never be able to survive without them otherwise. The rabbit didn't know, of course, because he couldn't fly himself, and if one of his children ended up blind they could just sniff around to find their way. Next they asked the wise owl if she knew of a way to help the little bird fly even without sight, but she was no help because owls can see in the dark so well that she couldn't even imagine not being able to see at all. Finally, worried that their sweet daughter would have to stay safely in the nest forever or die, they spread word far and wide asking for help. Finally, they received a visit from the oldest nightingale in the meadow. She was known for her beautiful voice, and she sang constantly as if in response to an invisible symphony."

"I like this part. This is where Mom started playing the relaxing music." Riley smiled and closed her eyes.

"Shh," Aidan admonished her. "Anyway, the nightingale was ancient and hadn't left her own tree in ages. When she arrived at the nest of the mockingbirds, she was weak and could barely stand at all. She asked the rest of the mockingbird family to leave, as she had a special message only for the little girl mockingbird. They did, and this is what the nightingale said: 'I'm going to teach you something that all songbirds know. A secret. This is something I must do before I go.'

"The little bird lifted her head to the soothing voice and asked, 'Will this secret help me to see?'

"The nightingale tilted her head in the way that birds do and said, 'In a way. I'm going to teach you about the melody of light.'

"'What's the melody of light?'

"'Without light, we wouldn't be able to see. Just like you can't see right now.'

"'Even owls?' she asked.

"'Even owls. There is always light around us from somewhere, even if it's too dark to be able to see clearly. But the secret of the songbirds is this: Light also has a sound.'

"The little mockingbird was interested. 'What kind of sound?'

"The nightingale paused as if listening to something. 'It's like a song. A continuously moving and changing song. That's why those of my kind are always singing. We can't help it. We love the melodies. We love the harmonies. These songs help us find our way, even in the darkness. They're always there, even when the light is so dim we can't see it with our eyes.'

"'Can other birds, birds like me, hear it?'

"The old bird nodded. 'Yes. But not so well as the nightingales. Most of the time the other birds are focused so much on what they can see with their eyes that the melody is lost.'

"The little bird waited for her to continue and then asked, 'Can you teach me?'

"The nightingale said, 'Yes, but it will take more than just listening with your ears. You also have to listen with your heart.'

"The little bird tried to listen with her heart, but that made no sense and she couldn't hear a thing.

"'I'll show you. You're too young to have known much of the world, but it is with our hearts that we really see, hear, and feel the world around us. I want you to think about your parents.'

"The little bird did as she was told.

"'What do you feel?'

"'I feel...warm. Happy.'

"The old nightingale smiled to herself. 'That's exactly right. Now, listen to the light. It's all around you. Your heart will hear it.'

"The little bird strained and listened, but she could only hear the breeze blowing through the leaves of her tree.

"'I don't hear anything except the wind.'

"With that, the old bird lay down and rested her head at the feet of the little mockingbird and said, 'I am very old, little one. I don't have much longer in this world. Just remember the feeling you have in your heart and keep listening. You will hear it. And when you do, let it guide your way in the darkness. It will always be there.'

"The little bird waited for her to say more, but the old nightingale would never speak again.

"The mockingbird put her wing out and rested it on the breast of the nightingale. It was still. She knew that the old bird was gone. She had used her last moments in life to share her wisdom and help a little bird in need.

"A deep and joyful sadness filled her chest. Her heart swelled with sorrow and appreciation. And then, without knowing how, she heard it. A soft and blissful song filled her ears, her feathers, and her heart. She could hear the light! She stepped up to the edge of her nest and turned her head this way and that, listening with growing excitement. She heard the other birds chirping in the distance, she heard the songbirds singing, she heard the grass growing at the base of the tree, and she heard her family cheering her on. Every inch of the light itself had a melody too and every melody wove together with the others in perfect harmony. Through the songs she could see the world around her.

"The little bird smiled and raised her wings to the air. She let the melody fill her...and she flew."

❖

Almost a year to the day after arriving at the Home, about a week before Christmas, a beautiful blond woman arrived in an SUV full of things Riley had never seen in person before. The smiling staff gathered the kids into the activity room as the woman laid out each strange and mysterious device on the table and floor in front of them. Riley's eyes danced over the fine lines, the shiny metal, the polished wood of each one, wondering what the differences were and what sound each would make. She didn't have to wait long.

Beaming, Ms. Suzanne made an announcement to all gathered in the room. "I have some really exciting news for all of you! This is Miss Geddis. She's the music teacher at Garrett Junior High, and she, the school, and our very own local Rotary Club have generously donated these instruments to our home! Not only that, but she herself is going to volunteer her time two days a week to teach any of you who are interested in learning how to play!"

There was a smattering of confused applause from the children who probably didn't know the first thing about music. Riley, however, felt her eyes widen with excitement. She had always been fascinated when she saw musicians on TV and when she heard music of any kind on the radio. It had been one of her only escapes when her aunt and uncle had been on meth-induced tirades in the living room. She and Aidan would crawl under their covers with an old clock radio and spend the night surfing through the stations, listening to the many different and distinct sounds that flowed from the speakers. Pleasant memories stirred deep within her as well. She remembered her mother sharing her love of classical music with them, even when they barely knew what music was. She would hold them as they fell asleep and tell them the names of the pieces that played. She'd say, "Listen to this one, kids. You don't need words to express what these songs can say with music."

Now Riley had the opportunity to learn how to play something herself and bring her mother close once again.

Miss Geddis took the facilitator's place in the middle of the room and smiled. "Hi, everyone. I want to thank you all for letting me join you here, and I hope that some of you are interested in learning how to play an instrument. Music is one of the best investments you can make in your life. It gives you a lifelong hobby, opens doors to organizations and friendships, it will help you do better in school—"

Groans from most of the kids.

"And playing music is just plain fun. So here's what we're going to do today: I'm going to tell you about each of the instruments I've brought with me, and if you're interested in playing one, I'll have you go and stand by it. I only have these few that were donated, so not everyone will get the one they wanted. I apologize, but hopefully, we can work it out so that everyone is happy."

With that, she started with the long silver stick that had about a million buttons on it. Riley soon learned that it was called a flute and it made a high-pitched airy sound that was pleasant, but just wasn't for her. From there the kids learned about the clarinet, the trumpet, the snare drum, the saxophone, the violin, and the trombone. Miss Geddis wasn't a learned musician on each instrument, but she got the point of each one across with ease. Each was interesting and beautiful, but it wasn't until she saw and heard the cello that Riley's heart melted. The sound was mellow and deep and it pierced her heart with each movement of the bow across the strings. What she heard when it was played seemed to echo the exact emotions that had been burning in her chest for years. As each note filled the air, Riley could feel an almost purifying cleansing throughout her whole body. She realized that her eyes had filled with tears as the woman played. The cello was Miss Geddis's primary instrument, and she made it sing. Riley knew exactly what she wanted.

❖

The clock on the wall had stopped. She could swear it. Every time she looked up the minute hand was in the same place! She tapped her foot in irritation as her teacher droned on and on about a book about animals on a quest to find their home that Riley had already read two weeks ago. All she could think about was that it was Thursday afternoon. Tuesday and Thursday afternoons were the days she got tutored on the cello by Miss Geddis. With Christmas past and three months of lessons under her belt, she felt she was finally starting to get the hang of how to hold her bow and could even play a couple of scales without having to look at her finger placement on the neck. Every spare minute she had was spent practicing in the activity room, much to the annoyance of her fellow foster kids.

Everyone else had seemed to be, if not excited, at least interested, in the prospect of learning to play an instrument, but as time went on, and they had figured out that it actually took a lot of hard work and practice, their enthusiasm had begun to wane. They played halfheartedly during their group rehearsal sessions, but only one or two ever played on their own time. That, and the other kids were always coming and going from the Home as they were welcomed into full-time foster families and new kids took their place. Riley alone had latched on to her instrument and actually loved the challenge of learning how to play properly.

Aidan, who didn't have a musical bone in his body, enjoyed playing Madden Football on the Xbox in the activity room while she practiced and he often helpfully told her how much she sucked—in a brotherly sort of way. But she knew he was kidding with her and was happy she had found something that she enjoyed doing. He could tell that having a hobby she loved helped her mood too. His support meant the world to her.

"That one sounded like a dying moose," he said with his back to her as a computer opponent sacked his digital quarterback.

"Shut up, Aidan. You try it. Miss Geddis just taught me the A minor scale and I'm already halfway through book one of Suzuki!"

"Gesundheit."

"It's a method, stupid. She says I'm going to be really good one day."

"Well, you're sure not good yet, so keep practicing!"

Heat flared in her cheeks as she grabbed her box of bow rosin off the music stand and threw it forcefully at his head, where it connected with a thud.

"Ow! Watch your temper! How many times do we have to talk about that?"

Riley took a deep breath. She did get angry so easily. "That's what you get for being mean. Just wait. I'm going to be in a symphony one day."

Aidan paused his game and turned around smiling while rubbing what was sure to turn into a large bump on his head. "I know you will, Nugget. You can do whatever you want to do. Mom and Dad always said so and I know so too."

Riley breathed out held-in frustration and smiled back meekly, thankful he understood and believed in her.

"But right now," he continued as he turned back to his game, "you sound like a rabid raccoon in a washing machine."

She rolled her eyes and sighed as she carefully placed her fingers back on the taped portions of the cello's neck that marked the proper finger placement, ready to start her scales all over again.

CHAPTER THREE

A s the months and years passed, Riley grew more and more fond
of her chosen instrument, and with that fondness came a much
greater proficiency. She was talented, and Miss Geddis knew it. She
had started offering free lessons to her alone on Thursday evenings,
much to the chagrin of the other foster kids. They didn't care about
music like Riley did; they were just jealous of the attention she was
receiving from an adult. Because of this, Riley was ostracized by
the few left that had once been her friends, and the bullies took
every opportunity to make her life hell. When Aidan wasn't around
to protect her, she often found herself on the losing side of a set
of stairs or with less hair on one side of her head after having it
violently jerked out by the jealous girls of the Home. She had to
plead clumsiness when Aidan noticed stray bruises on her wrists and
knees. The way she was treated infuriated her, but nothing she tried
seemed to help. Standing up for herself, hitting back, or even being
overly nice had no effect whatsoever.

Riley quietly pondered the reasons for the bullying one
evening in the last minutes before curfew. She had finished a full
play-through of "The Swan" by Camille Saint-Saens, and slow,
melancholy music always put her in a pensive mood. Her thoughts
were interrupted by three girls, who also happened to be in her
sophomore class, bursting through the door of the activity room,
laughing loudly. When they saw Riley staring at her sheet music in

a vain attempt to ignore them, they wandered over and jerked the sheet music off the stand.

"Hey!" Riley shouted.

"Whatcha doin', Ginger? Nerding out to some dead guy's music again?"

Riley glared at them and made a snatch at the paper, but it was quickly passed to another girl who, in turn, shredded it into tiny pieces.

Riley's blood boiled. "First of all, my name is Riley. You've known me for three years. If you're too stupid to remember something that simple then I have absolutely no hope for you."

The three girls made offended *uch* noises and took a step closer.

"Secondly, you shouldn't have done that."

"Oh yeah? What are you going to do about it, *Bush Fire*?"

Riley fumed. They were all in the same year in high school, but these girls acted like they were three years old.

"I'm going to ask nicely for y'all to continue practicing your signatures for your future welfare checks and leave me alone."

The girls were quiet for a moment, trying to figure out if they had just been insulted.

"Oh, *hell* no," said the girl who appeared to be the leader. She ripped Riley's cello out of her hands and threw it on the ground where Riley heard a sickening crack as the cello's neck broke into two pieces, held together only by the now slack strings.

Riley erupted.

Brandishing her bow like a bludgeon, she shot up from her chair and swung wildly at the girls who screamed and ran from the room, trying to protect themselves from the whip-like connections to their backs and heads.

When they were gone and Riley was alone, she looked down numbly at the shattered remnants of her only bow in her shaking hand. She let out a trembling breath and walked to her cello, lying quiet and broken on the floor. She knelt next to it as if it were a fallen comrade on the field of battle. She was crying quietly when Ms. Suzanne approached her and placed an understanding hand on her shoulder.

"I don't know why they do this to me," Riley whimpered.

Ms. Suzanne pulled her to her feet and hugged her. "I don't know either, but what they did was wrong."

She led Riley over to the couch and they both sat down. "You have your brother and your music." Riley could only gaze miserably at her broken companion on the floor.

"What am I going to do now? I don't think we'll be getting another cello donation any time soon."

"Can you use the ones at the school?"

Riley nodded. "Yeah, but we're not allowed to take them home. Not since one of the seniors stole and sold seven of the school's violins on eBay."

Ms. Suzanne was quiet for a little while, thinking. "You know, I think we may have a few extra dollars in our emergency fund. I'll get the cello fixed for you—"

Riley brightened.

"*But*," she continued, "I'm going to insist that you see the counselor who volunteers for us to help you get that temper under control. You cannot act out the way you just did."

Riley looked down at her trembling hands still clutching the splintered bow. "Okay. Sorry."

"Don't apologize. Be the better person."

Riley nodded.

"Now. I think not being able to practice for a few weeks is punishment enough."

Riley winced at the thought of being left without the solace of her music.

"And don't worry. Those girls won't get off as easily." Ms. Suzanne smiled, patted Riley on the knee, and left the room.

Riley collapsed back into the couch and threw the remnants of her useless bow across the room. What was she going to tell Aidan?

Unlike Riley, he had found his niche as a loud and gregarious jock. He had joined the high school's varsity football team as a sophomore and, now that he was a senior, he played as a starting linebacker. He had grown into a tall, muscular, and handsome young man just like their father had been and, despite the fact that he was

THE MELODY OF LIGHT

poor and still living in a group home, his effervescent personality and winning charm gained him many friends, and he kept a string of lovesick girls waiting in the wings, all vying for his attentions. Riley enjoyed watching him compete on the field, and he, in turn, loved to lie back on the couch and listen as she played her cello. He was big and he was tough, but he was still a loving, caring, and gentle big brother who would do anything for Riley.

While Aidan had been bulking up and becoming one of the most popular guys in their small San Antonio suburb, Riley had immersed herself in her music by joining first her junior high orchestra and, now that she was a sophomore, her high school orchestra as well as the local youth symphony. She was always first chair in every ensemble and easily passed the auditions for the regional and then state ensembles. She figured there was something to be said for her obsession, even to the detriment of social interactions.

She did have acquaintances, and even a few friends, in orchestra, and things were actually going fairly well for her when she was away from the Home. She liked school and was in the top percentile of her class. Of course, Aidan was always pushing her to do better. He was obsessed with the idea that she could make something of herself. She never wanted to disappoint him, so she let him help her with her homework every week and accepted it when he would get angry with her lack of interest in the boring subjects, wanting only to feel a cello resting against her ribs.

"Riley, you seriously have to know this stuff. It's on the SAT." He slammed his hand down on the open book in front of her to get her attention because her eyes had wandered yet again over to the sheet music for Bach's "Bourrée Suite No. 3."

She jumped and glared at him, but said, "I know, I know. When in the hell am I ever going to use the Pythagorean Theorem, though? I mean seriously. How many right triangles am I going to run into just begging to have their hypotenuse figured out?"

Aidan pinched the bridge of his nose in frustration. "That's not the point."

"Ha!"

"What?"

"The point...triangle...never mind."

He rolled his eyes and shook his head. "You can't pin everything on being a professional musician you know. It's not easy, and most people don't have the talent or the willpower to make it."

Riley glared at him. "Are you saying I don't have the talent or willpower?"

He sighed. "No. I'm not. I think you can do anything you set your mind to and you know that I'm your biggest fan. *But* nothing in life is guaranteed. You know that. I mean look at us." He gestured to the activity room that had become their refuge. "This isn't the lap of luxury. We have nothing. No money to go to college, no money period, no way out. Unless we get scholarships. You have to be great on your cello, yes, but you have to do well in school too. And you have to get high marks on your SAT."

The earnestness in his face made her hang her head in shame. He was right. She had no choice but to do her best in order to get a scholarship to a good music school. If she didn't...well, she didn't want to think about that.

She took a deep breath. "A squared plus B squared equals C squared. Right?"

He laughed and brushed back his shaggy light brown hair. "Yeah, that's right. Good girl."

"Thank you, sir. May I have my cookie now?" She batted her eyes at him with sarcastic saccharine in her voice.

"Don't make me smack you, young lady."

"Psh. I could take you." She took a light swing at him, which he batted away easily.

"Riiight. How about we work on getting you into a good college instead of your uppercut?"

Riley smiled and put on a fake ditzy accent. "Fine. But only because flipping burgers will be like, totally bad for my complexion."

Aidan rolled his eyes, but smiled and tapped her math book with a thick and calloused finger. "Math. Go."

❖

Riley looked over at the girl sitting next to Aidan in the audience. She was a pretty blonde, gazing up at him with stars in her eyes. Riley gave him a small thumbs-up from her seat next to the conductor on the stage. He laughed and winked.

This was her first major concert with the youth symphony, and he had brought a date. Riley could tell that the young woman couldn't care less about musical culture but was dying to impress Aidan. It made Riley smile. He was going to be such a lady-killer.

Soon the applause died down, and the conductor turned and lifted his baton into the air. Riley placed her bow on her strings, and with one swift downward movement, the forceful first notes of "Farandole" by Bizet filled the large room. Riley lost herself in the music, as she did every time she played. She became part of the fast-paced rhythm as her fingers flew over the strings of the secondhand cello she had used since childhood. When the song ended the audience erupted in applause, and she could see Aidan and his date, Brittany, smiling at her from the second row. She could get used to performing. There were worse ways to spend her time than being applauded by a room full of music lovers.

After the concert, she, Aidan, Brittany, and five of her fellow youth orchestra members all went out to eat Tex-Mex at the dive where Aidan worked part-time. His employee discount was much appreciated by the cash-strapped teenagers. The conversation soon turned to talk of college picks and life after high school. Riley was surprised to hear that most of her friends weren't interested in continuing their education and were going to work for their parents, go to a trade school, or just find a job wherever they could. It was strange for Riley to think about not going to college. Despite her circumstance and lack of funds, she had always assumed that college was the obvious next step for herself and her brother. Ms. Suzanne at the foster home definitely tried to implant the idea and work ethic into their heads. It was obviously important to her that the kids in her care know that they had the same opportunities as children with traditional families. Riley was thankful for that.

At the moment, all of the girls at the table had their eyes glued on Aidan.

"What about you?" a comely viola player asked him. "I just know you'll be on an NFL team somewhere. Maybe I should get your autograph now." She giggled at her supposed cleverness.

Aidan smiled and shrugged, always modest about his abilities. "I dunno. I'm not sure I'm good enough. I'll have to get a scholarship somewhere."

Brittany, obviously jealous of the other girls' dewy stares at her boyfriend, put her head on his shoulder and pouted, "If you go away to college, I won't get to see you as often." She ran her fingers down his arm and pressed her breasts firmly into his side.

Riley rolled her eyes at her friends. Brittany might have been pretty, but Riley was quickly discovering that she was just like all the other girls who liked her brother: sycophantic, lovesick, and so very shallow.

Aidan looked happy and smug, but changed the subject by pointing to Riley and saying, "This is the one who's going places. I know she'll get a music scholarship somewhere. I may have gotten the looks and the charm—"

Riley threw a handful of tortilla chips at him, making Brittany jump back as the crumbs flew all over her tight sweater.

"But she got the brains and the talent. And the temper."

Brittany glared at her as if she were stealing her boyfriend's affection, but her friends laughed in a forced way. They knew she was the best musician in the orchestra, and although her ability was in a different league, she had no airs of conceit or arrogance. Still, Riley could tell that they were envious and didn't like the idea of someone having more opportunities than they had. Every time the subject of life after high school arose, one of her friends would change the subject. Of course, this only increased the pressure on her, as she felt that she had to live up to everyone's expectations, prove that she was as good as they thought she was, and actually get into a decent college. Never mind the fact that she had to do extremely well on her SATs, stay in the top percentile of her class, pass a rigorous audition, qualify for a scholarship, *and* get financial aid, all without money or parental support. The obstacles facing her

THE MELODY OF LIGHT

were daunting and terrifying, so she did what any well-meaning high school student would do. She left the restaurant and went to a friend's house, where she lost herself in a haze of secondhand cigarette smoke and ill-gotten cheap beer.

❖

"So. When are you going to get yourself a boyfriend? I hear that trumpet player Antonio has a huge crush on you." Aidan relaxed back into the couch in the activity room as he fired up the Xbox.

"Oh my God, Aidan. Don't change the subject. This is really serious."

Aidan had just told her that he hadn't gotten the scholarship to Texas State. It had been his last potential offer. He had pulled his hamstring in the last half of the season and had only gotten to play for one quarter when the recruiters had come by. He was still trying to hide his disappointment, but Riley knew him better than anyone and could tell that he was utterly devastated.

"I'm not changing the subject. The subject is just over and done with. That's all."

The Madden Football start screen appeared on the TV, and he chose a two-player game. "Which team do you want to be?"

"I'm not playing that game with you right now, Aidan. We need to talk about this."

Aidan flew up from the couch and angrily threw the controller across the room where it landed harmlessly in a beanbag chair in the corner.

"*Why?* Why do we need to discuss this? I didn't get a scholarship. I'm not going to college. Big deal! I can do other things with my life." He lifted a large and heavy table by the window and slammed in back down to the ground in frustration.

Riley cowered in the recliner next to him.

"I'm not useless!"

"Aidan, I'm sorry. Please calm down." Riley trembled and felt queasy at his display of anger.

He stopped himself from punching the wall and then deflated, letting out a long sigh. He looked guilty. He walked back to the couch and slumped down in a heap. "I'm sorry, Nugget. It's not your fault. I'm sorry I yelled. I'm just super bummed and *super* pissed. I worked my ass off for that team for three years, and a goddamned pulled muscle just took a giant shit on my entire future."

Riley hesitated before offering, "You can still go to college, Aidan. Your grades are…okay."

Aidan shook his head. "I was only gonna go to play football. I'm no good at school. You know that. You're the smart one."

"What are you going to do then? You have to leave the Home when you graduate."

Aidan stood again and walked to the opposite side of the room to pick up the controller he had thrown. "I'm going to get a job. What else? Just like the other guys." He sat on the arm of her recliner and put his hand on her shoulder. "Listen. Don't worry about it. I'll figure something out. I always do. I have the whole rest of the school year to think about it."

Riley nodded reluctantly, and in an attempt to make him happy said, "I'll play as the Seahawks if you want. Go easy on me, though, okay?"

He smiled and punched her on her shoulder. "Never. I'm going to kick your ass as usual."

❖

The end of the school year was upon them before they knew it. Riley sat proudly in the orchestra watching the seniors file into the auditorium to their playing of "Pomp and Circumstance." Their high school wasn't very large, and it wasn't long before she saw Aidan make his way proudly to his seat. He looked over and waved, his graduation hat perched at a jaunty angle on his head. Even in his hand-me-down black robe, he cut a dashing figure, and Riley could see some of the female sophomores and juniors in the audience giggle and gaze longingly at him. The school was definitely going to be a different place without him there. He had everyone wrapped around his little finger. Sometimes Riley had trouble believing they were actually related. The differences in their looks and social aptitude were as wide as the sea.

After the seniors had taken their seats and all of the speeches had been given, it was finally Aidan's turn to cross the stage. The room erupted in applause and whistles as his name was announced even though the faculty had requested that the audience hold all applause until the end. Aidan turned to face the crowd, his arms outstretched, took a theatrical bow, and grinned slyly at his multitude of female fans. Riley shook her head in exasperation, but beamed at him. He loved to ham it up, and his charisma had won him the adoration of the entire school. She was so proud of him.

After the ceremony was over Aidan found Riley in the orchestra section next to the stage as she was putting her cello in its bag.

"Done!" he exclaimed proudly, putting the mortarboard that he had thrown in the air back on his head. "So. Your big brother did good, right?"

Riley laughed. "My big brother did *well*, yes."

"I know, dork. I just wanted hear you be an insufferable know-it-all one last time before I left the school." He punched her playfully in the arm and then pulled her into a hug.

When they pulled apart, Riley saw a gaggle of recently graduated girls waiting impatiently to talk to him, cameras and iPhones at the ready. She gestured with her head. "You'd better get going. Your groupies are about to wet themselves in their excitement to talk to you."

Aidan turned to look over his shoulder, and when he made eye contact with the group they all stood a little straighter and almost as one made a demure move to tuck their uniformly long hair behind their right ears. It was bizarre and hilarious at the same time. Aidan turned back to her.

"How do I look?" He put on a cartoonish smoldering look and Riley couldn't help but laugh out loud.

"Like a complete idiot. So by that I mean totally normal. Go on. Have fun. I'll see you later. Love you." She smiled and pushed him back toward the girls.

"Love you too, Nugget. Don't wait up." He winked devilishly and turned around, arms wide. "Ladies! We're free!"

CHAPTER FOUR

Riley's junior year passed in a blur of studying, practicing, concerts, practicing, avoiding the other kids both at the group home and at school, and practicing. She wasn't being bullied anymore so much as ignored. She figured that was fine. She had worried that not having Aidan around would make her more of a target, but the bad attention she received was relatively minor. People still made fun of her fiery red hair and subtle freckles with ginger jokes, but nothing ever turned physical, and she was thankful for that. At least she had grown into her face somewhat, and although she knew she'd never win any beauty pageants, she was happy enough with herself, and that was worth a lot.

Now that she was finally a senior, she had pulled away from social interactions even more. She had to make her final year of high school as successful as possible if she wanted to get into college. It sure didn't make it much fun, though. She still had her friends in orchestra, but she always felt like the perpetual third wheel, regardless of how many of them were together at any given time. She was the only one who had never dated anyone. She just wasn't interested. She was also the only one who had never had sex. Again, not interested (in the sex or the rash of teen pregnancies that had been going around). She didn't do drugs like some of her friends either. She was planning for her future while the rest of them seemed content with the present and the predictably dull life of the suburbs. This didn't leave a lot of room for discussions about things they all had in common. You could only talk about music and movies for so long.

It also didn't help that she could never do many things with them outside of school because she had no money. Occasionally, she'd accompany a group to one of their houses to hang out, but as the talk drifted, as it always did, to boys and sex, Riley found herself on the outside, trying to feign interest and trying to show that she was more than the music nerd they all saw her to be. Unfortunately, her ruse didn't often work and her so-called friends became more and more relentless in their teasing. They'd make fun of her single-mindedness, as if ambition and the yearning for a better life were bad things. They'd try to give her ambush makeovers and once even got close to forcing her to dye her hair. Nothing was as bad as the constant teasing about her lack of boyfriends, though. She had been called a lesbian more times than she could count. The fact that she had already started to figure out that part for herself made no difference.

Riley just tried to laugh it all off, terrified of losing the only connection to a social life she had, but the fire of anger always seemed to burn beneath the surface. They could be so nice to her sometimes, but while she was holding the proffered hand of their friendship, it seemed like the other was always hiding behind their backs, ready to slap her down. Riley didn't think she would ever truly understand people. It was so much easier to become a part of the little black dots and lines that ran gracefully across the pages of her sheet music. That she understood. That was her true language. That was the family she didn't have.

Aidan had moved out of the group home right after his graduation and now lived in a small apartment with two of his old football buddies near the center of town. It had become a local favorite hot spot for parties, and it was the most stereotypical bachelor pad imaginable. Riley only liked to visit when the other guys weren't home, otherwise the musty man smell and miasma of testosterone was stifling. She was terrified of what might be living in the month-old discarded pizza boxes, and when she caught sight of dirty gym socks and underwear on the floor, her stomach turned.

Her brother had gotten a job at a service station owned by his friend's dad, and he spent long days from sunrise until sunset learning how to repair anything from mopeds to Suburbans. Having him learn to be a mechanic made Riley thankful. It was a useful and necessary job that would allow him to have a lifelong career. Riley had been worried that he would get stuck doing something pointless. He didn't like to talk about his work much, though, and Riley could tell that he was unhappy. Girlfriends never lasted very long with him either. He was too restless to stick with one person for an extended period of time. Riley saw that her brother was slowly crumbling inside. He hadn't gotten what he wanted out of life so far, but he also couldn't figure out the direction he wanted his life to take. He never said it in actual words, but Riley's bond with him meant that he didn't have to. She knew his every thought just by the twitch of his cheek or the furrow of his brow. She wanted to help him, but his entire world was about helping her. Anytime she suggested that they rent a duplex or small house together when she graduated, he would fly off the handle and demand that she work hard enough to get into a good school and make something of herself. Having her stay in Whitehill was never an option. He was even setting aside every penny he didn't need to get by for her so she would have some funds for school. She couldn't persuade him otherwise. He was her brother, her best friend, her parents, and her benefactor all in one.

They tried to have dinner together at least once a week, and whenever she would ask about his week and how his mechanic training was going, he would gloss over it and change the subject to who won the Monday Night Football game or he would ask her about her grades. Nothing ever changed until Riley's Christmas break during her senior year. She stayed over at Aidan's apartment for the entire two weeks because both of his roommates were staying at their parents' houses, and Aidan had actually worked really hard to clean it up for her. She loved being away from the Home for such a long stretch of time and dreaded going back. She couldn't wait to get into college and leave the small suburb and her dreary childhood behind. Aidan never stopped pushing her, so it didn't surprise her when, only three days after celebrating their Christmas of one small gift each, video game playing, butter chess pie, pizza, and copious amounts of cheap wine in a box, he forced her back into what had become their weekly routine.

"Okay, Nugget. Get out your checklist."

"Are you serious? It's Christmas break, Aidan."

"Hey. If I can give up playing football in the park with the guys for an hour you can give up reading that stupid book for a while."

Riley held up the tattered book in front of his face. "Aidan, this is Virginia Woolf."

"And?"

"*A Room of One's Own?*"

Silence.

Riley rolled her eyes. "It's not a 'stupid book.' One, it's awesome. Two, it's an extremely important historical essay that argues for female creative and financial independence and therefore helped to foster real and empowering discussions about gender roles in society. Three, it's homework. I'm reading it for my English class."

"Okay. So it's not a stupid book. Let me try again." He cleared his throat. "Hey. If I can give up playing football in the park with the guys for an hour you can, just for a little while, give up reading that amazing piece of feminist literature that surely helped to bring about our current social enlightenment."

She laughed and tossed the book onto the couch. "Fine. Feminist manifesto perusal on hold."

She pulled a notebook out of her backpack and placed it on the coffee table as she sat on the floor, legs crossed underneath it.

"Let's go over it again." Aidan recited the list from memory. "SATs."

Riley sighed. "This is stupid. You know I've taken them and sent in my scores. We talk about it every week."

"Riley, I'm not going to let something bad happen because we forgot to do one stupid thing."

"SATs. Done and scores sent in to North Texas, Texas Tech,

Sam Houston State, the University of Texas, the University of Houston, Rice, and Texas State."

"Applications and essays?"

"Sent in with the SAT scores. Duh."

"Housing applications?"

"Sent in after my applications were accepted."

"Scholarships?"

"Scholarship applications sent for all schools except UT, which automatically considers all music students for one. Seriously, Aidan, you know all of this."

"Financial aid applications?"

"For the love of all that is holy, Aidan. All the damn paperwork is sent! Promise!"

"Auditions?"

Riley leaned back against the couch letting her head loll back onto the cushions. She spoke with her mouth open and slack. "Recordings sent to all but Texas State and UT."

"Why not those two?"

Riley sat up, her excitement winning out over irritation. "Actually, I wanted to talk to you about that. Those are the two schools I'm most interested in since I don't want to be too far from you here in Whitehill."

Riley noticed Aidan shift in his chair slightly. Something was wrong, but she would wait for him to tell her what he was thinking when he was ready.

"So when will you send in your audition recordings to them?" His voice was steady.

"Well, I actually wanted to ask if you could drive me to Austin and San Marcos to audition for them in person. It could be fun a weekend trip or something."

Aidan slowly nodded his head. "Yeah, I think we can manage that. If it's done soon."

Riley narrowed her eyes, but said, "Well, the local audition for cello at UT is two Saturdays from now. I already scheduled it. Yes, I knew you'd agree to take me. We can hit Texas State on the way."

Aidan smiled. "That will be perfect. Now. Grades?"

"Straight As." Riley looked away as Aidan gave her a knowing look. "Okay, fine. Except for Trig. I have a B in Trig. That's good, though. I had a C last semester."

Aidan smiled. "Yes, that's very good. I never even made it to Trig. I'm impressed."

"Okay. Are we done now?"

"Yeah. With the checklist, but..." Aidan looked like he was steeling himself.

"What? What's wrong?"

"Nothing! It's just that...well, I have some big news that I've been waiting to tell you, but I kind of have to now."

"Oh my God, you're pregnant."

Riley's attempt at levity didn't work.

"This is kind of serious actually, but it's a good thing. Honest."

"Well? What is it, then?"

"Okay. Don't get mad, but I've been doing a lot of thinking for the last two years..."

"Well done."

"Okay, tool." He reached out and lightly smacked the back of her head. "But seriously, you know how much I hate working for Eddie's dad, right?"

"Yeah?"

"Well, I don't make jack shit for the work I do. I mean I like the work itself. It suits me and I'm good at it, but I'm trying my best to save money for you and working that mechanic job just isn't cutting it."

"You're quitting your job?"

"Already quit actually."

"Why didn't you tell me?" Riley crossed her arms over her chest. "I mean, I'm not mad, but you know that you can tell me anything. What will you do now? Did you get a better job?"

"Well, like I said, I really want to be able to help you out when you go to college. I mean I know that you're a perfect candidate for a scholarship and financial aid, but you'll still need a lot of money for other things. Clothes and books and…makeup…and girly things… or something. I dunno." He shrugged uncomfortably.

"Aidan, don't you dare do this for me. I can't deal with that. I'm going to get a job too. I can pay for my own things. And makeup? Really? How long have you known me?" She looked at him with exasperation.

"Don't worry, greedy pants. I'm doing this for me too." Aidan smiled warmly.

"Okay fine. So what are you doing?"

Aidan took a deep breath and blurted out, "I joined the Marines."

The air seemed to have been forcefully ejected from the room. She couldn't breathe. All logical thought left her brain.

It seemed like an eternity, but Riley finally reacted. "You did *what*?" She jumped to her feet in delayed astonishment, bumping her knee loudly on the underside of the coffee table as she rose.

Aidan stood up with her and put out placating hands. "Shh. It's okay." He could probably tell that she was on the verge of one of her breakdowns.

"It's *not* okay, Aidan. What were you thinking? What about me?" She was shaking like a leaf.

Aidan's face hardened, and he stood up straighter, his shoulders square and uncompromising. Riley was moved by how confident and strong he looked.

"Riley, damn it, I'm doing this for both of us. I can't help you with the money I'm making here, and I feel like I'm wasting away. I want to *do* something with my life. Be someone. Be a part of something bigger than myself. As a Marine, I'll be somebody. It's a good job and it can be my career for the rest of my life if I want it to be. It's stable, my food and board is paid for, it's exciting, I get good training, and the extra money I make will help pay for your *goddamned college education*." His voice had grown louder as he spoke.

Riley vibrated with anger, but she realized that what she was feeling was more like abject terror. "Aidan, I…" Mortification befell her as tears sprang unbidden from her eyes.

He rushed to her side and sat her down gently on the couch. "Shh. It's okay, Nugget. You'll see. This will be a great thing."

Through her sobs she asked, "They could send you anywhere. I won't be able to stand not knowing what you're doing or how you are. Not being able to see you whenever I want."

"Come on," he tried to comfort her. "You'll be off at college having your own adventures. You won't have time to worry about your big brother. You'll be so busy playing your cello, taking all of those classes, meeting guys...or girls. Please. I'd only cramp your style."

Riley slowly calmed down and had a stray thought that Aidan had even figured out that she was interested in girls without her having to say anything, but an icy fear had gripped her insides. "But...but Marines do dangerous things. Bad guys *shoot* at Marines." The idea of someone purposely trying to kill him horrified and unnerved her.

"Well, I'll just have to shoot back. Come on." He put his arm around her shoulders. "No one can hurt me. I'm too damn handsome. I mean really. Do you know how much the lovely ladies would miss the otherworldly magic that is my..."

Riley groaned and elbowed him in the ribs. He made an oof sound and then grinned his lupine smile.

Riley sniffed. "God, you're such a perv. You're going to come home with an STD from some skanky prostitute in some Godforsaken corner of the planet or something."

Aidan laughed loudly. "Hey, you know I have safe sex. No diseases or babies for this guy! No glove, no love."

Riley covered her ears and made loud La La sounds. "Not listening! So not listening! TMI! Gross gross gross!"

Aidan laughed again. "Seriously though. I'll be fine. You'll be fine. It's a really great opportunity for someone in my position, and I can't think of anything better that I could do for my life. And yours."

Riley leaned into his muscular shoulder and sighed, still gulping from trying to stop crying. "But why the Marines? Why not the Air Force or Merchant Marine or...Peace Corps or something?"

"Riley. Have you *seen* the Marine uniforms? I'll be absolutely irresistible. I'll have a girl in every port."

Riley knew he was teasing her and rolled her eyes, but she could feel the muscles in her face lifting. Even when it seemed that her world was about to fall apart, Aidan could make her smile. She pulled away from him, blew her nose, and settled in for what was sure to be a long and painful conversation.

Sniffing and wiping her nose with a tissue he handed to her, she said, "Okay, Lieutenant Libertine. Cool down for a minute and tell me when you leave and where you're going and how long you'll be there and how I'm going to stay in touch with you and what you're going to be doing and—"

Aidan laughed and put his large hand over her mouth. "Slow down there, Sparky. One at a time." He let her go and turned to face her. "First, I'm going to basic training in three weeks, and I'll be at the recruit depot in San Diego. Recruit training takes thirteen weeks, and after that I get ten days' leave so I'll come and visit you here. After that, I'm sent to the School of Infantry at Camp Pendleton, but I don't know if I'll end up being an infantry specialist or something else." He shrugged. "If I go infantry it's about two months' worth of training. If not, it's one month at the SOI and then on to whatever specialty school I need. That timing depends on the specialization, and I don't know much about those yet. After all of that training is done, I'll get my orders for my first permanent duty station and will be there for about six months before I get deployed. That's standard anyway. I'm sure that part can change." When Riley didn't speak and just looked at him, he continued, "You know that I could just end up in Louisiana or something, right? They might not even send me overseas anytime soon, so don't worry too much about it until we know, okay?"

Riley snorted. "Yeah. Like I'd really worry about your goofy ass." Another tear betrayed her as it slid down her face.

Aidan sighed but slapped Riley's knee. "In the meantime, though, you're going to get a few late Christmas presents."

"Why? You don't have to get me anything else. This necklace

is definitely more than you should have done anyway." Her hand automatically went to the sterling silver bass clef charm and silver chain that she now wore proudly around her neck. "All I could get you was a used Xbox game."

Aidan waved her thought away. "Yeah. One that I've been wanting forever. You know I love it. And anyway, that's not the point. Come on. Follow me."

Riley looked at him quizzically, but followed him over to the window.

"You see that?" He pointed through the blinds to the parking lot below.

She scanned the few cars in the lot including Aidan's ancient and very worn yet functional Subaru. "What? The cars?"

"No. *Your* car."

She turned to look at him, her eyes wide. "You're giving me your car?"

Aidan pulled back from the window, a pleased look on his face. "Why?"

"Because I won't need it for a long time when I go away, and when I'm done with boot camp and get stationed at my home base, I'm just going to buy a motorcycle. It's a hell of a lot cheaper than a car. I'll save on gas, and if I get sent overseas it's a lot easier to find a place to store it."

Riley grinned before an obvious thought occurred to her. "Aidan, I haven't even taken Driver's Ed."

"Part two of late Christmas presents! I signed you up for the classes they offer at school. It's way cheaper and you don't have to go anywhere else. And..." He paused for dramatic effect. "Part three." He opened the closet door and pulled out a large hard-shelled case.

"Oh my God, you didn't."

"I did." He beamed. "Don't get too excited. It's not brand new or anything, but I talked to Miss Geddis, and she said that it's a high-quality one that has an amazing tone...or something."

Riley zipped open the case and gazed at the gorgeous cello inside. "This is too much."

"Nah. I got a pretty decent signing bonus when I joined up, so it's going to cover a lot of your first expenses, and you have to have your own cello if you're going to major in it. And to make life a little easier…here." He pulled a Visa card out of his pocket with her name on it. "I created a joint account for us. You can put your gas and books on here. Just let me know first if you need to buy something else. I'm not Brother Warbucks, and I don't want you to run this card up."

Riley was silent for a while, turning her first credit card over in her hands. "Aidan, you can't just give me everything you earn. You have a life too."

"Yes, I do, and check it out." He walked back over to the hall closet and pulled out a black leather jacket and shiny matching motorcycle helmet. He held them up proudly. "Pretty cool, huh?"

Riley sighed with exasperation. "You're going to kill me with worry. First you join the Marines, and now you're going to be a biker too. Aidan, for the love of all that is holy, *please* be careful."

"You know me." He winked.

Riley shook her head but smiled weakly. "Yeah. That's the problem."

CHAPTER FIVE

D o you want me to come in with you?"
Aidan and Riley were seated in a waiting room in the Butler School of Music on the University of Texas campus in Austin. Several string players were scattered around, manically going over their audition music with fingers moving silently in the air, but Riley was the last cello player that remained. She had nervously watched as cellist after cellist exited the audition room, some beaming from their performances, some breaking down in sobs over missed notes and butchered runs.

Riley's voice shook as she spoke. "You're not allowed and you know it. Anyway, this is all on me. I either play well enough or I don't."

"Well, I don't know much about music, but I think you're the best cellist ever." Aidan smiled helpfully.

Riley snorted in an anxious way. "Not even close, Bro. But thanks for the vote of confidence."

"Well, you sounded great in that last audition. I could hear you through the door."

Riley nodded remembering her decent audition at Texas State a few hours ago. "Yeah, that went better than expected."

"Why so mopey about it, then?"

She shook her head. "Not now. Too nervous."

An older music student poked her head out of the rehearsal room door. "Riley Gordon on cello?"

Riley took a steadying breath and stood up, paper rustling

loudly as she set the sheet music for the required Bach and concerto movements down on the chair behind her. She was used to learning music quickly and playing from memory, but this time it seemed like her whole life depended on the perfect remembrance of every note, every crescendo, and every bow movement. Never had so much been riding on her innate talent and good ear.

"Hey!" Aidan called after her. She turned around and saw him leaning back nonchalantly with his arm draped across the back of the couch. He radiated faith and confidence. "You kick ass."

Riley blushed as she turned back around and found the young woman who had called her name smiling back at her.

"Relax," she said. "You'll do great."

"Has everyone today done great?" Riley couldn't hide the quaver in her voice.

"No, but I'm sure you will. I can usually tell." She winked in a friendly way that Riley assumed was meant to reassure, but she was still more jittery than she had ever been in her life.

"Well, no time like the present, huh?" Riley stood up straighter and pretended to have confidence as she walked through the second set of soundproof doors the young woman held open for her.

❖

Riley hadn't said much after the audition was over, but Aidan had insisted that they take a student-led tour of the campus while they were there. As they had walked around the forty acres listening to the chipper young blond woman pointing out places like the "Six Pack," the Tower, and the West Mall, Aidan had made comments like "You'll probably study in the sun over there" or "Look at all of the student group tables on the West Mall. You should definitely join some. Make friends. Just make sure that your schoolwork comes first, though." His assurance that she would be accepted was absolute. Now, as they drove back to Whitehill, she could see Aidan glancing surreptitiously at her, probably trying to gauge her emotions. Finally, when they had been driving in silence for at least an hour he said, "Okay, seriously. How did you do?"

Riley shrugged and Aidan looked from her back to the road. "Don't worry if you messed up. Everyone does. And you sounded great at Texas State. It's okay if you don't get in to UT. I don't want you to be bummed about it. Whatever happens happens."

Sighing, Riley shook her head and looked down at her hands. "It was perfect, Aidan."

Confused, he glanced at her again. "What was perfect?"

"I was perfect. I played better than I've ever played anything. Ever. I was...perfect."

Aidan's face lit up and he removed his hand from the wheel to slap her proudly on the knee. "Rock! Why the look of doom and gloom, then?"

Riley didn't know how to put the fear, anxiety, and doubt she was feeling into words, so she said simply, "What if my best isn't good enough?"

Aidan sat quietly for a while before answering. "You may not think so, but I do understand some of what you're going through. My entire senior year was spent working out, practicing, and trying to prove to myself that I was going to be good enough to get a football scholarship. Turns out I wasn't."

"That wasn't your fault, though, Aidan. You got injured. I don't have an excuse if I don't make it."

"Well, from what I could hear, you're a shoo-in for pretty much any college you want. Why are you suddenly so stuck on UT?"

Sighing, she said, "Well, now that you're going to be based God knows where with the Marines, I don't really want to go to Texas State or any other college. I mean, don't get me wrong. I know that getting a scholarship *anywhere* will be a blessing for someone in my position, but we've spent our whole lives living small. Our town is small. Our home is small. Our family is small." She gestured between them. "Our opportunities are small. I want something bigger now. Austin is bigger. UT is bigger. I mean, you're doing something really big and amazing with your life. And me? I'm actually kind of..."

When she paused and looked out the window pensively, Aidan encouraged her. "You're kind of what?"

Riley turned her eyes back to his. "I'm kind of jealous of you."

He chuckled. "And you think moving to Austin is the answer?"

"I fell in love with Austin the moment I set foot in it. It's where I'm meant to be. If I don't get accepted to the music program, I'll…I dunno." She took a deep breath. "Let's talk about something else. I won't know for a long time anyway."

"Okay." He drove in silence for a few miles before commenting, "That girl that escorted people into the room was pretty hot. Maybe I should have applied to go to Texas too." He grinned.

"Jesus, Aidan. Do you ever think about anything except boobs?"

With no delay whatsoever, he replied, "Nope."

Riley smiled at his predictability.

"I tell ya what. Let's drive into San Antonio before we go home. It'll take you to the Riverwalk for a celebratory dinner."

Riley brightened considerably. She had only gotten to go to the Riverwalk twice in her life. Once when her junior high class went on a field trip to the Alamo and a few other Spanish missions in the area, and the other for a friend's birthday dinner when she was a sophomore in high school. "That sounds brilliant, but we shouldn't be celebrating anything. I won't know if I got accepted for another four months."

"We're celebrating you getting all of the applications done and your hard work on your performances. Riley, you've really kicked some serious ass these last few years. One dinner at the Riverwalk is nowhere near what you deserve."

"Well, when you put it like that…"

"Nugget?"

"Yeah?"

"Don't let what I'm about to say go to your head, but I'm so proud of you it feels like my brain is going to explode into a huge gooey, bloody mess. No matter what happens."

Riley turned her head to look and him and saw that he was positively beaming.

"Descriptive. And thank you." She stopped talking as her voice caught in her throat.

❖

"I'll call you as soon as I get there, okay?"

Riley nodded, trying to hold back her tears.

"It's a short, scripted phone call, but at least you'll know I'm safe. After that, I'll send snail mail with the address you can use to send me letters."

Riley just nodded again and looked at her feet. They were standing in the parking lot of a Days Inn near the San Antonio airport. Aidan and several other Marine recruits were to stay there that night and a bus would pick them up before dawn the next morning to take them through the MEPS process and then onto a plane to the recruit depot in San Diego. Riley now had her driver's license and had driven Aidan to what would be the start of his new path. Her heart was heavy, and she trembled with the fear of being on her own for the first time in her life.

"And anyway, it's only thirteen weeks until I get ten days' leave!"

Riley snorted. "Aidan, it will be the beginning of April. You're missing the last half of my senior year. What if I need you? For advice? Or something?"

"Just send me a letter. I'll always be here for you. You know that."

"You're going to miss my graduation when you're at the Infantry School thing."

"Yeah. I'm sorry about that one. Really. But I'll get to see you before you go to college."

"*If* I go to college." Riley was pouting and letting her frustrations get to her.

Aidan lightly popped her on the back of her head. "Shut up with that bullshit. Seriously."

"I'm sorry. I'm just…I'm scared that nothing will work out."

Aidan sighed and pulled her into a hug. She was engulfed in his arms, and her head rested on his strong chest. It was the closest thing she could get to a hug from a father. "No matter what happens,

I'll always be here for you. Whether I'm in Iraq or in the next room. Don't worry about what will happen. Just do your best, do what's good, and you'll know that you're doing the right thing."

Riley couldn't help the tears that slid down her cheeks. "I love you, Aidan."

"I love you too, Nugget."

❖

Riley stacked the new letter she received that afternoon neatly on top of the others that Aidan had sent her from boot camp. He only had one week of training left before he would be considered a Marine and would be able to take leave to visit her. She smiled as she remembered the phone call she'd received during her English class when he had arrived at the San Diego base. She hadn't cared that she let her phone ring during school. The device hadn't left her side since she had dropped Aidan off at that motel. Luckily, her teacher had a daughter in the Army and understood Riley's nervousness in regard to her brother's enlistment.

She had answered almost frantically when an unknown number came up on the phone as the class was discussing Dostoevsky. "Hello? Aidan?"

Even though he was yelling, he had been barely audible over the other chaotic voices in the background. He was reading a script, just as he had said he would have to do.

"This is Recruit Gordon. I have arrived safely at MCRD San Diego. Please do not send any food or bulky items to me in the mail. I will contact you in three to five days by postcard with my new address. Thank you for your support. Good-bye for now." The line had gone dead with a sickening *click*, but at least Riley knew that he had made it safely to his destination. She was still envious that he was getting to go out of the state of Texas for the first time in his life, but knew that he wouldn't get to enjoy what California had to offer while he was in training.

She pulled the oldest dated letter from the pile. She often read through them in chronological order when she felt alone and irritated, when her classmates had mistreated her, or when she felt like she was a failure. His words, regardless of their brevity or his unhappiness, always made her feel like he was still near, continuing to protect her, to listen to her, and to be her only connection to family.

Today hadn't been a good day. Other kids in school, the few who were going to college, that is, had already started receiving their acceptance letters. Riley hadn't received a single one yet. The people that were supposedly her friends had spent the entire day goading her about it; teasing that she would have to stay there with them in the pit that was their suburb. They just loved to tear her down. It seemed like they were afraid that Riley thought she was better than them. The truth was that Riley *knew* she was better than them, but not for the reasons they believed. It wasn't because she was an amazing cellist. It wasn't because she had straight A's. It was simply because she treated them well despite the poor way they often treated her. She was a nicer person, despite the constant simmer of anger beneath the surface. It sure as hell didn't make her life easier or happier, but she refused to stoop to their level. She turned her attention from her brooding back to Aidan's first letter from boot camp. She read:

Dear Annoying Little Sister (I kid because I love),

Well, Week 1 is over and done with, and we're about halfway into week two. The first few days were spent in processing, and even though I've watched the videos on YouTube and read about what to expect in boot camp, nothing can prepare you for what it's really like. I've never felt so insignificant and generic in all my life. I'm just one of many here. Actually, it's hard to even write the word "I." Here we're all "recruit." "These recruits" this, "This recruit" that. This recruit wants to punch his drill sergeant square in his pompous, loud face, but doesn't want to spend the rest of this recruit's life in the brig.

They strip away our individuality as easily as they stripped away our civilian clothes and hair. You know how much I loved my hair. It's okay, though. Turns out I still look incredibly dashing with a shaved head. Kind of badass, really. At least I know that if I lose my hair when I get older I'll still be irresistible. It's just not possible for me to look ugly.

Hey, I could see you roll your eyes from here. You know it's true, though. Speaking of, how are the lovely ladies of Whitehill? Is there some kind of mass-mourning going on without me there? Guess they'll all have to settle for lesser men.

There goes that eye roll again. Girl, you have to learn to control that.

Anyway, for the first few days, we didn't get any sleep at all and then had to do a physical fitness test. I passed with flying colors, of course, but damn, I'm tired. This is the first night since our main drill instructors have taken over that I've had a chance to sit and relax. Of course, you can never truly relax here. I hear the D.I.s screaming in my head even when I get the little bit of sleep they allow for us.

We've finally started the real boot camp phase. You know, the stuff you see in movies. We get up at the ass-crack of dawn and exercise. We run, we do push-ups, God, so many damn push-ups, we run some more. The chow is pretty good, though. Most of the guys complain about it and want some good ol'-fashioned home cooking or even fast food, but since you and I never had real home cooking, it all tastes the same to me—although I wouldn't complain if they gave us a pizza and beer every now and then. God, I want a beer.

We've also started the classroom training. Bet you didn't know that I'd be going back to school, huh? They're teaching us about basic military etiquette, ranks, uniforms, the culture and history of the Marines, etc. That isn't a door, it's a hatch. That's not a bathroom, it's the head. We do serve with the Navy, you know. Everything is nautical. Kind of cool really. The Marines have an awesome history.

We have to memorize everything. And I do mean everything. The D.I. has been in my face more than I can stand asking me to recite the 11 General Orders for him. I have to say it perfectly or I push. Of course, if I look at the D.I. when I'm not supposed to, I push. If I fall out of step in drill, I push. If I take longer than ten seconds to take a piss, I push. If I do everything 100% correctly and think that I've finally done something well, I push. My arms are so damn sore. The football training and mechanic work still didn't prepare my body for this shit.

That's about all I can write for now. I can't keep my eyes open. I just wanted to send you a letter to let you know how "this recruit" is doing. I'll try to write at least once a week. Please don't send any care packages because the D.I.s will just confiscate the stuff anyway, but I'd sure like to hear from you. I'm making some really good buddies here, but there's nothing like a letter from family to remind us of what we have outside of this hellhole.

Do well in school and know that your kick-ass big brother loves you,
Aidan

Riley folded the letter and placed it neatly back in its envelope. She pulled out the next one. This one was much shorter.

Dear Riley,

Well, I'm in Week 3. Same ol' shit except now we've added in the hand-to-hand combat training and bayonet stuff. That's actually kind of fun, but the D.I.s just don't let up. I'm so frickin' sick of getting screamed at all the time. I know what they're doing. I know they have to break us down to build us back up, and at the same time they're getting us used to the stresses of war, but that doesn't make it any easier to take.

The thing that actually bothers me more than anything is how offensive the D.I.s can be. You and I grew up in

the Home with all sorts of different kinds of kids. I mean, truthfully, we were the minority there, you know? And these D.I.s, man, they insult every kind of person imaginable. It doesn't matter if the D.I. is white, black, Hispanic, Asian, or covered in polka dots. They're all absolutely perfect so they can tear down everyone else. I've been called a useless fag, a little girl, white trash. Don't even get me started on the way they talk about women. I have to wonder how they train the female recruits over at Parris Island. This is the stuff they don't show as much in the movies. If you go on YouTube and watch videos about what it's like, they won't show you really bad stuff—the bigoted stuff and the threats of physical violence. The only acceptable thing about it is that it is actually completely fair. No one is left out. Equal opportunity bigotry, I guess.

Would you believe that we even have a gay recruit in our platoon? Most of the guys here are surprisingly okay with the gay thing as long as it's not rubbed in their faces. There are a few judgmental assholes, of course, but they're just assholes in general. It doesn't matter to the D.I.s that he's gay, though. To them we're all fags, women, pieces of shit. And this guy (his name is Craig, btw) is actually one of the best recruits here. He's way into the Marine culture. His mom is a Marine. His dad is a Navy chief. Both of his grandfathers were Marines. And his maternal grandmother was even a SPAR in the Coast Guard back during WWII. This guy lives and breathes the military. It makes me feel kind of lame for just joining on a whim. The halfway intelligent guys in our platoon all look up to him as a leader. The idiots can't see past the gay thing. Oh well. Their loss. He's my closest buddy here, so if they don't like it they can go to hell.

Anyway, sorry to sound all pissed off. This is just harder than I thought it would be. I do want to thank you for your letter, though. It was so good getting to hear from you. I'm sorry that those bitches in your class are getting

*you down. You are so much better than them. In all ways.
And don't worry. They'll change their tune when I walk up
in my uniform. They won't mess with you after that!
Take care of yourself!*
    Aidan

The next letter in the pile was the shortest she had received.

Dear Riley,
    *What in the hell have I done? This is only my fourth
week, and I don't know how much more of this I can take.
Thirteen weeks? Are you shitting me? This is the most
hellish place imaginable. I'm so sick of being told what
to do and when to do it for every goddamned second of
my life. I'm going crazy. The Marine Corps can kiss this
recruit's ass. The only things that are keeping me on the
right side of sanity are you and my buddies. Craig, Rafael,
and Lamar are my best friends here, and without them I
probably would have washed out by now. I'd do anything
for those guys.*
    *I have to give you a lot of the credit, though. Your
last letter made me smile for the first time in…so many
days. Thanks for keeping an eye on things back home for
me. I'm really proud of you for making the State ensemble
again. I knew you would, of course. I'm sorry I'll have to
miss the concert this year, though. That is unless I decide
I've had enough of this bullshit and just hop on a bus
home tomorrow.*
    There is a definite possibility of that happening…
    Aidan

Riley hadn't liked reading about him being miserable.
Especially when she knew that he was doing this partly for her. Still,
the letters kept coming, and with every one, his mood and excitement
improved. He was truly becoming a Marine. The military knew how
much pressure a person could take before they broke completely

versus breaking just enough to be molded into a fighting machine intent on their own and their friends' survival in the face of dauntless enemies. Riley didn't necessarily agree with everything they did or everything they were going to have to do out in the field, but was glad that Aidan was finding his way.

She put the letters back in the shoebox of heirlooms. It was true that her day had been terrible, but re-reading Aidan's letters had helped to put things in perspective, as she had known they would. If he could get through boot camp, she could damn sure get through her senior year of high school.

She smiled as she thought, is there really a difference?

Chapter Six

Dear Aidan,

I know you'll be home soon, but I couldn't wait to tell you. It's happened. I got in. I got in to the frickin' University of Texas School of Music. I'm sure you're imagining me freaking out right about now, but I swear I'm in shock. I can't believe I made it. They're so selective. I just…I don't know how I got in. Aidan, I even got one of their scholarships. It's not a full ride or anything, but it's going to help a hell of a lot!

With the financial aid I'm getting, the money you're so generously giving me, and whatever I earn at the part-time job I get when I move to Austin, I'm going to be set. Well, I'll never be rolling in it, but I'll be able to get by. That will be a weird feeling! Well, it will be nice until I have to pay back my loans for years afterward.

And to top that off, I even got placed in one of the newest, nicest dorms. Remember that huge one that looks like a prison? Not mine! You know that beautiful one that's closest to the music school, right next to Clark Field, and right across the street from the stadium? Yeah. You can see me smiling, huh? It's called San Jacinto or San Jac to the students.

On another subject, I'm so excited that you'll be home soon. You sounded so bummed that it's going to be before my graduation, though. Don't be. I'm ready to leave, trust me. The ceremony isn't a big deal. And since you so annoyingly asked, no. No one has invited me to the prom and no one will. I'm not bothered, though. You know I can't dance. It sounds awful anyway. Why would I want to spend all night with people who are anywhere from fake nice to downright bitchy to me all dressed up and pretending like it's the best night of their lives? No thanks. Not my style. There's a viola player that I'm friendly with who isn't going either (her parents are super strict and won't allow it—some religious thing), so we're going to go to a movie instead. Hopefully something brainless with lots of explosions and no high school drama. So don't worry about me. I know it's weird for you to have such a geek for a sister when you were Mr. Popularity, but I'm fine. Honestly. I prefer the quieter, artistic side of life.

That doesn't mean that I won't totally kick your ass if you piss me off, though.

I'm so excited to get to see you again. Please come home in your uniform. The girls at school will just die. It sucks that you only have a week before you have to go to your other infantry or whatever training.

Anyway, good luck in your Crucible thing. I know it's going to be the hardest thing you've ever done, but I have zero doubts that you'll get through it, and when you get your Eagle, Globe, and Anchor you'll be a frickin' United States Marine. I'm so proud of you, Aidan. You honestly have no idea. Yes, I'm still a little pissed about it. Yes, I'm so worried about you I don't know how to deal with it, but I want you to know that I love you and couldn't be happier that you've found something that will earn you the respect you deserve and a job that will hopefully make you happy.

Please call when you can and tell me how everything went. I miss you and will see you soon!

Love,

Your little sister, the TEXAS LONGHORN! Hook 'em!

Two weeks later, when Aidan stepped off the aging Greyhound bus in the center of town, Riley practically flew over the concrete that separated the station from the street. He was wearing a uniform that consisted of a green coat and pants with a khaki shirt and tie underneath and topped off with a soft pointed garrison cap. When Riley reached him she threw her arms around his neck and he easily picked her up off of the ground as he straightened.

She was struck by how much he had changed in the months that he had been gone. He had been strong and burly before, but now he seemed slimmer and even more muscular, if that were possible. His face was slightly narrower, but with more pronounced lines as if even his jawline had benefited from the training.

"Hey, Nugget." Aidan smiled as he set her gently back on the ground.

"Well, shit, Aidan. Look at you." Riley put her fists on her hips and looked him up and down. "You look damn handsome, you know?"

Aidan laughed. "I told you! Chicks dig the uniform!"

"Come on. Let's get out of here."

He stopped her with a hand on her shoulder as she turned to leave. "Stop. First things first." He pulled a set of dog tags out of his pocket and put them around her neck.

She looked at them and saw that one was a copy of his official dog tag and the other had more unofficial information.

Riley Michelle Gordon
Cellist
University of Texas

"Congratulations, Riley. I wish I was smart enough to tell you how proud of you I am, but I just can't figure out how to put what I'm feeling into words. I feel like my chest...like it's a balloon... or like it's been hit with a mortar made of pride...or something like that."

Riley laughed. "That works."

"Anyway, I made those dog tags for you so that we can always be together, even when we're apart. I don't want you to ever forget that you have a big brother somewhere in the world that loves you and thinks you're the smartest, coolest, and most talented girl ever."

She threw herself into his arms and sniffed as she wiped a tear on his uniform jacket. "Thank you."

"Come on. People will start to think that I actually like my little sister or something. I've got an image to uphold here."

Riley laughed and they turned to walk to the motel.

Aidan no longer rented the apartment with his friends and he didn't want to set foot back in the Home, so he had rented an extended-stay suite near the bus station for the week. As they were walking, Riley glanced at him again. His large green bag was slung over his shoulder, and a flash of WWII soldiers returning home popped into her head.

"Okay. So tell me about the bling," she asked.

"The bling?" He looked down at her, confused.

"The shiny bits." Riley pointed at the ribbon and medals on his chest, and Aidan laughed.

"Oh my God, if the guys heard you say that we wear 'bling'…"

She poked him in the ribs. "Just tell me what they mean. What's that?" She pointed at the red and yellow ribbon.

He looked down at his chest and tapped the small colored bar. "That's the National Defense ribbon. Everyone who completes boot camp in any of the services gets it."

"And that one?" Riley pointed to the silver medal underneath it.

"Rifle marksman qualification badge. Turns out your big brother's a damn good shot!"

"Well, that's good to know. Must be all of those years of shooting bad guys on the Xbox."

"It does help with hand-eye coordination." He smiled.

"And what about this?" Riley patted the yellow chevron patch on his sleeve.

"That means this recruit has…" Aidan sighed and shook his head, but beamed. "That means that *I* have earned the rank of private first class."

"Is that good? Can you order people around?"

He laughed. "Oh God, no. But it does mean that I was one of the top in my class. Most guys are just privates when they get out of boot camp unless they have prior JROTC experience or something. It's an honor to get PFC right out of the gate."

"So it means you kicked ass, then."

"Yes. It means I kicked ass. Craig got it too. I mean, of course Craig got it too. He's the perfect Marine. If you don't care about the gay thing. Which I don't. Duh," he said, gesturing to her.

"Well, you look totally hot, PFC Gordon."

"Not looking bad yourself, Nugget."

Riley snorted. "Uh-huh. Lovely young suitors line my walk every night vying for my womanly attentions."

"Don't worry about it. Just wait 'til you get to college. Whatever happened in high school will be totally forgotten."

"Well, the selective amnesia can't come soon enough. I'm so over this shit." Riley kicked a rock across the pavement as she walked.

"Is it really that bad?"

"I don't want to worry you or make you think that I'm weak, but it has gotten pretty awful since you left."

Aidan stopped and turned Riley to face him, a stern look on his face. "What's happened? Who do I need to kill?"

Riley sighed, but smiled at his usual over-protectiveness. "That might be going a *little* far, Bro. And it's just petty stuff, really immature bitchiness. They call me ugly. They throw things at me when the teacher's not looking. I mean they're not even creative with their bullying. It's kinda sad really."

"You realize they're jealous, right?"

Riley snorted. "Jealous of what? My supermodel beauty? My vast fortune? My impressive lineage?"

"Don't make me smack you. You know damn well that you're infinitely smarter and more talented than those losers. They just feel intimidated."

"It doesn't seem that way."

"Trust me. I've seen it a million times. When you get to UT, you'll find people like you. People with brains and a future. Just wait it out." He put his arm around her shoulder and they started walking again. "And in the meantime, if you need anyone's ass kicked you just let me know. I'm kind of a big deal now."

Riley laughed at his usual arrogant sense of humor.

❖

The ten days of Aidan's leave passed in a blur of beer, pizza, his old high school buddies whisking him away to parties, and a steady stream of female visitors who stayed the night with him after Riley went back to the Home. She tried not to think about that part. Still, she knew he deserved this break and couldn't blame him for making the most out of it before he had to go back to training.

That conversation hadn't been a fun one. The first night that he had come home he had taken her out to dinner at her favorite Italian restaurant and had explained his next steps.

"So, I have Infantry training next."

"The short version or long version?"

"Long version," Aidan said with his mouth full of lasagna.

Riley slammed down her fork. "Aidan, that means you're going into the Infantry, doesn't it?"

He swallowed. "Yes, but listen…"

"No! You told me that it was possible if you did well on your tests and in boot camp that you could get placed somewhere that wasn't as dangerous! Communications or something."

"That's true, and while my ASVAB scores were pretty decent and I did really well in boot camp, the Infantry stuff is what I've fallen in love with. Look, I'm not going to be a rifleman. I'm going for the LAV crewman specialization."

Riley glared at him. "LAV crewman." It was a statement, not a question, but she knew that he would explain.

"Light Armored Vehicle. I'll start out as a driver, then if I do well I can move to gunner, and if I'm awesome at that—as if

I wouldn't be—I can become the vehicle commander. Riley, how cool will it be to tear around the desert in a massive armored go-kart on steroids?"

Riley stared at him, deadpan.

"Look. It's what I want to do. And it's not all fun and boys playing with cool toys. It's mostly maintenance and mechanic stuff really. But I'm good at that. I have experience with that, and I think it will serve me well. And look. It's an armored vehicle. No, it's not one hundred percent safe, but would you rather I be running around outside, kicking doors down, and doing fancy Captain Kirk rolls in the dirt?"

Riley considered what he was saying. Yes, it was true that he had training as a mechanic and that had to be useful in the position he wanted, but it seemed to her that the LAVs just made larger targets.

She sighed. "You know I'm not going to feel great about anything that you choose to do if it sends you overseas to fight."

"I know." He passed her the last piece of garlic cheesy bread as a peace offering. "But keep in mind that this is what I really want to do and I want you to be happy for me."

Riley couldn't stay mad at him. She loved him too much. She took the bread, set it down on her plate, and leaned forward. "So just do me one tiny, small, miniscule favor, and I promise I'll never bring it up again."

"Anything."

"Come home safe."

Aidan grinned and held up his hands, gesturing to himself. "This is *me* we're talking about. The world would stop spinning if I weren't here to keep it going."

Riley sat back and huffed. "It's really a shame the Marines couldn't instill some self-confidence in you. Guess they didn't want you to get cocky. Oh wait…"

He winked at her and waved the waiter over. "Two créme brulees, my good man. We're celebrating. My little sister is going to college!"

CHAPTER SEVEN

Riley frowned as she took in her single sad suitcase. Her entire life could fit into one piece of luggage. That was depressing. She placed her now framed diploma on top of her folded shirts next to the heirloom box and zipped the suitcase shut. She registered the quiet stares of the other girls, but they were new and young and she didn't know them well.

She hefted her suitcase off of the bed, grabbed her cello, and edged her way past the quiet younger girls into the hallway where the ladies who ran the Home waited to tearfully hug her good-bye. Riley couldn't help but well up knowing that she had no intention of ever returning to Whitehall to see them again. That part of her life was over. She was moving on. But still, these women had been the only good part of living in a foster facility. They honestly cared about the children that were brought to them. It wasn't their fault that the overburdened foster system kept them too busy to lavish individual attention on each child.

After a few words of encouragement and farewell, Riley packed up her car and pulled out of the dirt driveway for the last time. Pressure squeezed her chest while elation tingled her stomach. She crossed the threshold of the gate and she didn't look back.

❖

The door of the studio apartment she had subleased from an engineering graduate student who was traveling through Europe for the summer clicked as she unlocked it. She hesitantly peeked inside, worried that the student might still be home, but she saw that, although basically furnished, the apartment was completely bare. The previous occupant had obviously packed up her personal effects since she wouldn't be home for three months—and probably because a stranger would be staying in her apartment.

Riley walked in and threw her suitcase on the double bed. For a moment, she just stood in the center of the disconcertingly quiet room, her ears straining for the familiar noises of children playing, crying, or throwing tantrums. All sounds she hadn't even realized she had grown accustomed to at the Home. Now that they were gone, she realized how much she enjoyed the silence. It would be nice to just...*be*...here. No one would interrupt her thoughts. No one would force her to escape to a run-down activity room just to have some time to herself. She was free.

At least for the summer.

In the fall, she would move into her dorm on campus and would share a room with another person once again. Even though she had been forced to sleep in a room with multiple people for most of her life, she was still nervous about living with someone in college. What if her mystery roommate hated her? What if she complained about her practicing her cello? What if she was a complete bitch? What if, what if, what if.

Riley shook her head. There was no need to worry about that right now. Whatever was going to happen was three months away, and there was nothing she could do about it anyway.

She made an irritated *tsk* noise and inwardly scolded herself for worrying about such superficial things when she knew how incredibly lucky she was to have the opportunity to go to college at all, and at her first choice with her dream major at that.

"Be useful," she said to herself as she opened up her suitcase and carefully unpacked its meager contents and placed them in the dresser next to the bed. She set the ever-important shoebox of heirlooms in the top drawer where she could access its contents whenever she got lonely.

Afterward, she pulled out her cell phone and made a list of all of the things she would need to buy immediately from the store. The bed had no linens, she had no towels, the kitchen was completely bare except for an old bottle of mustard and a packet of baking soda in the refrigerator, and she had to go out and buy one nicer set of clothes for all of the interviews she was bound to have as soon as she started looking for a job.

When the list was complete, she sat on the window seat next to the nightstand and took a moment to gaze out across the tops of the live oak trees that grew in front of the small apartment complex.

She took a deep breath and smiled. "Day one. Let's go."

❖

Riley face-planted onto the bed. It was stiff and barely jiggled as her weight fell on it.

"Ow," she said, her voice muffled by her newly purchased comforter.

It had been a long couple of days. All of her shopping was now done, and she had even been to four job interviews. Her fingers were crossed for the sales position at the local musical instrument store, but she feared that with her lack of work experience she would only get offered the stocker position at the small local organic grocery store…if that. But no, she couldn't worry yet. She had only been on her own for two days, and she had three months to get used to her new city before she moved into the dorm.

As she was pondering what she was going to do with herself in the next weeks, her cell phone rang. She jumped up and grabbed it off the side table, hoping it was Aidan checking in to see how she was doing. It was a number she didn't recognize.

She answered the call and smiled as she learned that she had been hired as a barista at the small coffee shop only a few blocks from the UT campus. She told the woman on the phone that she would indeed be able to start tomorrow and jammed her fist silently into the air in triumph.

Two days in Austin, two days as a real life human being, and she already had a job. Surely that was a world record. She hung up the phone and looked around the bare room. What now?

"Celebrate."

She got up off the bed and rummaged through the three bags of groceries she had brought home. She set two bottles of sarsaparilla, a frozen tikka masala dish, and Blue Bell strawberry ice cream on the counter. That, paired with a night spent streaming episodes of *Battlestar Galactica* on her computer, made for a pleasant evening indeed.

❖

Working at the coffee shop turned out to be a perfect job for her. She always had to work the late shift, but she didn't mind. It gave her time to play her cello without disturbing anyone during the day.

"Don't look now, but that skinny brown-haired girl is back. Table four."

Riley turned from the sink behind the coffee bar to look at the isolated table by the bookshelf. The coffee shop was busy despite it being just after midnight, but the brown-haired girl with the glasses was the only one looking directly at her.

"Girl, what'd I say?" Koji, her flamboyantly gay and super-hyper coworker, slapped the back of her head. It was too late, though. She had been caught looking by the familiar young woman in the corner. Riley turned around quickly, unable to hide her embarrassment.

"You know, she never used to come in as often before you started working here," he said, nudging Riley with his hip as she continued vigorously scrubbing the dirty blender in the sink.

Riley shook her head. "I've only been here for two and a half months, and she doesn't come in any more often than our other regulars. People do like coffee at night too, you know. College town and whatnot? And we're right next to campus."

Koji pursed his lips. "Mmm-hmm. You can keep paddling up denial until you reach the sea, but that girl likes you. I catch her staring all the time. When she orders coffee from you I can see her struggling to say something else, but she chickens out."

Riley blushed, but didn't say anything.

"You should go talk to her."

"Right."

Koji clicked his tongue. "It's not like you don't have an excuse. You could ask her if she needs anything else. A refill, some biscotti… the intimate companionship of an adorable blue-eyed redhead such as yourself."

"It would be so obvious. No, thanks. And…shut up."

He turned around as customers approached the register, but said over his shoulder, "Okay, but you're missing out. That girl is cute…in a nerdy, mousy, geek chic, I-bet-she's-wild-in-private kind of way."

Riley just shook her head. Still, she chanced one last glance over at the shy girl in the corner. Their eyes met, and they both looked away quickly. Riley tried to hide the smile that formed. Maybe she should go talk to her…later. Much, much later.

❖

"I can't believe that I finally get out of training after *all* these months and I'm still doing grunt work," Aidan whined as he carried two heavy boxes of books up the dormitory stairs. "How could you buy so many books in only three months?"

"Oh, stop complaining. I have, like, four possessions to my name. It's not like this is hard for a solider like you."

"Marine," he huffed.

"Sorry. A *Marine* like you."

"Just remember that you promised we can go out after we're done moving you in. No way in hell am I going to hang out in a college town for a week without meeting some of the ladies. We've gotta go to Sixth Street! Craig and Rafael texted me already about the shit they're getting into back home, and believe me, it's a hell of a lot more fun than this."

Riley turned around in the middle of the stairwell and glared down at him. "Aidan, *damn it*, you can go if you want to! It's not my fault your leave happened to fall at the same time as the start of school!" She stamped her foot in frustration.

"Whoa! Temper, Sis! You know I'm just kidding. I'm happy to help you move in. Really."

Riley deflated. She hated losing her temper so easily. "I'm sorry. I just feel guilty. Your buddies are off having fun and you're stuck with your volatile little sister."

"Riley." Aidan peeked out from behind the boxes he was holding. "Don't feel guilty. I love you. I wouldn't miss this for anything, and please keep moving because these boxes are hella heavy."

"Oh. Sorry." She turned and carried her cello up the rest of the way to the third floor.

She found her room number, and when she opened the door, she was startled to see that the girl whom she assumed to be her new roommate was already completely moved in. Her eyes widened as she took in a bed draped with a bright purple satin bedspread against the far wall, lacy pillows, a study desk that was completely covered with cosmetics, large pink wooden Greek letters nailed into the wall, and posters of half-naked male soccer players taking up the rest of the real estate.

"Oh God." The words slipped out before Riley could stop them.

Her new roommate heard her and leaned forward to see who had walked in. Her smile broadened as their eyes met. "OMG, roomie?"

Riley smiled nervously and set her cello case against the wall. "Looks like it." She walked in and set her box on her own uncomfortable-looking bed and then offered her hand. "Hi, I'm Riley. Riley Gordon."

Riley noticed that the girl's white-blond hair sparkled in the light from the window. She knew that her own probably looked lifeless and dull. Riley felt downright homely next to this girl.

"It's so good to meet you, Riley! I'm Brooke." She took Riley's hand and pulled her into an uncomfortably close hug. "Oh, we're going to have so much fun I just know it!" She swayed back and forth as Riley struggled to breathe. It was only when Aidan walked into the room that she stopped suddenly and let out a small gasp.

Riley turned her head with difficulty and explained, "That's my brother Aidan. He's helping me move."

Aidan smiled and moved past them to set the rest of the boxes on Riley's bed. Brooke's demeanor changed dramatically. She let go of Riley and slowly sashayed over to where Aidan stood in his tight USMC T-shirt that showed every muscle in his arms and chest.

"Hi, Aidan." Her voice had lost its bubbly quality and was now slightly lower and infinitely more breathy.

Riley rolled her eyes. *Here we go again.* She wished she had a hundredth of the charm and good looks of her brother. It was so annoying knowing that no matter what she did he was always going to be the one that would be the center of attention. Where Aidan was adored, Riley was ignored.

"Do you go to school here too?" Brooke asked hopefully.

Aidan smiled, "Nope. I'm in the Marine Corps." He pointed unnecessarily to his shirt. "Just helping Riley get settled before I have to go back."

Brooke looked enamored. "Oh, a Marine. How brave! Well, don't you worry about anything. Riley and I are going to be BFFs, and we're going to have the best time ever, aren't we?" She looked over her shoulder.

Riley smiled halfheartedly.

Brooke turned back to Aidan. "See? I'll take good care of her. I'm a sophomore so I can show her the ropes. Hey, how about I show you guys around right now?" She smiled at Aidan, who looked to Riley.

Seeing her nervous face, he replied, "I appreciate it, but we're actually going to go hang out for a while. I have to leave in a couple of days, and I don't know when we'll get to see each other again."

Brooke looked disappointed, but said, "Totally cool. You two have fun. Just be sure to come and say bye before you go, okay?" She batted her eyelashes at him.

Aidan spoke to Riley. "Do you want to unpack now or can you do it later?"

Riley wanted to get out of that room. She had been there all of two minutes and the girliness of it was already stifling. "I can do it later. Will you walk with me over to the music building? I need to pick up some music before class starts."

"You're a musician?" Brooke asked. Riley thought she heard a note of trepidation in her voice.

"I am. Cellist. Performance major." Riley looked at her and smiled with embarrassment. Would this obviously popular girl think that was too geeky?

"Oh!" There was a pause. "Will you be…practicing in here?"

"I don't know. Maybe a little. Why?"

Brooke's smile turned a tad fake. "No reason. It's just…I mean…it's a small room and…you know…noise and stuff."

Riley glanced at Aidan, who shrugged in a "leave me out of this" sort of way. She looked back to Brooke and stated, somewhat defensively, "I'll make sure you're not here. I don't want to be a bother. They have practice rooms at the music building anyway."

Brooke's demeanor changed instantly. "Excellent! Well, anyway. Welcome to Texas and I'll see you guys later!" She looked at Aidan when she said it. "Have fun!"

Riley smiled politely. "Thanks. See ya."

❖

When they were out of the dorm and walking past the enormous gothic-style football stadium toward the music building, Aidan said, "So. She seems…fun."

Riley was trying not to think about it. It was unfair of her to judge someone based solely on a five-minute conversation. She shrugged and simply took in her surroundings as she walked. Students clad in burnt orange and white were everywhere.

"Maybe she'll calm down a little when I'm not there. I can't help that I'm so damn distracting."

When Riley didn't say anything, he playfully bumped her with his hip as they walked up the hill to the school of music. "Come on. You're exactly where you wanted to be. I need you to be happy about this or I'm going to worry my ass off while I'm gone."

Riley turned and smiled at him. "I am, Aidan. I couldn't *be* happier. I mean, look at those trees." She gestured to the gorgeous greenery surrounding them. "It's beautiful here, it's one of the best universities in the nation, and they've accepted me. Me! Little Orphan Nothing without a penny to her name. This is—" Her voice caught in her throat. "This is the best thing that has ever happened to me. I am...*so*...happy."

Aidan smiled and put his arm around her shoulder as they walked. Riley *was* insanely happy, but she would have given anything in the world for Aidan to take this journey with her. Having him constantly by her side had been her only saving grace as they had grown up, and the thought of making such a drastic life change alone terrified her. Still, she knew that they would still have their emails and video chats. They might be few and far between depending on his deployment, but she knew that they would be her lifelines when things got too hard.

❖

That evening Riley took Aidan to the coffee shop where she worked. She hadn't been able to get out of her evening shift, so Aidan was content to spend the four hours keeping her company and working on some of the emails and financial things he had to get done before reporting to his new unit and duty station in Twentynine Palms, California. They would be visiting Sixth Street—the street full of bars, blues joints, and crowds of intoxicated college students—as soon as her shift ended. She had promised, after all.

"So why the name Metro Haus?"

Riley shrugged as she pulled the handle on the espresso machine to make him his macchiato. "I think it's a combination of two other coffee shops that are closed now. That's what I heard anyway. I think the owners are UT alumni who had a fondness for them. I like it, though. It's homey."

After she set the hot mug in front of Aidan she was pulled forcefully into the back room by Koji.

"Riles, who is that gorgeous man you're helping?"

"My brother."

Koji looked genuinely shocked. "He's *your* brother?"

Riley noticed his confused glance at her face and body. "Don't look so surprised. I might get my feelings hurt or something." She glared at him.

"Oh!" He looked embarrassed. "No! I mean—"

"Don't bother." She shook her head. "I already know."

Riley walked back out to where Aidan sat, and she stopped dead in her tracks. Aidan noticed and followed her gaze to the table in the corner.

"Who's that?"

"What?" Riley jumped and looked at him.

"You stopped as if you'd seen a ghost. Who's that girl?"

"No one. A regular."

He turned around again.

"Don't look!"

Too late. The brown-haired girl was looking at them both. She blushed and looked down quickly at her iPad where she pointedly poked at the screen.

Aidan turned back around, a lupine grin on his face.

"You like her."

"What? No! What?"

"Come on, Riley. You have a little bit of color in those cheeks."

"Shut up! No, I don't." She could feel her cheeks getting warmer. Traitors.

To Riley's horror, Koji chose just that moment to invite himself into their conversation. He leaned on the counter and whispered to Aidan conspiratorially. "That girl comes in almost every night that Riley works. Like clockwork. Your sister has an admirer."

"Koji? Are you kidding me right now?" Riley was mortified.

She knew that the boys were just teasing her, but the truth was that she did actually think the girl with the glasses was pretty cute and there was just no way that she was going to let them in on that little secret. They'd be sure to embarrass her even more.

Koji just laughed and motioned to the girl who was now surreptitiously watching them over the rim of her coffee cup. "You guys would make just the cutest little lesbian babies together!"

Riley turned her back to the corner table and pointed her finger in Koji's face. "Don't start. Not now." She brushed past him and said, "Since we're both off the clock now, I *was* going to ask you to come out with us tonight. Do you want to do that or stay here and think of more childish ways to humiliate me?"

She untied her apron, threw it on the counter, and walked out the door. She knew that they would both follow right behind.

❖

"So, Koji. How's my little Riley as a barista?" Aidan asked.

Koji smiled and threw back a shot of tequila. "Not bad. The customers seem to like her."

"You mean the *girls* seem to like her." Aidan giggled at his own joke.

"Guys. I'm right here," Riley said irritably.

Aidan and Koji had decided to spend the evening at an Irish pub adjacent to Sixth Street. Riley could get in without being twenty-one, and Aidan had wanted to hear the live Celtic band. The only problem was that, now that the boys were both drunk, their conversation had turned to her.

"I'm your designated driver, you know. I could just leave your asses here and make you walk if I wanted to," she said in a huff.

"Aw, c'mon, Sis," Aidan said as he put his arm around her. "We're just teasing you. I think it's cute that a chick's into you."

"Can't we talk about something else?" Riley didn't know why she was so annoyed by this subject. Somewhere in the back of her mind, she guessed that it might be because she thought it would be the greatest thing in the world if a cute woman was interested in her, but she didn't want to deal with the disappointment when it turned out to not be true.

"Okay, okay," Aidan said as he moved his arm from her shoulders and took another long drink of his lager. "Koji, what about you? Have you worked at the coffee shop long?"

"About a year. I hadn't been there all that long when Riley started this summer."

"Are you a student at UT?"

Koji made a "sort of" motion with his hand and said, "Used to be. After my junior year, I kind of had a crisis of purpose. I'm taking a year off to figure things out."

Riley hadn't known this. She felt unsociable for never having asked him about it before. "What made you have a crisis of purpose?" she asked.

Koji sipped on his glass of water before answering. "I was a government major on track for pre-law, but then"—he made a snapping motion—"I realized that was what my parents had pushed on me. I mean, nothing's wrong with that and I'm not mad at them or anything, but it's just not something I want to do."

"What do you want to do?" Aidan asked.

"If I knew that, I wouldn't be taking a year off and working at a coffee shop." He smiled.

Aidan nodded. "I understand. I was training to be a mechanic before I decided to join up. It was fine and I liked it, but it just wasn't…enough. If that makes sense."

"It does indeed. I dunno. I think I might actually be leaning toward hospitality at this point."

"Being nice to people?" Aidan asked, brow furrowed.

Riley slapped her forehead.

Koji replied, "Hotel management, catering, restaurant owner, that kind of thing."

"Oooh," he said. "That sounds cool."

"Still thinking about it, but it sounds more like what I'm into at this point. Either way, I've given myself until the spring to make a decision. In the meantime it is my life's goal to make sure Riley doesn't have a moment's peace."

"Thanks. Really," Riley deadpanned.

"I'm glad she has you as a friend." Aidan was serious now. "You seem like a good guy. I was worried about her being too shy to make friends."

"Again. I'm right here. Right. Here." She waved her arms to get their attention.

"Oh, girl, please. You know he just cares about you. Enjoy it. I don't have any siblings, and my parents are too busy traveling around the world with their truckloads of inheritance money to pay me any mind." His face darkened. "I'd give anything for a brother or sister who cared that much about me."

Riley felt abashed. She never questioned Aidan's protectiveness of her. He had every right to worry now that she was on her own for the first time. "I get it. You're right. Just…lay off the teasing. It's embarrassing."

Aidan and Koji grinned with the same Cheshire Cat smile, and Riley knew that would never happen.

CHAPTER EIGHT

What had she gotten herself into? Riley was only two months into her freshman year of college. She was already addicted to coffee and ramen, and she spent every waking hour reading boring textbooks, listening to professors drone on about whatever the hell thing that was ratified in who knows what year during the war of blah-ty blah, writing essays, trying to figure out equations, learning about the history of music, and, as she was currently sight-reading, memorizing and practicing new and particularly difficult cello études for her performance class. This was all on top of practicing her music for the symphony orchestra rehearsals.

Draping herself over her cello, she sighed loudly. She tried to slow her breathing and relax. Panicking about her massive workload wasn't going to help anything.

She jumped as someone tapped on the narrow glass window of the practice room door. Looking up, she saw a familiar face. It was Tori Pearson, the senior violinist who had escorted her in to her audition before the start of the school year. She also just happened to be one of the hottest girls Riley had ever seen. It was always difficult keeping her eyes off her during their orchestra rehearsals.

Tori had jet-black hair that she wore in a kind of pixie-meets-punk short cut where the bangs draped down over her right eye. She was petite, but fit, and her black skinny jeans rode so low on her hips that Riley's eyes were inadvertently drawn to the pale skin that showed under the too small vintage Flogging Molly T-shirt she wore.

Riley jumped again as Tori's second knock brought her back to her senses. She looked from Tori's stomach to her eyes guiltily and saw a hint of a smile on her face. Embarrassed, Riley set her cello down and opened the door. "Sorry. I'm kind of out of it. I haven't slept much lately."

Tori smiled. "No worries. Riley, right?"

"Yeah. Riley." She knew her name!

"I'm just clearing out the practice rooms. The building closes in thirty minutes."

"Okay." Riley didn't want her to leave now that she had the opportunity to talk to her, so she scrambled for something to say. "Do you work here too? I mean, in addition to going to school?"

Tori nodded. "Yep. It feels like I should just set up an apartment in one of these." She gestured to the small practice room. "I'm here way more than I'm at home. Anyway, it's as good a job as any. It saves me time and money commuting between class and work. Just keep them both in the same place!"

Riley stood in silence. Tori intimidated her. Not only was she older and mind-numbingly cute, but she was also one of the best violin performance students at the university.

Tori raised her eyebrows as the silence stretched on and pursed her lips in an expectant smile. "Soooo…"

Riley shook herself. "Oh! Yeah. Sorry. I'll pack up. I don't think I can keep my eyes open any longer anyway." She berated herself for making such an awful impression.

"Cool. See ya."

"See ya."

She watched Tori walk down the hallway and peer into the other practice rooms before turning around a corner and out of sight.

"Well, that was lovely," Riley said with irritation as she put her cello into its case and angrily stuffed her sheet music inside. "The witty and charming conversationalist Riley Michelle Gordon strikes again."

❖

She entered her dorm room as silently as she could in case Brooke was trying to sleep, but found, not for the first time, that her roommate was gone. It seemed that as the days passed, Brooke was spending more and more nights out late going to parties or doing God knows what until well past midnight. Riley couldn't fathom having time for schoolwork with the kind of party habits that Brooke seemed to have. Still, she didn't mind. Brooke probably already thought she was mentally unstable after all the times Riley had woken her up screaming from nightmares of cigarette burns and belt beatings. Those were always fun.

She tucked her cello and backpack neatly in the corner, changed into her pajamas, and then double-checked her schedule for the next day. Calculus, Orchestra, Music Theory, and Astronomy. Riley sighed as she set the alarm on her iPhone and crawled under the covers. Twelve thirty-five a.m. She could still get six and a half hours of sleep. At least it was better than the four she got last night.

❖

Riley was startled awake by the slamming of her dorm room door. It didn't take long for her head to clear enough to know that she was pissed off. The last thing she needed once she had finally fallen asleep was a rude roommate who didn't know the definition of consideration. She was about to give Brooke a piece of her mind when she heard a soft giggle, some stumbling into the wall, and then the low voice of a man.

You have got to be effing kidding me. Riley stayed perfectly still on her side facing the wall.

"What about her?"

Brooke's voice, her words slurred, whispered, "Don't worry. She sleeps like a log…unless she has a nightmare freak-out. She never notices when I come in late."

Riley's eyebrows creased in anger. *Just because I don't yell at you every time you wake me up doesn't mean that I don't notice.*

How had Brooke snuck a guy into the room in the first place? Should she say something to them?

She heard them move to Brooke's bed on the other side of the room and... *Oh God.*

Soft rustling and kissing noises were followed by the distinct sound of a zipper being lowered.

Riley was mortified. She didn't know what to do. She wanted to protest, but couldn't find the courage. Embarrassment and horror paralyzed her.

The étude she had been learning started playing in her head. She turned the mental volume up as loud as it would go, but it couldn't drown out the awful sounds. It looked like it was going to be another sleepless night.

❖

"Riley."

Riley sat up quickly and blinked, a drool mark left on the table where she had fallen asleep. "Wha?"

Tori laughed. "You were out like a light."

"What time is it?"

"Five thirty. Your theory class ended an hour and a half ago."

"Shit!" She had only wanted to rest her head for a few minutes after class before having to go to the coffee shop. "I'm late for work."

"Where do you work?"

Riley started shoving her paperwork back into her backpack. "Metro Haus."

"Oh yeah, I know that place. Good coffee cake."

Riley nodded as she zipped her bag and stood to leave.

"I'm headed that direction. Need a ride?"

Riley stopped and stared. Her brain was still foggy from having been woken from a dead sleep, but a small surge of nervous adrenaline brought her back to her senses. "Uh. Yeah. Sure. If… that's okay. If it's not too much trouble."

Tori smiled and motioned with her head to follow. "Not a problem at all. I only live a few blocks from there. It's on my way."

Riley followed gratefully. "I can't believe I crashed like that. Thanks for waking me."

"I almost didn't. You looked like you needed the rest."

"I did. I *do*, but you know, work and stuff."

Tori glanced at her as they walked. "You work too hard, you know."

Riley shook her head. "Can't get what you want unless you work for it."

"I suppose that's the way we should all think. I think it's easier when college is new. Not as many distractions."

Riley thought about Brooke. She was only one year older, and she had more distractions than cat at a laser show with a free catnip buffet. "It's not that I don't *want* distractions. I just don't want anything to interfere with what I'm trying to accomplish. I was given a scholarship, and I don't want to let people down. Myself included."

Tori nodded. "I get that. I think it's really admirable actually."

Riley felt a twinge of heat in her cheeks.

"But I think you're working too hard anyway. I always see you in here, practicing, studying…sleeping." She nudged Riley with her elbow. "Look, some of the grad students are throwing a party this Saturday. Annual midterm thing. Why don't you come? It's going to be pretty epic. It's at the Iota house."

Riley almost stopped walking. She had never been invited to a party before. Not a real one anyway. She'd been invited to hang out with people, and she'd been to birthday parties, but she imagined that this would be a *real* party. One like she had seen in the movies. She thrilled to the possibility of being a regular person for once. Not some angry, work-obsessed shut-in. She was in college. This was supposed to be the best time of her life.

"Yeah. Yeah, I think I will. Sounds fun."

Tori clapped her on the back. "Yay! Proud of you. I'll loosen you up yet."

This time Riley couldn't hide her blush.

❖

"You're wearing *that*?" Brooke asked that Saturday night as she got ready for her own outing.

Riley regretted telling her about the party. She looked at herself in the mirror. What was wrong with jeans and a Texas School of Music T-shirt? It was a party thrown by music majors, after all.

"You'll never get laid wearing something like that."

Riley spluttered, "What? I'm not…I don't want…no! I mean…I don't—"

"Oh, calm down." Brooke laughed. "But seriously, why not sex up the outfit a bit? It's your first college party, right?"

Riley nodded, suddenly nervous.

"Here, we're about the same size. At least borrow one of my tops and let me do your makeup."

Riley looked at her hesitantly. She couldn't fathom wearing the kind of revealing clothes Brooke wore or plastering on that many pounds of makeup.

Brooke held up her hands placatingly. "I won't overdo it, I promise."

Riley decided to submit. This was one of the first times Brooke had actually been nice to her. Maybe this would help thaw their somewhat icy relationship.

Only thirty minutes later, Riley looked at herself in the mirror again and barely recognized the young woman who stared back. Brooke had stayed true to her word and had managed to simply accentuate her features without making her look too "made up." Brooke had also tamed her wavy red hair with the help of a lot of mousse. The top that Brooke gave her to wear was a fitted black designer blouse that accentuated her curves nicely. She felt a little odd and exposed in the attire, but had to admit that she did look a bit more attractive. She was also thankful for the long sleeves as they covered the small burn scars on her arms.

She thought about Tori checking her out, and a smile passed over her lips.

Brooke noticed and smiled. "Better, right?"

Riley nodded. "Better. Thank you."

"Good. Now go and have fun." She opened the doom room door to leave, but turned before walking out. "Oh, and you might want to find someone to crash with tonight. This room will be... busy."

As the door clicked shut, Riley sighed with frustration. Of course she had only offered to help so that she could get Riley preoccupied with her own extracurricular activity. Her selfishness knew no bounds.

❖

Riley had never been to the Iota house on fraternity row, but she knew immediately that she was in the right place. The music blared from the open doors and windows and, even though the night was still young, she had to step over frat guys in unintentionally matching white Texas T-shirts and khaki cargo shorts, sprawled out drunk on the front lawn.

Yep. Just like the movies.

As she entered, she saw a large group of students in various stages of undress gathered around a large graduate student she recognized as one of the symphony orchestra's tuba players being held up by his friends. It was the first time she had seen someone do a keg stand, and the point of it completely eluded her. This didn't seem to be the case with the rest of the students, though, as they cheered and goaded him on as if he were competing for an Olympic medal.

"Hey! Riley!" A barely discernible voice fought past the wall of sound to Riley's already overwhelmed ears.

She turned and saw Tori waving her over from the landing at the top of the stairs. "Come up!"

Riley was relieved to see her. She wasn't one to strike up conversations with random strangers, much less ones that appeared to be stoned or hammered or both. She grabbed an empty blue Solo cup from the stack next to the conveniently placed keg in the foyer, filled it to the top with a pale and watery lager, and climbed the stairs to meet Tori.

The landing was as full of people as the downstairs area, but the music was a fraction quieter. Tori led her through the people milling about and motioned for her to go into the room at the end of the hall. When she did so, Riley noticed that it was a game room complete with dart board, pool table, and a custom-made Longhorn beer pong table. Most of the room's occupants surrounded it, Solo cups full of beer in hand, laughing when one of their buddies missed a shot. At least conversation would be somewhat possible in this room.

Riley followed Tori to a group of students she knew from class and orchestra. She was relieved to know that she wasn't going to be surrounded by total strangers all night.

"See, guys? Told you she would come. This is Riley Gordon, the freshman who *nailed* her audition. I mean, hardcore nailed it. Keep an eye on her. She's the best I've heard in a long time." Tori put her arm around Riley's shoulders as the other students moved over to make a place for them on the collection of couches in the corner of the room.

Riley tried to stifle the shiver that had run through her body at Tori's friendly, but physical gesture. She attempted to cover it up by raising her hand in a slight wave to the group. "Hey."

They waved back, and Tori pulled her down to join her on the vacated section of couch. Tori removed her arm from Riley's shoulders, and Riley felt a pang of disappointment at the loss of contact.

A loud cheer erupted from the beer pong table so Riley missed what the dark-haired saxophone player said, but she gathered from the following remarks by the group that she had been complaining about a globally disliked music composition professor.

"Watch out, Riley," the dark-haired girl said, "you'll have to take his class in two years. He's a nightmare. It doesn't matter how good your compositions are. He'll rip them apart."

Tori replied, "You know it's only because he lost that best film score Oscar to a former student of his, right? That's the only reason he gave up composing for film. He doesn't want to compete with us."

A baritone player spoke up. "Maybe he'll retire soon. He's got to be about a hundred and thirty by now."

"Ain't tenure a bitch?" the saxophonist responded.

"Have you written much?"

Riley turned to the speaker, a violinist named Alan who looked surprisingly like a young Marlon Brando.

Riley shook her head. "Nothing yet. Every time I try to write my own music it comes out as something that's already been done. I just don't think that will ever be my strength. I'd rather play anyway. That's what I love. I don't care who wrote the music. I just want to be the one bringing the sounds to life and make people feel it."

A few of the musicians in the group nodded in agreement as another loud cheer threatened to drown out their conversation.

Tori turned her head to look at her. "I think a lot of music students, this group excepted, of course"—she motioned to the students on the couch—"sometimes forget about that. There are a lot of politics in the music business, and so many people want to be on top. Like with anything I guess. But sometimes they forget to go back to the basics and play or compose or conduct or whatever, for the pure love of it."

She placed a warm hand on Riley's knee. Riley embarrassed herself by jumping a little, but Tori didn't seem to notice and gave her knee a squeeze. "Don't ever lose that, okay?"

Riley couldn't speak so she just nodded, and the conversation turned to other topics like school rivalries, irritation with the constant construction around campus, and some horrible happenings in some Third World country. Riley liked this group. She didn't have to say much, but still felt welcome and like an equal, even though she was several years younger than most of them. They kept each other's beer cups full all night with designated keg runs, and Riley lost herself in the buzz of alcohol, thumping rhythm, and good conversation. The best part, though, was that Tori hadn't moved her hand, and she didn't until they all left the frat house together in the early morning hours.

❖

Riley had never watched the sun rise. Not really. She had seen the light change from the window in the Home, she had gone to early morning orchestra rehearsals as the sun lit up the sky on dark winter mornings, but she had never really sat and watched the sun as it gradually painted its dark canvas with muted reds and pinks, then transformed to deep oranges, and then finally settled on a brilliant Texas blue.

This is what she saw for the first time as she sat on a lookout called Mount Bonnell, and she was awed by it.

"Nice, huh?" Tori asked, her head leaning sleepily on Riley's shoulder.

"Beautiful," Riley responded, unable to take her eyes off the sky, the vista of low hills, expensive homes, and the sparkling lake below her.

Tori sat up and turned Riley's face toward her own with the calloused, yet smooth fingers of a string player. She placed a soft, yet lingering kiss on her lips and then reclined to rest on her elbows, legs stretched out and eyes shut to enjoy the growing sunlight on her beautiful face.

Riley sat stunned. She couldn't move. Had that just happened? Her face was still turned, now staring at the empty space where Tori had been. It wasn't until she remembered the other four people with them that she stiffly turned to look back at the view. She didn't really see it this time, though. Every nerve in her body seemed to be routed through her lips. She could still feel Tori on them and she could think about nothing else.

"All right," Alan said loudly, thoroughly breaking the spell. "Who's up for pancakes at Kerbey Lane?"

There were murmurs of general approval, and their small group stood up slowly, the effects of an entire night and morning's worth of drinking starting to take their toll.

Riley stood and joined them, and when she looked at Tori she saw nothing different in her eyes. Had she imagined it? Did Tori not realize how much that kiss had meant to her?

Their eyes met, and Tori smiled, but looked apologetic. "Don't worry. The hangover will wear off. Nothing a little hair of the dog and buttermilk pancakes can't cure."

Hangover? Hair of the...What about the kiss? What did it mean?

"Okay," was all she could say. What she meant was, *Please kiss me again. Kiss me and don't ever stop.*

❖

Aidan,

Sorry I'm just now getting around to emailing you back. School has been crazy. I'm loving it, so don't even start your worrying again, but it is a lot of work. I don't think I sleep enough. Or at all. Is it normal to see unicorns riding unicycles on the West Mall? Nah, didn't think so either.

Have you settled in to your new unit? Do you mind still being in California? I hope they give you time off to go to the beach and stuff. I know you must be enjoying the "scenery." Yes, I'm talking about all the hot California girls with big fake boobs and nonexistent bikinis. Those exist in real life and not just on reality TV, right?

I do need your help, though. Aidan...I was kissed this morning. Like, a for reals kiss from that senior student you thought was hot at my audition. Her name is Tori and she's...I dunno. I don't know if we're friends or if she actually likes me or what. I have no experience with this stuff. All I know is that I think she's just about the hottest, coolest person I've ever met. And those people don't usually like me. What do you think? God, I hope she likes me. Why would she kiss me if she didn't? Did she feel sorry for me? Was it because she was still drunk? Do you think someone dared her to do it? She didn't say anything about it afterward; just went on as usual and made it seem like it never happened. I just don't know. Maybe I should forget about it. Should I? What if I pretend that it didn't mean anything and she's just waiting for me to tell her I like her? What if I tell her I like her and it's all been a joke or a big mistake? Help! I'm so not good at this!

Anyway, sorry to bother you. I know you're probably busy doing...whatever you do out there...blowing shit up or something. Thanks for the pics. You guys look great, and it's nice to be able to match names with faces. Keep 'em coming!

Love you!

Riley

❖

Sis,

Okay, first of all, our base in Twentynine Palms is in the frickin' desert. The ocean is like, four hours from here or something, so no, I haven't been living it up surfer-style. There's not much "scenery," as you put it, either. We head down into Palm Springs on our leave sometimes, but that mainly makes Craig happy because it's such a gay Mecca. Growing up in Whitehill, I never thought I'd ever go to so many gay bars. But just so you know, even though I don't swing that way, I'm still a hit with the dudes. It's good for my ego. Or would you say it's bad since my ego is so huge to begin with? We have fun, though, and I will say that gay guys often bring their straight girl friends to the bars so I guarantee you I haven't been lonely! Ha! I can see your "ew" face from here.

But seriously, I'm really glad that we beat the odds and Craig, Rafael, and I got stationed in the same platoon. It's kind of rare to stick with the same guys from boot camp. Now that we're together we'll all be deployed together too. That will make it a hell of a lot easier to go overseas. And no, we don't know where we're going yet. We'll be here until after Christmas for sure. There are a lot of us new guys in the unit so they have to make sure we know what we're doing.

The LAV training really is great. Of course, we still spend a lot of time working on the vehicles, cleaning and replacing parts, repairing stuff, etc., but when we get to work on maneuvers, tactics, and yes, blowing shit up, it's all worth it. I kind of wish you could come out and see everything, but you'd probably hate it. I'll send some more pics of us in the LAVs in my next email.

Okay. Now to the fun stuff. THAT HOT PUNK CHICK KISSED YOU?! God DAMN I'm jealous. But on the other hand...nice goin'! You know? I think it must run in the family. You're just a late bloomer.

I know, I know. Stop f-in' around. Listen, I think you're majorly overthinking this. Maybe she likes you (as if she couldn't). Maybe she was just lost in the moment. I know it was huge for you because it was your first kiss (as far as I know), but for most people it's not that big a deal. I kiss plenty of girls, and I guaran-damn-tee you that I'm not out to marry a one of them. You're just a different kind of girl. Old-fashioned. Maybe she doesn't know that. I don't know. I can't really help other than to tell you that if you feel like she's interested, go for it. It'd be good for you to come out of that thick shell for once. Of course, if she hurts you I'll be down there in a second to show her how protective big brothers can be.

Anyway, try not to do that thing you do, where you overanalyze everything until there's no meaning left, and just take things as they come. If she wants to hook up, enjoy it. If you're not into that—like I am—and you want something with more meaning, then let her know. Never

ever do anything that makes you uncomfortable, always be true to your own feelings, and if you need anything at all you know that I'm here.

Be safe, have fun, enjoy yourself, and keep working hard like I know you do.

Proud of you, Nugget.

Aidan

CHAPTER NINE

O ver the next month, Riley started hanging out with Tori more
often, practicing their symphony music together, listening
to old recordings of famous conductors and orchestras, or simply
finding nap space on one of the music building's many couches,
but the subject of the kiss hadn't come up even in awkward glances
or subtle innuendos. It was like Riley had dreamt it. She enjoyed
her new friend, but every time she looked at her she thought about
the way her lips had felt, and she wanted more than anything to
slam her against the wall of an empty practice room to see what real
kissing could feel like. It made being around her difficult. Tori never
seemed to notice, though, and if she did, she never let on. She was
always her cool, chill self, and that, in itself, was refreshing.

Riley needed a calming influence in her life. She felt
overwhelmed so often with her workload she thought she might fail,
and that, in turn, made her angry with herself a good portion of the
time. She wouldn't fail. She couldn't. She had a goal set for herself
and, by God, she *would* succeed.

Lost in her thoughts, she opened the door to her dorm room to
find the usually pristine side that belonged to Brooke in shambles.
She saw a bra and a notebook fly past the wall and walked in to see
Brooke, completely in tears, tearing through all the belongings in
her drawers.

"What's going on? What's wrong?" Riley asked worriedly.

Brooke turned her head, and black streams of mascara lined
her usually flawless face. "My necklace!" She choked back a sob.

"The diamond pendant from my necklace is missing!" She held up a broken gold chain.

Riley had never seen her like this and didn't quite know what to do. "How big is it? I can help you look."

Brooke turned back to the destruction of her well-organized underwear drawer. "It was my grandmother's! She gave it to me when I came to college. It's been in the family for ages!"

Riley put her backpack on the bed, got on her hands and knees, and started looking on the floor. Brooke continued to cry and slammed the drawer shut.

"They're gonna *kill* me."

"When was the last time you saw it?"

Brooke grabbed a tissue and blew her nose before hiccupping, "Two nights ago. I wore it on a date with Chad."

Ah. Chad. Riley knew *way* too much about him from his few nighttime visits to their room.

"Did you…take it off…I mean…maybe it broke when you guys…" Riley didn't want to say it.

Brooke sat on her bed in a slump. "I don't know. I mean, it *has* to be here. I found the chain on the floor next to the bed." She pointed at her feet.

Riley got up from her knees and patted Brooke's shoulder awkwardly. "I'm sure it's here somewhere. Don't worry about it now. Things usually turn up when we're not looking for them anyway."

Brooke nodded and lay down onto her purple pillow. She sniffed pathetically. "Will you get me a chocolate milk from downstairs? It makes me feel better when I'm upset."

Riley paused. "Yeah. Sure."

She waited for an offer of money to pay for it, but it never came so she turned to leave.

"And popcorn." Brooke called after her.

Riley's brow creased. Popcorn, *please.*

"And some M&Ms! No peanuts!"

Riley heard this just as the door shut. She pulled out her wallet and found the last ten-dollar bill from her recent paycheck. She had just spent the rest of her money on a new box of rosin for her bow and a few new strings. She wouldn't get paid again for another two weeks.

She shook her head. She was sorry that Brooke had lost something that meant so much to her, but it was getting harder and harder to handle her constant lack of consideration. She couldn't get a full night's sleep when she needed it the most because of Brooke's late-night arrivals and rendezvous, she was rarely paid back for shared necessities, and Brooke had yet to say please or thank you for anything. Riley didn't know how much more she could take. She knew she should say something, but her temper always made her terrible at confrontation. She could never discuss things that bothered her calmly and rationally. Her anger always won out, and she usually just spluttered and ended up saying something stupid or contrary like, "Nuh-uh! *You* suck."

Riley sighed as the elevator descended to the ground floor where the dorm's café/convenience store was located. She hated this kind of stuff. Why couldn't people just treat each other nicely? Still, something had to be done. Not right now, of course. She didn't want to kick Brooke while she was down. But soon.

❖

That night, she expressed her frustrations to Koji.

"Girl, your roommate sucks. You need to put the kibosh on that shit before it gets any worse. She takes advantage of you and you're being way too doormat-y about it. Doesn't it piss you off?"

"Yes!" Riley slammed the coffee cup she had been cleaning on the counter by the sink. "I just…I dunno. I hate confrontation. I'm not good at it."

Koji jauntily put his hands on his hips. "You need to promise me you're going to tell that rude bitch where to stick it."

Riley looked at him with a stony expression and said, "Stick it, Koji?

"Yes. *Stick. It.* As in, 'Hey, rude bitch who treats me like shit, you may go and stick any appendage of your choosing into an orifice conveniently also of your choosing so long as it is dark, musty, and putrid.'"

"You're disgusting, Koji."

He winked at her and said, "Proudly so. But I have something that will make you feel better."

"What?"

He motioned behind her and said, "Customer for you at the register."

He then spun her around by the shoulders and gave her a little shove straight at the girl standing there waiting to place an order.

It was the cute geeky girl with glasses who usually sat in the corner. Riley immediately flushed. Koji hadn't been at all subtle and Riley tried to gain her balance with some semblance of grace.

The girl smiled shyly and fidgeted.

"H-Hi. What can I get ya?" Riley asked, trying to be cool.

"Café mocha, please."

"Sure. Just a sec."

Riley turned to make the drink, and Koji followed her while whispering in her ear, "Come on. She obviously wants to talk to you. Say something to her!"

"Shut up, Koji!" she said in a hiss. She knew that the girl must be watching their overt whispering. "She just asked for a drink! What am I supposed to say?"

"I don't know! Be sociable or something." He glanced behind him, caught the girl looking, and wiggled his fingers at her in a wave. "She has history books with her. Say something about that. You like history. She likes history…unless she's just taking the regular prerequisite history classes, but I don't think so. I'm getting a total history buff vibe."

"How do you know *I* like history?"

"I can tell. You're a nerd like her. Nerds like history. Just say something to her!"

The hisses of their whispering sounded as loud as shouts to Riley's ears. "For the love of all that is holy, just gimme a minute!"

She shoved him to the side as she mixed the coffee into the chocolate syrup she had poured. She then heard something that made her stop mid-stir.

"Hey! What's your name again? We see you in here all the time so it seems like we should know it by now. I'm Koji, by the way." He was putting on his friendliest flirt voice that he usually used with the cute frat boys.

"Beth," she said quietly.

"Hey, Riley!" Koji called out much louder than was necessary considering their distance. "This is Beth. Your customer. Just so you know." He then turned back to the girl. "Beth, this is Riley, *your* barista."

She was glad her back was turned because her face was so hot she knew that it must be beet red. "*Got it. Thank you*," she said through gritted teeth.

She heard him say, "She'll be right over with your coffee."

Clenching her jaw, she finished the drink and made a mental note to murder Koji as soon as she got off her shift. Still, she was curious about the girl who always sat in the corner. She saw her at least once a week, after all. Maybe it was time to talk to her. At least as a friendly customer service thing, she rationalized.

She turned and placed the mocha in front of the young woman. "Beth?"

Beth smiled, and Riley noticed, for the first time, her brilliant green eyes. The glasses she wore didn't take away from their sparkle at all. Riley was caught off guard for a moment.

"Yes, thank you." She lifted the cup to her lips and sipped the steaming liquid.

Riley continued to stare at those amazing eyes. She couldn't help it. When Beth put the cup down, Riley noticed that a thin line of whipped cream traced her top lip.

Beth smiled and said, "This is really good."

Riley grinned. "Thanks."

Beth didn't seem to notice the whipped cream so Riley made a small movement, pointing at her own lip. "You have a bit of… yeah."

Beth's eyes widened and she grabbed a napkin to wipe her mouth. She lowered her eyes with obvious chagrin as her cheeks flushed pink. "Thanks," she said quietly.

Great. Now Riley had embarrassed her. *Say something, idiot,* Riley admonished herself.

"So. You study history? I like…history stuff."

Lame lame lame.

Beth looked up gratefully. "Yeah. History major."

"What's your favorite…time period…to study?"

Beth brightened considerably. Riley knew she had hit on the right subject. How did Koji know these things? "It's not my favorite *time* to study. It's my favorite *place.*"

"Place? Like, French history or something?"

She shook her head. "No. Ocean."

"The history of the ocean?" Riley was confused.

"Maritime archaeology. Sunken ships. Lost civilizations."

"Oh! Like *Titanic* and Atlantis."

Beth nodded enthusiastically. "Exactly! Except there's so much more to it, and honestly, most of it isn't big and exciting. The smallest fragment of pottery or the rustiest nail can tell us so much about the civilization that created it. And the fact that these things have been hidden from us for centuries and that we're only now technologically advanced enough to discover them is just so exciting."

Riley noticed how her eyes lit up when she spoke about the subject. "That sounds cool. I've always wanted to go to the ocean."

Beth looked surprised. "You've never been?"

Riley shook her head. "Nope. Landlocked near San Antonio most of my life."

"That's sad."

"Well, I suppose I don't really know what I'm missing, so I can't be too sad, right?" Riley smiled.

"You should go. I should—" She cut off her sentence abruptly. Riley felt that she had been about to invite her to do something. "I mean, I grew up by the ocean. I could…I dunno. Tell you about it sometime. Or something." She had grown quiet and shy again.

Riley smiled. Was this girl wanting to get to know her better? Was this an opening? God, she was bad at reading people.

"I'd like that."

They smiled in awkward silence for a moment before Riley remembered to look at her watch. "Eleven o'clock. Shift's over. Home time."

Beth looked disappointed, but tried in vain to hide it. "Okay. Have a good night. Thanks again for the coffee."

Riley smiled and gestured to the barista bar behind her. "That's what we're here for."

She waved and walked to the back where she saw Koji duck back behind the door. He had been watching the whole interaction.

"Okay, what the *hell?*" Riley asked as she shut the door behind her.

"What? I thought you needed a little help." He shrugged.

"Help with what? Making a mocha?"

"Oh, don't play stupid. That girl has been coming here to see you almost every night you work for months and you're both too shy to talk to the other. It was getting painful to watch. Someone had to do something."

"Maybe she just likes our coffee." She poked Koji in the stomach.

He scoffed. "I don't know why you're so upset. She's cute. Why not get to know her?"

Riley leaned against a cabinet and shrugged. "I dunno. I'm not…interested…right now, I guess." Her thoughts turned to her confused feelings about Tori. "There's this other girl."

Koji gasped. "You've never said anything! Oh my God, spill it!"

Riley rolled her eyes. "Now you know why I never said anything. And besides, there's nothing to tell. She's a senior violin performance major, she's insanely cute, and she intimidates the hell out of me with her impossible coolness."

"Does she know you like her? Does she like you?"

Riley turned to hang her apron on the designated wall peg and shrugged. "She's hard to read. I think she likes me as a friend, but I can't tell if there's anything more."

Koji tsked. "Poor Beth."

"Who? Her?" Riley motioned to the main room of the coffee shop.

"Yeah, her!"

"Koji, I've spoken like four sentences to her."

"All I'm saying is that she *isn't* hard to read. It's my professional opinion that you should give her a chance."

Riley put her hands on her hips in exasperation. "Professional what?"

Koji smiled. "Professional, irresistible, gay Lothario."

"Good night, Mr. Drama."

Riley walked out of the shop through the back door, her thoughts a jumble of questions and insecurities. Surely Koji was exaggerating about Beth's interest in her.

What was so special about Riley Gordon? She wasn't a sexy athlete, her looks were girl-next-door at best, and there wasn't much at all about her that she thought anyone would find in the least bit interesting. Still, a small flutter of…was it hope? Or pleasure? Tiny beats of butterfly wings tickled her stomach and she grinned to herself as she walked back to her dorm.

❖

The next morning, Riley woke to a text from Tori. Riley checked the clock on her phone and sighed. It was the first morning she could have slept in all week. Brooke was staying at Chad's and, although she normally worked on Saturdays, she had the day off since the coffee shop was booked for the day for an independent film shoot. She opened the message.

Sorry so early, but the quartet I play in is down a cellist (stomach flu). We're playing a paid gig tonight at a wedding and are desperate. Practice in an hour in the big room. Can you help us out? I'll owe you big time!

Riley blinked the sleep away from her eyes and sat up. She looked at the stack of books on her nightstand. Books that were required reading for her English class on Monday. *Oh, what the hell.* Maybe it would be worth it to have Tori owe her…something.

Sure. Be there in an hour, she texted back.

OMG, thank you! Ur the best!

Riley grinned and got up to get dressed.

❖

The music the quartet would be playing wasn't too difficult. Riley did struggle to fit in with the more seasoned musicians who all knew their parts by memory, though. She tried to ignore the irritated glances thrown her way by the second violin player. He obviously wasn't impressed with her ability to sight-read and play professionally on short-term notice. Tori tried to smooth things over, though. It was either Riley or no cello at all. No one else they had asked had responded.

"I think that's enough, guys," the viola player said after three hours. He was one of the nice ones Riley had met at the party. "We're just going to wear ourselves out."

Riley stayed silent.

"You're right. This is as good as it's going to get. No one listens to us at these things anyway," Tori offered, trying to be helpful. "Riley, you've done great. Don't be nervous."

It must've shown.

Riley just nodded and put her cello back in its case. She realized as she zipped the cover closed that she had forgotten one important question. "What am I supposed to wear?"

Tori smiled as she opened the door to leave. "Formal wear. We're all in black, but it can be a dress or a nice suit. I go for the suit myself. Meet at six tonight in the Balcones Country Club main ballroom."

Riley tried not to panic. She didn't have many nice outfits, much less a formal black one. She nodded and waved good-bye, but as soon as Tori and her friends left the room, she called Koji. When he answered all she could say was, "Shopping emergency! I need your help!"

His voice sounded appalled on the other end of the line. "What makes you think that just because I'm gay I'm a fashionista?"

Riley said nothing.

"Just because I *am* a fashionista doesn't mean that you have to assume it." He laughed. "Okay. What do you need and when?"

"Black formal suit by six. Five, really."

"Oh, snap. Meet me at the Barton Creek mall in forty-five."

"Thanks, Koji." She hung up the phone and ran as fast as she could carrying a giant cello case back to her dorm to put the cello up and grab her car keys.

When she arrived in the mall's parking lot she texted Koji, hoping that he wouldn't be late to meet her like he was late to work almost every night.

Here. Where r u?

Banana Republic. U won't believe the amazing saleswoman I found to help.

Cool. Be there in a sec.

She looked at her watch. Two o'clock. She had plenty of time.

She entered the mall and checked the directory to find the Banana Republic. It was just around the corner. She made her way over, mulling her finances over in her head. She would have to put the suit on her joint credit card because she only had a few dollars to her name. If she was lucky, she would just break even with the money she earned playing at the wedding.

She entered the store and found Koji in the sale area at the back of the store.

"Hey. Thanks for meeting me on such short notice," Riley said, giving him a hug.

"No worries. You never have to twist my arm to go shopping.

And look"—he held out a black suit jacket and matching pants—
"I already found a nice-looking suit for you in your size and the
saleswoman is in the back checking for a white shirt."

"How do you know my size?" Riley asked, reaching for the
jacket.

"Natural gift. Some people are a good judge of character; I'm a
good judge of size and age. I could be a carny."

Riley turned the price tag to face her. "A hundred and thirty
dollars! Just for the jacket? Koji, I can't afford that!"

Koji's face fell. "But it's on sale. It was originally two hundred
and seventy-five."

Riley felt ashamed. "I mean, it's just that I don't have that kind
of money. I was thinking that I would spend fifty dollars max. Isn't
there anywhere cheaper?"

Koji shrugged. "Yeah, I guess. I just automatically go to places
that have...you know...good things. I'm sorry. I didn't think."

"If it helps, you can use my employee discount." The voice
came from behind them.

Riley turned to see Beth from the coffee shop smiling and
holding a folded white button-up shirt.

Koji elbowed Riley in the ribs. "See? I told you I found a nice
saleswoman for you."

"Oh!" Riley smiled with embarrassment. "I didn't know you
worked here. Did you?" she asked Koji.

"Nope. For reals!" he said when Riley looked at him skeptically.

"I just started last week, actually," Beth said. "Needed some
extra money for school and a pretty hardcore coffee habit I've
picked up. But yeah, I have an employee discount if that helps." She
smiled sincerely.

Riley couldn't believe how nice this girl who she had just met
was being. "Thank you! I mean, I still don't think...I don't know if
I can afford it even then, but..."

Koji interjected, "Don't you need a nice formal outfit for your
orchestra concerts?"

Riley nodded. "I was going to pick up something secondhand."
She immediately regretted saying that out loud.

He shook his head. "No. You need something nice that's yours and that will last you a long time. You need this." He held up the suit. "I'll even donate to the cause. In exchange for you working a couple of my shifts, of course."

Riley smiled. Maybe he was right. She did need something nice to wear after all. And with friends as generous as this, how could she possibly say no?

"Okay. But I really can't thank you guys enough."

The two stood side by side and smiled. Beth said, "Koji told me that this is for a quartet or something and that you play cello. I'd love to hear you play sometime."

Riley was happy to do something for Beth in exchange for her generosity. "You name the time and place and I'll be there."

Beth flushed and handed the shirt to Riley to try on.

❖

After she had paid for her suit and was leaving the store, Beth stopped her. She stumbled over her next words apprehensively. "Will you be at Metro Haus tomorrow? I mean, I hope you don't mind my asking."

"I don't and I will be. Eleven a.m. to six."

"Okay. I might see you there then. I need a caffeine fix when I study Ancient Roman Civ. So…yeah. Just wondering."

Riley smiled. She wasn't used to people being interested in her whereabouts or interests at all. "I'll have your mocha ready. On the house. I'll even throw in my favorite apple fritter. Thank you again for helping me out with this. It really means a lot."

"Just have a great show tonight. Or wedding. Or whatever. Break a leg I guess I'm supposed to say."

"Maybe it should be break a string," Riley offered as Koji snorted. She threw a *shut up* glance his way. "Anyway, I have to get ready. Thanks again and I'll see you tomorrow. It'll be nice to have you there. The day shift is boring."

Beth's face lit up as she waved good-bye.

They left the store and Koji burst out laughing.

"What?"

"Oh, girl, she has it *bad* for you. And you like her back." He poked her in the ribs.

"What? No! Koji, she was just being nice. I'm just being appreciative."

He shook his head. "I know flirting when I see it, and *you*"—he wagged his finger at her—"were flirting."

"Was not!"

"Were too."

"I don't even know *how* to flirt."

Koji put on a high-pitched voice that was supposedly an imitation of Riley. "I'll have your mocha ready. And an apple fritter. And my phone number. And I'm sooo glad you'll be there tomorrow! I do miss you so when you're gone! Every day of work without you there I feel a giant hole eating away at my soul."

"Yeah. That's exactly what I sound like and exactly what I said. Funny *and* an impressionist? How can you be this good at so many things?" Riley said sarcastically.

"Mom always said I was special."

"She got *that* right."

❖

The wedding performance went off without a hitch, and even the second violin player congratulated her before they said good-bye to each other in the parking lot.

"I still don't know how to thank you for doing this on such short notice, Riley," Tori said sincerely.

Riley decided that it was better to not offer up alternative payment suggestions.

"I enjoyed it. I've never played in a quartet before. I'm sorry I messed up that one line. I misread the repeat."

Tori shook her head. "No one would notice that except you. You found your place again really fast. Anyway, thanks again." Tori turned to her car before remembering something and saying, "A few of us are going to the staged concert version of *Candide* on Tuesday night if you want to join. There's a guest tenor in it who's supposed to be really good."

"I don't think I can. Money's a bit tight." She smiled apologetically.

"Psh. Don't worry about that. I'll cover you as an extra thanks for tonight. We'd love to have you there."

Riley smiled. "Yeah. Okay. Sounds fun."

"Perfect! We're all meeting at the music building at six p.m. to carpool."

Tori pulled Riley into a tight hug, and Riley tried to not go completely stiff. Her heart raced as she felt Tori's body pressed firmly against her own.

"'Night, Riley," Tori said as she pulled away. "See you at rehearsal Monday."

Riley didn't trust herself to speak, so she just smiled and waved good-bye.

CHAPTER TEN

Riley leaned against the counter at the coffee shop, daydreaming about the feel of Tori's body on her own, thankful that the shop was almost empty. Koji had the day off, and her only other coworkers were the weekend manager and a new girl who was more interested in flirting with him than in making a good cup of coffee.

A loud thump next to Riley caused her to jerk her head from her hands quickly as she looked toward the noise.

"Sorry!" Beth said with embarrassment. "I didn't mean to scare you."

Riley smiled. With all of her musings about Tori, she had completely forgotten that Beth was going to drop by that day. Her stomach flip-flopped when she saw her. Beth's light brown hair was tied back in a ponytail and a few strands had come loose. Beth tucked them behind her ear in irritation. Her glasses had traveled a bit too far down her nose as well, and she used her finger to push them back into position. Her cheeks flushed as books she had set on the counter toppled to the floor. The look on her face mirrored how Riley felt when she embarrassed herself in front of Tori. On Beth, however, the consternation was downright adorable.

Riley's eyes crinkled in absolute delight. All thoughts of Tori were swept from her mind as Beth picked up the books and then fumbled to get settled on the stool at the counter where Riley stood. Riley couldn't peel her eyes away. She wanted to watch her all day, no matter what she was doing. This wasn't a feeling like she had with Tori. Tori was sexy and alluring, out of reach and intimidating. Beth was the kind of woman she could see herself snuggling on the couch watching a movie with, going on adventures with…spending the rest of her life with.

She swallowed hard and said cheerily, "Hey! Let me get that mocha ready for you. And the apple fritters were *just* dropped off from Ken's Donuts, so they're still super fresh."

"You really don't have to do this."

Riley turned around to make the drink because she really wanted to hide her shaking hands. "I want to. You helped me out of a tight spot yesterday."

As Riley made the drink Beth asked, "How'd it go? The quartet thing."

"Pretty well, actually. Made a bit of extra cash. Cash that will go to that suit, of course, but it's money well spent, I think."

Riley finished the mocha and set it and the fritter in front of Beth. "Go ahead. Try it."

Beth bit into the apple fritter and her eyes shut in pleasure. With her mouth full, she managed to get out, "Ohmygod."

"I know, right?"

"Best apple fritter ever."

Riley beamed as if she had created the recipe herself.

Beth swallowed and then pushed the book she had accidentally slammed onto the counter toward Riley.

"I brought this for you. It's a history of music at sea. It talks about how sailors used music to alleviate boredom while away from land for so long, the types of instruments used, sea chanties"—she shrugged—"stuff like that. Anyway, I thought you'd like it since you're a musician. Gives us a common topic."

Riley picked up the book and leafed through it. "This is really cool! When do you need it back?"

Beth took another drink of her coffee and swallowed. "I don't. I have a huge collection of books like this already. I've been collecting since I was a little girl. Mom works in a maritime museum. I won't miss it."

Riley was impressed as she flipped through a few more pages. "This actually does look really interesting. I love anything having to do with music."

"Besides…" Beth paused, "it may teach you something you don't know about the ocean and sailing and, well, I think you should go some time."

"To the ocean?"

Beth nodded in reply. "My parents live in Galveston. I could…I dunno…if you're ever interested in going down there…for a trip… or something. I mean, if you need someone to show you around I go back at least once a month…" She trailed off at the end of the sentence and stuffed a much-too-large piece of fritter into her mouth in an apparent attempt to keep herself from rambling.

Riley grinned. Beth had gotten nervous again, and it was the cutest thing Riley had ever seen. Also, the thought of taking a real road trip—something she had never done before—to see the waters of the Gulf of Mexico was intriguing. She couldn't deny that she found the idea of spending more time with Beth even more so.

"That sounds like fun. I might take you up on that sometime."

Beth tried to act like it was no big deal, but she smiled, and Riley thought she could see a slight tremor in her hand the next time she took a sip from her cup.

❖

Riley and Beth talked for the rest of her shift, and when they both had to leave to do homework, it seemed like neither of them wanted to say good-bye. Riley felt an actual pang of loss when her new friend walked out of the front door.

"Well, this is unexpected," she muttered to herself as she slung her backpack over her shoulder and started her walk to the library for the evening.

She didn't know when she'd see Beth again and they hadn't even exchanged numbers or anything yet. She consoled herself with the knowledge that she would get to see Tori at rehearsal the next day and at the *Candide* performance on Tuesday night. She had been more than excited about the prospect of spending another evening with Tori, but somehow her enthusiasm was now a bit muted.

The image of Beth struggling to make a good impression popped into her head again. The butterflies returned to her stomach, and she didn't care that she was grinning stupidly to herself as she walked.

This was unexpected indeed.

❖

The next week Riley devoured the book Beth had given her, much to the detriment of her regular homework, and Riley found herself obsessing over it. She researched instruments, downloaded MP3s, and even learned to play a few easy tunes by ear on her cello. Every night at work, she waited for Beth to come into the shop so she could impress her with all that she had learned, but she never showed. Had Riley done something wrong? Had she offended her the last time they had spoken? She replayed their conversation over and over again in her head, but she couldn't find anything that could possibly have run her off.

She even considered going to the mall to see her at Banana Republic, but she didn't want to give off a stalker vibe.

"It's just a trip to the mall. Don't be stupid." Koji tried to reassure her after she hadn't seen Beth for seven days.

"Koji, I've spoken with her what…three times? Ever? What's wrong with me? I want her to like me so badly."

"She does like you so badly."

"She doesn't know me yet."

"She wants to. Don't freak out about it. Anyway, what about that other girl you're into?"

Riley shook her head and kept scrubbing at the already pristine counter. "I feel like I'm going crazy. I've never had one crush in my life. Not one. And now I can't think about anything else. I so don't need this right now."

Koji clapped his hands to his face in mock elation. "My baby's all grown up and has entered the mysterious and delightful realm of womanhood!"

"Don't be an asshole. I'm really worried about this."

He deflated. "Why in the world are you worried? It's so normal for you to be interested in people."

"But what about my schoolwork? I just can't concentrate on anything. Koji, I *have* to do well. I'm on scholarship, I have financial aid, and I have nowhere else to go. If I can't do what I need to do I'll…" She swallowed hard. "I'll be lost."

Koji took the soaked rag from her, threw it in the linen bin, and turned her to face him. When he spoke he said every sentence as if he were reading bullet points. "Welcome to college. These are going to be the best years of your life. Everything is new. Everything is exciting. Some of these new, exciting things will hurt a little. And that's okay. It's just part of the experience. You work harder than anyone I know. Relax a little. Enjoy what you're feeling. You'll remember it the rest of your life."

Riley had never seen Koji so straightforward and serious. It was disconcerting.

"O…Okay."

"Good!" Koji clapped her shoulders and then did an overly dramatic pirouette. "Your fairy godmother is now going home. I have a date with one of the bartenders from Oilcan Harry's!" He flitted into the back room and was gone.

❖

Aidan,

I swear I don't mean for this to be a regular thing, but I'm having girl issues. Three to be precise. If you're getting tired of my whining, just let me know. Otherwise, HELP!

Girl issue #1: My roommate is a selfish bitch. She never pays me back for stuff, she brings her nasty boyfriend to our dorm room late at night and has sex with

*him with me RIGHT THERE pretending to be asleep.
Frickin' disgusting. She makes snide comments about me
all the time unless she needs me to do something for her,
and she's just inconsiderate about everything. I've already
asked about getting transferred to another room, but
nothing is available. I have to wait until the whole year
is over. It's only November. How am I going to survive
that? I've started sleeping on the couches in the music
building whenever I have a sliver of free time because I
just don't want to go back. I mean, I've lived with other
girls my whole life, and most weren't the nicest, but either
my tolerance has been slowly eroded or this girl just has
the talent of getting on my last nerve. Maybe a little of
both. I want to talk to her about it, but my biggest fear
is that it will make our situation even worse. We do have
several months to go. So what should I do? Put my foot
down, ask nicely, and expect nothing, or just ignore it and
get through it?*

*Girl issue #2: Tori (the hot girl) and I are friends
now and we get to hang out sometimes, but most of the
time we only talk in the music building or we hang out
with a group. She's never mentioned what happened that
morning she kissed me and, although I'll admit I'm not
good at seeing it, I really don't think she has more interest
in me. Kinda bums me out. I get butterflies every time she
gets close to me, but I just don't think she's into me. That
brings me to:*

*Girl issue #3: Beth. Yep. There's another one now. I
know what you're thinking, but no, I'm not like you. I'm not
used to having a string (if two can be considered a string)
of girls that I'm interested in. And I'm ESPECIALLY not
used to one of them liking me back. And yes, I'm pretty
sure that Beth is interested. You've seen her actually.
Adorable nerdy girl with glasses at the coffee shop. You
and Koji were being dicks about it if you'll remember.
Well, as much as I hate to admit it, I think Koji was right.*

*She finally came up to talk to me a few weeks ago, and...
well, she's really, really nice. Super smart too, and you
know how hot I think that is. She's into studying sunken
ships or the history of fish or something. I'll admit I was
a little nervous and didn't quite pay the best attention to
our conversation. I was too busy trying not to look dumb.
Anyway, we haven't talked all that much, but I just feel like
I want to see her again. Every day. I dunno. It's getting
pretty tiring actually. When I'm with Tori, I'm all jittery
and can't stop thinking about how damn hot she is, and
when I'm at the coffee shop, I find myself looking at every
customer who comes in, hoping it's Beth. Koji did give me
some good advice about not letting it get to me, that it's
normal, etc. etc., but I still want to know what you think.*

*Also, I know it's only two weeks away, but I don't
suppose they have any last-minute options for you to
take leave at Thanksgiving, do they? I really miss you.
I keep the heirloom box under my bed, and I've been
taking it out a lot lately. Nothing's changed, of course,
but seeing your dog tags and the stuff that belonged to
Mom and Dad...I dunno. It helps me keep you all close,
you know? I think Brooke thinks I'm crazy, looking at the
same old things over and over again. I don't care. I'd tell
her how special the stuff is if I thought she'd give a rat's
ass. Anyway, don't worry about me too much. It's not like
I have any real fondness for the holiday. You can only see
the Home's pageant so many times, you know? But still,
if they'll let you have leave, it'd be nice to see you. We
have a week off of classes. I have plenty of catching up to
do, of course, and I've kind of been doing a lot of for fun
reading and studying about the ocean stuff so that Beth
knows I'm interested in what she likes. But anyway, yeah.
I hope you're well.*

Love you!

Riley

❖

Riley,

Everything's great here. Same ol' same ol' really. We pretty much train nonstop. Well, that and work on the LAVs. I swear, I don't know how they can break down so often. I've gotten really good at the mechanic stuff now. I mean, way better than I was when I worked at the garage.

No, I don't get any leave for Thanksgiving. I'm sorry :(A couple of the older guys do, but us noobs are stuck here. Don't even ask about Christmas. I have no idea. I've talked to some of the guys who have deployed before, though, and it's looking pretty likely that we'll get our orders in the next two or three months. I'll finally get to go overseas!

Don't panic...I know how you are. The good part about that is I'll get a full week's leave off before we go. So maybe I'll get to see you in March or so?

Now, on to the fun stuff.

Girl issue #1: Your roommate sounds like she needs a good slap across the face, but since neither one of us would do that, your option is to let her know how you feel. You don't have to put your foot down...at first. If she has any decency, she'll realize how she's made you feel and apologize for it. If not, well, that's when you get serious. I know you can't switch rooms this year and it might be difficult, but you're both adults and I'm sure you can work something out.

Girl issue #2: Mmmm. The hot chick. Honestly, Riles, I think you need to let this one go. It seems like you're banging your head against a wall trying to figure her out. It's taking up too much of your energy and sanity. It's okay to still find her insanely attractive. It's okay to want to ravish her in the music building every chance you *get. Hell, I would want to do the same thing. But don't look for anything more. She's eye candy. She's a buddy. If something is meant to happen, it will. If not, well, just enjoy the way she makes you feel and appreciate her friendship. Putting that into practice may not be so easy. I get that, but try anyway.*

Girl issue #3: Now HERE's the interesting one. I do remember that girl, as a matter of fact. And yes, Koji was right, you guys would totally make precious lesbian nerd babies together. (I just dodged the shoe you mentally threw at me so HA). But really, I could tell she was interested in you just from that night. Now it looks like she's ready to act on it and I say go for it! If she's this cute, smart, and nice, why in the world are you wasting time pining over someone else? She sounds perfect. You need someone like that in your life. It sounds like you're really interested in her too, and even if nothing romantic comes of it, she could be that friend you really need. If she turns out to be more than that I'll be the proud big brother of the cutest couple at UT.

You go get to know Beth and keep me updated! I've been without a woman for weeks now, and I need to know that at least ONE Gordon is happy with someone.

Love ya, Sis,
Aidan

CHAPTER ELEVEN

I'm going after work, Koji." Riley's hands were planted decidedly on her hips as she stood with her back to the Metro Haus cash register.

"Excellent!" He paused. "Where are you going?"

Riley's arms fell in exasperation to her sides. "To the mall! I talked to my brother, and I've decided that it's time to stop being a wuss about Beth. She likes me…I think…and yes. I think I might like her too. I want to get to know her better."

"Congratulations, here's a cookie. But what does that have to with going to the mall?" he asked.

"Haven't you noticed that Beth hasn't been in to the coffee shop for a week?"

He shrugged. "I've been off most of the week."

"Well, I…I need some…socks, and I thought that since I was going there anyway I could maybe, you know, swing by Banana Republic to see if she's there or something."

Koji looked at her with unimpressed eyes. "You need socks," he said plainly.

Riley nodded.

He stared at her for a few seconds before asking, "You don't need socks, do you?"

She paused and then said sheepishly, "No, I do not."

Koji shook his head.

"I knew it! If she's there I'm going to look like a creeper, aren't I?"

This made him laugh. "After her stalking you every night in

here for months? Unlikely. I think you'll make her day if you just show up randomly. Although the likelihood of her being at work is pretty slim."

"Well, I'm going to take that chance. I…I dunno. I just want to see her again."

Koji grinned and clasped his hands under his chin. "OMG you are just *too* adorbz."

Riley swiftly kicked him in the shin and flipped him off as she left the coffee shop to the sound of his pained giggling.

❖

Okay. No stalker vibes. Just looking for socks. What am I doing? I don't know what I'm looking for in the first place. What do I expect to happen? A friendship? A relationship? I could do with the first, but I'm sure in no place to be able to handle the second. Why am I even thinking these things? Why would she be interested in me anyway? Am I actually interested in her? There's no way she can see something in me, and even if she does she's bound to pull into disappointment station as soon as I open my damn mouth and she sees the mess that is my life. Shut up, stupid brain. Why do you always over-complicate things? Why can't you be normal? What's wrong with you? No wonder you've never had any good friends.

Riley pounded her fist onto the steering wheel. "Shut up!" she yelled to the emptiness of her parked car. She took a deep, long breath and then sighed. "And now I'm talking to myself. Neurosis 1, Riley 0."

Instead of continuing her internal diatribe, Riley exited the car, not stopping until she was only a few stores away from Beth's Banana Republic. Here she stopped short, almost getting run into by the elderly woman walking behind her.

Just stopping by to shop. I was in the area. Socks. Haven't seen you at the coffee shop. How are things? Do you want to maybe hang out sometime?

She rehearsed the conversation in her head one last time and walked into the store.

When she didn't see Beth in any of the sections, she was almost relieved. She tried to pretend that the relief outweighed the disappointment. Letting out a wavering breath, she turned to leave. She walked out of the store with her head down and slowly started the journey back to her car.

"Hey!" a familiar voice shouted from behind her.

It was Beth. She was standing outside the store with her backpack slung over her shoulder. Riley couldn't hide the relieved and nervous grin that formed on her face.

"Hey," she said as she waved.

"What are you doing here? Need more suit stuff or were you just dying to come and see me?" Beth laughed as if that was absurd, but there was a hint of earnest hope in her tone.

Riley paused. "Socks."

"Oh." Beth frowned and looked at Riley's empty hands. "Didn't find any you liked?"

Riley's cheeks flushed. This wasn't going the way she had wanted. She shook her head.

"Okay. Well, I'm off work now, but if you want any suggestions on other stores…I mean, there's a Dillard's over there," she said, pointing to the other end of the mall, "or the Gap back that way." She thumbed over her shoulder.

"Thanks." Riley was completely unable to speak. What had come over her? Beth waited for her to say something else, but then gave up.

"Well, I'm on my way back to campus, so…see ya later." Beth hurried away as if flustered.

Shit.

"Wait!" Riley jogged after her. Beth turned, a hopeful expression on her face. "Since I'm in the area," she tried to remember her speech, "you wanna have dinner or something?"

The heat in her ears was insane. Why did this scare her so much? She wasn't asking Beth on a date or anything. She just wanted to get to know her better. Right?

To Riley's immense relief, Beth's face broke into a wide and immensely attractive smile. "I'd love that."

❖

Beth took them to a Tex-Mex chain restaurant outside the mall where they settled into a booth and started crunching on the obligatory chips and salsa.

"I haven't seen you at the coffee shop in a few days," Riley ventured.

Beth nodded. "I was actually on a short research trip with one of my professors and his TA. They're working on a project together about the effects of the Loop Current on deeper manmade reefs in the Gulf of Mexico. They needed a lackey, so I volunteered for extra credit. Gave me a chance to visit home too since we were based in Galveston."

"That sounds cool." It really did too. "Was it fun?"

"It was, actually. My dad offered them the use of his boat as a dive platform so that they could go check things out. It was nice to spend a couple of days out on the water again. But anyway"— she leaned back—"I'm back now until Thanksgiving and can freely partake in any coffee-based beverages you're nice enough to make for me."

Riley smiled. "You must really like our coffee."

Beth paused, pensive. "There is something about your shop that I do like very much, yes." For a moment, she stared straight into Riley's eyes, but then shied and looked down at the empty basket of chips.

Riley didn't know how to respond to that, so she attempted to hide her blush with a large swig of the Sprite she was drinking.

"So. How are things in your world?" Beth asked.

Riley set her glass down and shrugged. "College has been... confusing for me. But things are pretty good overall. I can't really complain."

"Making friends?"

She shrugged. "There's Koji at work, a couple of people in the music school, and Tori." Her ears turned pink.

Beth shifted as if nervous to ask the next question. "What about that guy? The one you were with at the coffee shop at the start of school. You two seemed...close."

Riley smiled. Beth was trying to find out if she was seeing anyone. If any other girl had asked about Aidan, she would have assumed they were interested in him. But not Beth. As bad as she was at reading people she could see this. She decided to not let her in on the truth just yet. Just to see what happened. "That's Aidan. Isn't he just unbelievably hot?"

Beth's face fell. "Oh. Yeah. I mean, if that's your type. You guys are...cute together." Her expression showed that she didn't think they were the least bit cute together.

"Our parents thought so."

Beth looked confused, so Riley decided to put her out of her misery. She leaned forward and said, "Aidan is my brother."

Beth looked happily surprised. "Oh. Oh! Yeah, of course he is. Well then, you guys *are* cute together."

Riley sat back and shrugged. "Aidan is the heartthrob. I'm the brain."

"I think you're a lot more than that."

The comment was so straightforward that Riley blinked and found herself dumbstruck.

Beth continued, "Something about you..." She looked muddled. "I'm not good at this, but what I guess I'm saying is that I want to know more about you. You seem...guarded. Like you're afraid to let people in to see the real you."

"Maybe I'm just shy."

"Yeah," agreed Beth. "I get that because I am too, but there's something else." She gazed at Riley deep in thought and then must have realized what she was doing. "I'm sorry. I'm not trying to pry. You just...intrigue me. That's all. I'm sorry."

Riley shook her head. "No need to be sorry. I'm flattered that you're interested in learning more about me. That doesn't happen often." She smiled but said nothing more because she was still afraid to share her background with Beth. She felt more comfortable with her already than she ever had with anyone else, but her walls were still a fortress of self-protection and not even Beth had the power to breach them quite yet.

Beth must have realized this so she changed the subject. "So. How are you liking Austin so far?"

Riley smiled. "It's so much better than Whitehill I can't even begin to tell you. Of course, I've really only hung around campus, but even sitting at Metro Haus is better than Whitehill. It doesn't take much."

"Have you ever been to a Longhorn football game?"

Riley shook her head.

"Okay, that's on your must-do list as a student here, and Austin is out there waiting too. There's lots more to see. Have you been to the state capitol?"

"Nope. Unless you count just looking at it down Congress Avenue."

"What about Lady Bird Lake?"

"Crossed over it a few times."

"Have you seen the bats?"

"What bats?"

Beth feigned being appalled. "The Congress Avenue Mexican free-tailed bats!"

Riley looked skeptical. "Yeah, you just put a whole bunch of random words together and lost me."

Beth laughed. "Austin is home to the world's largest urban bat population, and they live under the South Congress Avenue Bridge. That's only in the summer, though. What about swimming in Barton Springs? It's too cold now, but add that to your list. Let me think of what else…" She paused and chewed on her bottom lip pensively. "Live music?"

"Other than class?"

"Austin is the live music capital of the world! Okay. I know what we're doing this weekend."

Riley looked surprised.

"Oh. Sorry. I mean, are you free this weekend? To do some

sightseeing? I'm a great tour guide. If you want." She looked hopeful.

Riley beamed. "Totally free."

Beth looked relieved. "Perfect. I promise I won't let you down. We're going to have a blast."

It was hands-down the most pleasant evening Riley had ever had with a friend. Before the meal was even over, she found herself counting down the hours until the weekend tour.

❖

Nothing could have prepared Riley for the two days she spent with Beth. True to her word, Beth had proven to be a excellent tour guide, and Riley could now say that she had been an enthusiastic part of the screaming crowd of 80,000 at a home football game which the Longhorns won, she had taken a tour of the state capitol building, and she and Beth had even gone kayaking on Lady Bird Lake after having a picnic in Zilker Park on a breezy and chilly Sunday afternoon.

Now, following a live acoustic set by a local musician at Emo's, they sat out on the porch of the Dog and Duck pub sipping on virgin piña coladas and eating French fries. Riley still felt slightly awkward around Beth because she didn't know if her growing feelings for her were starting to show. Beth, however, seemed more outgoing and open than she ever had.

"See what I mean?" Beth continued their conversation as Riley poured more malt vinegar onto the fries. "Live music capital of the world. There were so many shows to choose from tonight, but I've heard that artist before and thought you might like her."

"I did! I had no idea there was so much to do beyond campus. I mean, Aidan, Koji, and I went to Sixth Street once, but that was just kind of meh. The boys drank most of the time and it was fun to hang out, but for the most part, I think I'm more of the quiet type. I'd much rather go to a show or watch a movie."

"Oh! That reminds me. Another Austin must-do is the Alamo

Drafthouse theater. They serve you food while you watch the movie. Uh-mazing. They play a lot of indie and art house films too, so there's always something cool happening."

Riley smiled and asked, "Are you inviting me to a movie? Haven't gotten sick of me yet?"

Despite her outward confidence, Beth blushed. "Yes to the movie. Definitely no to the second."

Here they were, flirting again. And with every passing minute, Riley was feeling more and more attachment to her. What worried her was whether her feelings were simply relief that she had finally found someone who liked her so much or whether she was actually starting to have real feelings for Beth. She had never really liked anyone before...except Tori, of course, but this felt different. She didn't want to stop looking at her in case she missed one of her cute grins. She didn't want her to ever stop speaking because everything she said seemed to have the weight of the world riding on it.

This was definitely turning into a pretty major crush, and every second cemented the attraction.

"Thanks, Beth," Riley said sincerely.

"For what? Asking you to a movie?"

"For all of this. You've been really cool and I appreciate that. I had a blast this weekend. Best weekend I've ever had in my life if I'm being totally honest." She shrugged sheepishly.

Beth laughed. "You must have had a really boring life then!"

Riley's smile fell and she looked down to her fingers as she fidgeted with her fork.

Beth noticed because she said, "Oh. I'm sorry. I didn't mean to offend you. I didn't mean it. You said you had it tough growing up, and I shouldn't open my stupid mouth about things I know nothing about. Please forget I said anything, and God, I'm stupid. I'm sorry."

Riley looked up to see Beth red and shame-faced. She really seemed horrified that she had said something offensive. Feeling sorry for her, Riley reached out and took Beth's hand in her own, giving it a small squeeze. "No need to be sorry. Really." She didn't want to go into details about her childhood. Not yet. Instead she said, "No, my childhood wasn't the best, but it could have been much, much worse. I saw and heard about much worse where I grew up. And hey," she said, brightening, "even if I had grown up going to Disneyland every day of my life, this *still* would have been the best weekend I've ever had and that's because of you."

Beth smiled appreciatively, but she had grown quiet again as if afraid of saying the wrong thing. Riley didn't want that at all. She was enjoying their growing level of comfort with each other and definitely didn't want her issues to come between them or drive Beth away.

Realizing she was still holding Beth's hand, Riley let go abruptly and placed her hands in her own lap. "So. How are your classes going?" she asked to change the subject.

"Ugh." Beth groaned as she tilted her head back and became more animated again. "My sophomore year is harder than my freshman year. And I'm assuming next year will be even worse and on and on and so goes life."

"Surely it's not that bad."

"No. It's not. Just a lot of work. There are parts of this year that are better than last, though." She smiled at Riley affectionately. "What about yours?"

Riley's cheeks warmed and she leaned back in her chair and took a deep breath of the clean Texas air. "My year is definitely better than last too, but there's not much competition. I..." She paused, wondering how much she should say. "I struggle with things, with how I feel about what happens in my life. It's not always easy, but I will say that people like my friends Koji and Tori...and now you... you guys have made all the difference in the world. This may have been just a tour around town for most people, but to me it was proof that there's more out there for me. I just have to be willing to go for it."

Beth smiled and they gazed at each other for a long while. Finally, the spell was broken when four drunk patrons stumbled out onto the porch and started singing terrible renditions of classic rock songs at the tops of their lungs.

Riley winced and said, "I think that's our cue."

Beth nodded and stood to leave. "Agreed. It's late anyway. I have class early tomorrow."

Riley joined her. "Me too. Nothing says 'good morning!' like a monotone lecture about the politics of the Civil War Reconstruction period."

"Snooze. I get it. I have Chem first thing. It's such a great idea to have labs with volatile chemicals with students who are either half-asleep, hungover, or even still drunk from the night before in some cases."

They got into Beth's car and started the short drive back to campus.

Beth yawned as she drove. "God, I'm exhausted. And really out of shape!" She rolled her neck from side to side trying to stretch it out. "I didn't realize how much work kayaking would be after not doing it for a year."

Riley realized that she too was tired and could feel the welcome soreness beginning in between her shoulder blades. "Me too, but I needed that. I don't get up and move nearly enough."

"Anytime you want to go again just let me know."

Beth pulled over on the street next to Riley's dorm. She seemed timid again. "So."

"So." Riley smiled, feeling like every limb was in a stupid position. "Thanks again. Really. I had a blast."

"No problem. I'll see you soon?" It was a hopeful question.

"Definitely. Have a good day tomorrow. Don't study too hard."

Beth snorted. "That's like telling steel ships not to oxidize and rust on the ocean floor." At Riley's blank stare, she shifted uncomfortably and said, "Sorry. Oceanography student."

Riley laughed. "'Night, Beth. Thanks again." She got out of the car, shut the door behind her, and turned to walk away. She swore she heard Beth curse to herself as she drove away. Riley knew that feeling intimately. She chuckled to herself.

Walking back to her dorm room, Riley felt a little lighter. The demon of fear and uncertainty that lurked in her chest had quieted some, but still made sure his presence was acknowledged. Still,

Riley actually felt excited at the possibility of gaining a best friend. She knew Beth could be that person for her. Never had she connected with someone so easily. Maybe she should stop worrying so much. Things weren't looking so bad after all.

She opened the door to her room and was relieved to see that Brooke wasn't there. Maybe she would spend the night at her boyfriend's place again. Riley still hadn't gathered the courage to talk to Beth about how she felt regarding their situation, but at least now she had the time to spend alone working on an English essay.

Riley opened up her laptop and pulled the power cord out of her backpack. She crawled under her desk and plugged the cord into the wall, but then something caught her eye. There was a brief reflection of light from the edge of her desk on the side that ran along the far wall. She picked up a small object from where it had gotten lodged in the rug. What she held was a small diamond in a gold setting. She had just found Brooke's lost pendant! Excitement flooded through her. Brooke was going to be so happy about this that Riley was sure that any difficult conversation they had to have would be so much easier. Maybe Brooke would even start to respect her a little now.

Riley stood with a smile and placed the diamond in a decorative bowl on Brooke's desk. She also wrote a note telling her where she had found it and expressing her joy at having Brooke not have to worry about it anymore. She knew that Brooke would probably find it tomorrow afternoon.

Riley plopped down into her own desk chair and powered on her computer, ready to write her English paper and feeling wary, but immensely satisfied with the way things were starting to go in her life.

CHAPTER TWELVE

The next afternoon, after she was done with her classes, Riley entered her dorm room and found Brooke sitting cross-legged on her bed, her computer open in front of her. Riley smiled broadly, glancing at the bowl where she had left the found pendant. It was gone so she knew that Brooke had gotten it back. She looked at Brooke for thanks, but saw only a fake smile over pursed lips.

"Hey! Did you see that I found your necklace?" Riley ventured anyway, hoping for a better reaction.

Brooke nodded curtly. "Yeah. Thanks."

Riley's smile fell. Why did Brooke look so angry? "Oh. Good. I hope…I hope you feel better now."

Brooke nodded again and looked back to her computer screen, typing loudly.

Riley was so confused. She had pinned so many hopes on her good fortune of finding the necklace helping to repair their relationship. She didn't know what else to do, so she put her backpack down, grabbed her music folder, and quietly left to go to the music building for rehearsal. She seethed with anger. Nothing she did would ever be good enough for that girl.

❖

"Riley."

She looked up from her music, the cello still resting snugly between her legs. Orchestra rehearsal had ended, but Riley had stayed behind to work on a section of music that all of the other, more experienced cellists seemed to have no trouble with. Riley felt like she was trying to tie her fingers in knots just to get half of the notes right, and she was furious with herself.

"What?" she asked irritably.

"Whoa, Miss Piss Pants. What's up with you today?"

Riley looked up to see Tori standing next to her. "Oh. Sorry. It's just this stupid run. I can't get it right. I'm the only one too. My inexperience is showing."

Tori actually laughed. "Youngest cellist in the university's top orchestra and you're struggling with a run. Look at me cry my face off." Tori was still holding her violin, so she played a melodramatic and depressing melody.

This made Riley feel overdramatic, so she laughed at herself.

"Come on. Movie night. You and me." Tori picked Riley's music up from the stand and put it away in the waiting folder.

"What?"

"Did I or did I not say that you needed to relax?"

"You said—"

"Just get up. Or is your dance card too full to make time for me?"

"My dance...what?"

Tori rolled her eyes. "God, we need to get you out more."

❖

"Three and a half stars," Tori said as they walked from the movie theater to a local bar by campus.

"Out of five or out of ten?"

"Out of fifty."

"Damn. I'd say at least a four with that scoring system."

Tori shook her head as they crossed the street. "I'm sorry I subjected you to that. Who knew a movie about a Nazi-fighting vampire chick could be so bad? I figured that a free movie at the Union would be worth it, but no amount of gratis could make up for those two lost hours of my life."

Riley shrugged. "Still better than continuously banging my head against the wall in the music building."

"Well, here's to a better rest of the night." Tori put her arm around Riley's waist as they walked into the bar.

Tori led her over to a table occupied by several other women who were also in various stages of proximity to each other. Riley noticed the other patrons of the bar, mostly fraternity types, staring and smirking at them.

Oooh, Riley thought. Right.

"Ladies, Riley. Riley, ladies." The women at the table waved and made room for them to sit down.

"You're starting to get to them young, Tor," a tall woman with a shaved head said from the other end of the table.

Tori rolled her eyes and whispered in Riley's ear, "Ignore them. They're crass sometimes."

"Oh, I'm crass *all* the time," said the woman, who had obviously overheard.

Riley smiled with embarrassment. She had never hung out with a group of lesbians before. She had known she was gay for a long time, but with no crushes and no girlfriends, it honestly never made any difference in her life. Right now she felt uneasy. Not because she was surrounded by lesbians, but because she felt like she didn't fit in. These girls were like Tori. Older, experienced, and way too cool.

"Okay, guys, we're here. What are we talking about tonight?" Tori asked as she poured Riley and herself a pint of Shiner from the pitcher on the table. Riley reached for the chips and queso to give herself something to do with her hands.

Apparently, this was a weekly get-together for this group. What they talked about were subjects that 1) Riley knew nothing about, and 2) made her uncomfortable. These women were obviously very wise to the ways of the Sapphic world, and Riley learned all too quickly that she was extremely lacking in her education on these matters. She supposed that she shouldn't be shocked by the things they talked about, but she realized that she had been raised in a rather sheltered environment—at least where sexual matters were concerned. Still, she tried to feign interest and figured that anything she learned that night might well come in handy in the future.

❖

By the end of the evening, with her buzz fading sleepily, Riley felt better. The women were nice despite the whole TMI factor.

"So. What'd ya think?" Tori asked as she slid her hand into Riley's on their walk back to campus.

"They're cool. Too cool for me, I think, but cool."

"You're adorably quaint sometimes, you know that?"

Riley laughed. "Am I that backward?"

"No. You're just getting into things. You may be all innocent in public, but my money's on you being a beast in the—"

"Holy shit, you are *not* about to say that!"

They were walking next to the large brick wall of the Biomedical Engineering building when Tori stopped abruptly and gently pressed Riley up against it. Riley swallowed hard. She knew what was coming next. Tori slowly leaned forward and brushed her lips very lightly against Riley's cheek. Riley opened her mouth to say something, not to protest, not to stop her, but just to fill the empty space between them. Nothing came out. Tori moved her lips to Riley's mouth and kissed her for a long while. Riley was more shocked than anything, but it was definitely nice. Still, she was thinking about it too much. Was she doing it right? Was Tori disappointed? What did this mean about their relationship?

When Tori pulled away, she looked smug. "There. Lesson one."

Riley didn't really know how to respond. She didn't know if Tori was being condescending or not, so she just asked, "Did I pass?" Might as well play the game.

"Oh yeah. A-plus." She smiled. "Lesson two is ready when you are." She leaned in and kissed the side of Riley's neck.

Riley shuddered and felt heat flow through her.

"Come over to my place tonight." It wasn't a demand, but it was obvious that she wasn't used to the offer being declined.

Riley stared at her and Tori laughed. "Don't worry. You're

perfectly safe. I won't do anything…unless you want me to." She winked slyly. "We can just hang out."

Riley was terrified. Terrified, but intrigued. Besides, what did she have to look forward to in her dorm room? If Brooke was there she was just in for another uncomfortable night of silence, or worse. Better to spend the night with someone she trusted and who actually cared about her.

"Yeah. Okay," she found herself saying.

A short while later, they walked into Tori's apartment, and Riley saw many generic first apartment trappings. Cheaply framed posters featuring music festivals and bands like the Violent Femmes and The Libertines, and prints by Van Gogh lined the walls. The couch was covered with a frayed orange throw, and empty beer bottles sat haphazardly on the small counter of the kitchenette. The only things that made this room more familiar to Riley were the stacks of music theory books, piles of random sheet music, and a violin case propped up in the corner. Of course, the case had band stickers plastered all over it as if it were the guitar case of a rock star.

Riley smiled and sat on the couch where Tori motioned as she went into the kitchen to bring her a beer. She scanned the room again and said, "I can't figure you out."

"Oh yeah? How so?" Tori asked as she popped the tops off two Ziegenbocks.

Riley gestured to the room around her. "Well, for one, I can't figure out the violin thing. Why not guitar? Why not bass or even piano? You don't seem very…classical. More…Joan Jett?"

Tori handed her the beer and sat down so close that she leaned against her. "Beethoven was the rebel of his day. His music was so passionate at a time when emotions were kept smashed down inside that women flat-out fainted when he played for them. Berlioz shocked the French musical establishment by turning forms and harmonies on their heads. When Stravinsky debuted *The Rite of Spring* in 1913, the audience rioted and tried to stop the performance. The dissonance of the piece freaked them out.

"The only difference between the classics and modern music is the year. Tchaikovsky and Iron and Wine. Wagner and Morrissey.

Verdi and Sarah Bettens. Music is music. I love it all. But to answer your question, violin because that's what I'm best at playing. I mess around a little on the guitar and piano, but there's something about the feeling of a bow grabbing onto that string and making such a clear and resonant sound. I'm sure you get it too."

Riley nodded. "I definitely do. Nothing like it."

They sat in silence for a minute before Riley scanned the room again, her eyes falling on a picture of Tori hugging an attractive brunette of the same age. "Who's that?"

Tori smiled. "Meghan. My girlfriend. She's on a soccer scholarship at Bryn Mawr."

Riley was stunned. Tori had a girlfriend? What about all the—

"I know that look," Tori interrupted Riley's thoughts. "Don't worry. We've been together since our first year of high school. We've agreed to have fun and be open while we're both at school. Just nothing with strings attached. As soon as we both graduate, we're getting married and thus will begin the happily ever after."

Riley attempted to not look shocked. The evening had already been surprising, but she hadn't expected this news at all.

Reading her expression, Tori frowned. "You know, I think I should've told you before. Stupid of me. You're new to all this, and I just realized that I've probably confused the hell out of you. I'm really sorry if that's the case. I didn't even think. I do like you, you know, and if you were to want anything else to happen between us, I'm still good with that. But if not, no worries. You're my friend first and foremost." She smiled kindly and put a bit of space between them, apparently trying to make Riley more comfortable.

Riley wasn't at all uncomfortable, just…confused. "But…what about…" She didn't know how to articulate it, so she simply said, "What about tonight? I mean, what if I do want to…you know… continue?" She didn't know what she wanted yet, but experimenting with Tori definitely didn't sound all that awful.

Tori smiled. "Tonight I'm with you, and it's all about you. I have a lot of love to give and every ounce of it is genuine. Tonight, as one of my favorite songs says, I will love you forever. But I would never do anything unless you wanted me to."

Riley nodded slowly, understanding. She supposed that explained Tori's openness about physicality a bit more. She did feel pretty special knowing that Tori was attracted to her, and it was almost as if a weight had been lifted from her shoulders. Whatever their relationship was going to be, Riley didn't have to worry about Tori not liking her, but at the same time, she also didn't have to worry about anything long-term.

Beth's face flashed in her mind.

Ah.

In that one moment, Riley finally knew without a shadow of a doubt. She found Tori attractive as hell, but it was Beth who had taken hold of her heart.

Tori brushed her hand across Riley's knee. Riley felt a tremor of desire pass through her, but said reluctantly, "Maybe when I'm ready. Not yet. I'm also more of the…I dunno…long-term monogamous type? I mean, I've never been in a relationship, but I kind of assume that I am." She smiled apologetically.

Tori nodded. "Got it. But if you change your mind, you know where to find me." She leaned back against the armrest of the couch, looking sexier than Riley had ever seen her, and she almost changed her mind right there on the spot.

"Sooo tempting." Riley let her eyes wander over Tori's body.

Tori barked a laugh. "So we're cool then?"

Riley smiled. She really did like this girl who had taken her under her wing and felt even more comfortable with her now that everything was out in the open. "More than cool."

Tori said, "Let me put some music on. I think you'll like it. Indie stuff."

She moved to an old record player across the room. She pulled an album off the shelf and held it up for Riley to see. "This one has the feel of folk music from the 1960s, but it was released last year. Brilliant new artist from England."

"They still make records? Like, LP records? My parents used to have some of those."

Tori snorted. "Yes, they do. Albums just sound too clean nowadays. You don't get the real feel of the music unless you listen to them this way. Not every album comes out on vinyl, but a lot of them do. I kind of have a collecting problem."

She put the needle down on the record, and after the initial scratch and soothing crackle, the music started. She then walked over to the couch and sat down, putting her arm around Riley's shoulders. Riley rested her head peacefully on Tori's chest.

They listened to a few songs in silence and then Tori asked, "Are you feeling better about things now?"

"What do you mean?"

"I mean you always look so sad. Or angry. Or...worried, I guess. You're an awesome girl, and I want to make sure that you have fun in life too. Parties, friends, love, music. You always seem to retreat inside yourself. I want to help bring you out. I worry about you."

Riley sat pensively and traced circles lazily across Tori's thigh. "I'm not unhappy. I'm always..." She thought for a moment. "Scared."

"What are you scared of?"

"I almost don't even know anymore. Failure? Destitution? Exposure? What if I can't cut it? What if something happens to my brother in the Marines? What if I fail at everything I try? What if someone sees through this quiet façade to the shit that torments me at night?"

She didn't know why she was telling her this. Maybe it was because she was the first person to ever specifically ask. Still, it felt liberating.

Tori sat up and turned Riley's face toward her. "Everything you're feeling is valid."

This wasn't what Riley had expected her to say. The people who knew a little about her past just told her that everything would be fine and to stop worrying even when she gave them only the smallest glimpse into her psyche.

"Everyone has those feelings," Tori continued, "but the trick is learning to bring the good feelings to the forefront. Do you think I don't worry about failing? I'm from an area of Dallas that even the cops are afraid to patrol. I grew up with no money, no dad, and a mom who didn't have time for me because she worked three jobs just to pay for our apartment, our food, and my violin lessons. She saw musical ability in me from day one and worked her ass off to make sure she could get me out of that hellhole. Music was the only thing I could do well so music is what we chose as my escape route. Every damn day of my life, I worry that I'll never be good enough. Every damn day, I get scared that I'll never be able to pay her back for all of her sacrifices."

She ran her fingers down Riley's cheek, and Riley leaned into the caress. It felt so nice to have such close contact with someone. "Universe, let me be a violinist in the Dallas Symphony, or in Omaha, in Portland, I don't care. As long as I prove that I can make something happen for myself." She lightly kissed Riley on the lips and then whispered, "I see myself in you sometimes. And it breaks my heart. My job, whether you like it or not, is to help you see the good. The fun. Hell, even the dangerous. Life is nothing without joy, and you can't let the fear win."

She leaned back again, leaving Riley wide-eyed and moved.

"What do you want, Riley Gordon?"

Riley couldn't find an answer.

"One word. Just one."

"Happiness."

"See? That wasn't so hard, was it?"

"I hate being angry."

"Okay. What's something that makes you happy?"

"Music."

"Good, you've got that in the bag. What else?"

Riley surprised herself when she said, "Beth."

Even Tori's eyes widened although she looked amused. "Who's Beth?"

Riley stammered, trying to force the already spoken word back into her mouth. "Friend. Kind of. Just met her really."

"Well, Jesus, Riley, why didn't you say that you were interested in someone?" She was smiling broadly.

"I...I didn't know."

"You didn't know you liked her?" She playfully slapped Riley's knee.

Riley shrugged. "Not really. Well, yeah. I mean, I've tried to not think about it too much. Too busy. And I have to admit that you weren't near the bottom of my thoughts either." This she said quietly, with obvious embarrassment.

Tori rolled her eyes but seemed pleased. "Woman, this is exactly what I'm talking about. These are the kinds of things you don't want to wait to act on. Does she know you're into her?"

Riley shook her head vehemently.

"Is she into you?"

Riley nodded shyly and couldn't help the smile that formed.

Tori rolled her eyes again. "Good Lord. I guess it's up to me to give you a swift kick in the ass. You baby dyke types are adorable but oh so slow. Question one. Is she into music?"

"I think so. We haven't talked about it much."

"Well, you'd better hope she is. Two. What's happening Sunday night?"

Riley was confused by the question. Tori knew that they had the first symphony orchestra concert of the year that night. "Our concert at Bass. Why?"

Tori looked at her, nonplussed.

"Oh. Right. Invite Beth to watch the concert."

Tori winked and patted Riley's knee with friendly condescension. "Very good. You might just get the hang of this yet."

Riley blushed at her ineptitude.

"And after?"

Riley looked at the ceiling, thinking. "Dinner at Trudy's?"

"Perfect. Nothing formal."

"Tori, you're telling me to ask her out on a 'for reals' date? I don't know if I can do that."

"C'mere." Tori motioned Riley closer so she leaned in, their faces almost touching. "If you can do this"—Tori once again pressed her lips onto Riley's, causing yet another shudder of pleasure—"you can ask the girl you like out on a date."

❖

Riley spent the night at Tori's house but, although they slept in the same bed, nothing else happened between them. It was Riley's first time sleeping snuggled up to someone else, though, and it was one of the nicest experiences she had ever had. The warmth of another person who cared about her was just about the best feeling in the world.

The next morning, Tori left for the music building and Riley went back to her dorm to pick up her books and papers for her first classes. She couldn't wait to tell Aidan about her new revelations so she called him as she walked. As usual, he wasn't able to answer his phone, so she jogged the rest of the way, and as soon as she entered her dorm room, she opened her computer and typed an email to him.

> *Aidan,*
>
> *Okay. Now you really won't believe what's going on. I won't go into too many details, but let me summarize.*
>
> *Tori: Has girlfriend, but in an open relationship. We made out; it was awesome. But now she's decided to mentor me because I've realized that I've fallen for—*
>
> *Beth: I just can't get her out of my head. I've never met anyone like her. She's interesting, she's brilliant, she really seems to like me, and she has such a normal, girl-next-door cuteness that I just can't stop thinking about her.*
>
> *I'm scared to death though. I've already gotten too comfortable with Tori, but now that I know there are no strings there, I feel better about it. I will feel awful if I pull perfect, sweet Beth into the shit-show that is my brain, though. It's not fair to her. But despite all that, Aidan, I'm going to ask her out on a date. I won't say it's a date...I mean, friends ask friends to see them in concert and then to dinner too so maybe it will be ambiguous? Anyway, despite my brain trying to get me to stay away, I'm going*

for it. Until I chicken out and run away screaming, that is. I'll let you know how it goes.

God, I sound like a broken record, don't I? And as I write this, I realize what a pain in the ass I'm being. I'm whining about nothing. Two girls like me? When in a million years did I ever think this would happen? I'm doing well in my classes, not all As and Bs, but well enough I think. And I have three close friends now. Why am I bitching and worrying? If I had an answer for that, I wouldn't be consulting Dr. Aidan Email, would I?

Oh. One last thing. Brooke is still a rude bitch and I hate her face.

The end.

Riley

That evening, while Riley was cleaning her station at the coffee shop getting ready to go home, a now familiar face sat down at the bar.

"Hey there," Riley said as she removed her apron.

"I was hoping I'd catch you at the end of your shift," Beth replied.

"Oh yeah?" Riley leaned against her side of the counter, lessening the space between them.

"Yeah."

"Okay. You caught me." Riley smiled teasingly.

Beth, who had at first seemed confident, suddenly shied again. "Well, I just wanted to know if you wanted to hang out again or something. We do still need to go to the Alamo Drafthouse. I just finished a paper for an early final and wanted to celebrate. One less thing to worry about, you know?"

Riley's brow furrowed. She wanted nothing more than to hang out with Beth. The problem was that she was already behind on two papers, studying for three tests, and had hit a complete dead end on an original composition for one of her music classes.

"I can't," Riley said apologetically.

Beth's face fell, but she tried to hide her disappointment.

"That's cool. Just thought I'd drop by and see if you were bored. I think I might go to the free movie at the Union tonight instead, then. Some Norma Shearer film from the thirties."

"I'm sorry. I'm just really bogged down with schoolwork."

"Yeah. Totally get it. No worries." Beth smiled sympathetically.

Riley knew that this was the perfect opportunity. "I want to make it up to you. What are you doing Sunday?"

Beth pulled out her iPhone and checked her calendar. "I have to put the finishing touches on an Oceanography project, I work from twelve until four, and then I'm free." She looked up expectantly.

Riley took a deep breath. "Perfect. We have a concert on Sunday night, the symphony orchestra I mean, so…I just wanted you to know in case you wanted to come and watch. I mean, you said you wanted to see me…us…play. So…yeah. Sunday night at seven thirty. If you're interested."

Beth beamed. "I'd love to see you play."

"Cool! So uh…if you want to grab a bite to eat afterward or something…I thought maybe we'd both be hungry by then…or something."

Beth was positively glowing. "Yeah. That sounds fun. Where should I wait for you?"

"I'll meet you in the lobby. I'll need to drop my cello off at my dorm, but after that I'm good to go."

"Riley?"

"Yeah?"

"I'm really sorry to be slow or naïve, but I just have to know… for my own sanity…" she took a deep breath, "is this a date? Because I would really love for this to be a date."

The nervousness had returned, and the desperate look on Beth's face tugged at Riley's heartstrings. She reddened, but said, "Yeah." She cleared her throat, as it seemed to have closed. "It's a date. If that's okay with you, of course."

"Oh. My. God." Koji's voice squeaked from behind them. He had just arrived to take over the night shift from Riley. "You two. You two, oh my God. Oh my God, you two." His face looked like it was going to split in half from smiling so widely.

"Oh, Jesus." Riley's head fell onto her folded arms. Beth just smiled and waved.

"I've just witnessed a real life Little Lesbian House on the Prairie or some shit. Could you two *be* any more adorbz and old-fashioned?"

Riley stood up straight and glared at him, "Well, we can't all be Grindr and one-night-stand addicts, can we?"

"Girl, you can't insult me with truths. I own it." He smiled even more broadly.

"Beth, I'll see you Sunday. I'm sorry about my uncouth friend here."

"Can't wait." Beth stood to leave. "Thank you for inviting me."

"No problem. See you then." Riley waved and immediately turned to Koji. "Not. One. Word." She then retreated to the back room where she could catch her breath. Beth couldn't wait! She had gotten the courage to ask her out, and she felt invincible for the first time in her life.

Her phone buzzed in her pocket, and she smiled as she saw Aidan's name on the caller ID. She hit the Answer button.

"Aidan!"

"Hey, sis. Just read your email. You are seriously blowing my mind with this girl stuff."

"You will *not* believe what I just did."

❖

Riley sat back down with the rest of the orchestra after the conductor had motioned for them all to take a bow. The concert had gone extraordinarily well, and the epic final notes of Stravinsky's *Firebird Suite* still hung in the air as if reluctant to give up the limelight. *Firebird* was one of Riley's all-time favorite pieces, and she was thrilled that they had played it as the final piece of the night. It reminded her of herself: she always felt aflame. From her literal history with fires, to her constant descents into depression and anger, Riley wanted nothing more than to rise from the ashes and embers of her past and find the part of her life where she could shine in triumph. She felt she was on the right path, but was also keenly aware that she was missing something. She was doing as well as she could on her own, but needed that one extra spark. A beacon. Something or someone to make sure she stayed headed in the right direction.

As she contemplated this, the house lights came on, and both the audience and the orchestra gathered their belongings and started filing out. Riley hadn't seen Beth, of course—the concert hall was much too large for that. But she knew she had been there.

A fluttering started in her chest in anticipation of what was about to be her first date. She quickly packed her cello into its case backstage and made her way to the lobby. She double-checked her suit, the same one she had purchased with Beth's help, and followed other orchestra members through the doors. Her eyes were immediately drawn to Beth, who stood alone near the glass walls of the entrance. She wore a cobalt blue dress that fell just below her knees, and a black knit sweater covered her shoulders. Her hair was tied back in a loose ponytail, and she had on just a touch of natural-looking makeup. She nervously held a small clutch in both hands, close to her abdomen as she glanced around the room.

Riley stopped and swallowed hard. The feeling she got in her stomach every time she saw Beth magnified itself by hundreds. Seeing her like this made her tremble.

She tried to smooth her hair, as it had become disheveled when had lost herself in the music she played onstage. Just as she was about to walk over to her, a voice said in her ear, "Don't tell me the delightful young lady standing alone as if waiting for her princess is Beth."

Riley jumped as Tori put her arm around her shoulders. She blushed because she had been caught having very private thoughts about just that young lady. "Yeah. That's her."

Tori smiled. "Riley, she could not be more delicious. You were right."

Just then, Beth's eyes fell on the two of them. She smiled, but Riley could see her unsure glance at Tori, who was still standing with her arm wrapped intimately around her shoulders.

Tori leaned in once more and whispered, "Don't do anything I wouldn't do."

Riley smiled. "Is there anything you wouldn't do?"

"Other than men, not really. Now go have fun." Tori gave Riley a friendly push, and she approached Beth from across the room.

"Hey," Beth said shyly when Riley stood in front of her. "The concert was amazing. I mean really amazing. I love classical music, but I've never seen it performed live. It adds a whole new dimension. Like the music is alive. I mean, I guess it kind of is when people are playing…live. Sorry. I'm rambling. But yeah, I loved it."

Riley beamed. "I'm really glad you were able to come. And you look," Riley's eyes traveled down Beth's form, "beautiful." It embarrassed her to say it out loud, but it was the truth.

Beth flushed a deep red and said, "You look quite dapper yourself."

"This?" Riley ran her fingers down the collar of her suit jacket. "It helps when the saleswoman dresses me. So. Ready for dinner?"

"Yep. Starving."

"Let's just stop by my dorm room first. I need to drop off my cello and change into something a bit more casual."

"Sure. I'd love to see your room."

Riley's stomach fluttered. Maybe one of these days she would be kicking Brooke out of their room for the night.

As they walked the short distance to her dorm, Beth asked questions about the music that had been performed, the differences between certain instruments, and about Riley's experience playing in the school's premier orchestra as a freshman. Riley was thrilled that Beth was interested in and thoughtful about her chosen path and answered everything with pleasure.

When they entered her residence hall, Riley noticed a few disdainful looks thrown her way by some of the girls from her floor who were studying in the common area. That was odd. She had never even talked to most of them. She glanced at Beth, hoping she hadn't noticed. Beth was looking at the notice boards and decor and luckily hadn't seen. Riley decided it had been her imagination and continued on to her room.

Brooke wasn't in the room when they arrived, and for that, Riley was eternally grateful. She didn't feel like introducing the girl she was falling for to the girl she loathed. She quickly put her cello away and changed into jeans and a button up shirt. It was casual, but nice enough to match the cute dress that Beth was wearing.

After changing and suffering the glares of her dorm mates yet again, Riley and Beth drove to the Trudy's by campus and settled in for an evening of amazing chips and queso and conversation.

After the obligatory banter of nervous first-daters, Beth leaned forward and asked, "So I know that you're an amazing cellist, you make a mean mocha, you have a brother, and that you hated your childhood, but that's about it. I'm now registered for Riley 101. Go." She leaned forward and smiled expectantly as if she really did want to know everything there was to know about Riley's life.

Okay. It was looking like tonight was going to be that night. Time to share. How much was she comfortable sharing though? Riley looked into Beth's eyes and saw curiosity and sincerity. It might be nice to let someone in, but she wasn't comfortable revealing *too* much. She wanted to impress her, not show her the depth of the inner demon's domain quite yet. But she would be truthful. She couldn't imagine being anything but to Beth. Still, she couldn't let her see the pain her past caused her every single day.

Riley settled in for the edited-for-TV version of a long and sometimes painful history.

When her story ended, Beth looked reflective and resolute at the same time. Riley had been expecting pity or judgment or uncomfortable awkwardness. That was what usually happened when her so-called friends at school had heard small snippets of her past. But Beth was different. She almost seemed…what was it that Riley observed? Was it strength? It was as if Beth was sitting up straighter. Like she had grown. Not in size, but in presence. Despite not having had a real example of it in her life, Riley thought Beth looked almost motherly. But not the doting, baby-talking, makeup and PTA sweater wearing kind of motherly. She looked like a protector. A defensive, solid, unyielding force that made Riley stare in awe.

Finally, Beth spoke, and her voice was soft and steady. "The fact that you're sitting here across from me, on a scholarship for music at one of the nation's most famous universities, with a history of abuse, and holding your own basically by yourself...I can't even begin to tell you how impressed I am. I knew the first time I saw you at Metro Haus that there was something special about you, but I never could have guessed the extent of it."

The demon inside that had stirred with the telling of her story retreated in confusion. Riley didn't know how to respond, so she just stared blankly.

Beth seemed to come to a decision. "What are you doing for Thanksgiving?"

The randomness of the question threw Riley off. "Uh. Nothing really. I have a couple of papers to write and finals to study for. Why?"

"What about Thanksgiving dinner?"

Riley shrugged. "Ramen and chips and hot sauce in my room. My whore-bitch of a roommate will be out of town, so cheers to that." She held up her glass in a mock-toast.

Beth took a deep breath as if steadying herself for a difficult question. "Would you like to come home with me?"

Riley blinked.

"I mean," Beth shifted, "if you don't have other plans and don't want to spend it alone...well, my parents always have more than enough food, and I thought...you know...you might want to see the ocean and get away from school for a bit."

Riley was in shock. This girl she was just starting to get to know was inviting her to her home in Galveston? Even after getting a peek at her mental baggage? People just didn't do nice things like that for her.

"You don't have to...it was just a thought." Beth shifted in her chair and her hands fidgeted nervously.

Finally, Riley smiled and said, "That sounds amazing actually. I'd love to."

Beth's face lit up like the sun, but all she said was, "Cool. I'll let my parents know."

The rest of their dinner was spent discussing travel plans for the upcoming holiday—Beth would be driving and playing tour guide—and what Riley was going to see during her first time at the coast. She couldn't believe it, but she was starting to feel more comfortable with Beth than she ever had with anyone in her life, except Aidan. This worried her. She didn't need distractions from achieving her goals, and she sure as hell didn't want to drag someone into the chaos that was her inner turmoil. No one should have to deal with that. Brain storms, demons, doubts, insecurities. Her baggage was heavier than most, and the thought of burdening this adorable, sweet girl with it almost caused her to have a panic attack right there at the table.

This was happening too fast. The fact that this was happening at all suddenly set off a cacophony of alarm bells in her head.

Don't lose sight of why you're here.

Don't burden her with your problems.

Don't let anything stand in your way.

Don't let yourself get hurt.

Don't take her down with you if you fall.

Don't let her see your weakness.

Don't, don't, don't, don't.

But she was. She would try to fight it, but she already knew that it was futile. Right now the thought of having someone to share things with, to just hang out with, and to confide in was winning in the epic bout of insecurity that was taking place in her mental arena.

"So yeah. It's only a few days and there's not a ton to see, but I'm really excited to share it with you. You've made my night; my whole month." Beth's eyes sparkled.

Riley took a deep breath and tried to hide her unease. "I can't wait." She smiled nervously and tried to enjoy watching Beth finish her tacos.

Chapter Thirteen

There it is." Beth put an arm around Riley's shivering shoulders. Before them stretched the seemingly endless waters of the Gulf of Mexico. "Whatcha think?"

"It's…big," Riley said ineloquently.

Beth laughed. "Yeah. It's big."

"But I mean, it's beautiful too. It looks like it goes on forever."

"Wanna stick your toes in?"

"It's freezing outside!" Riley pulled her flimsy jacket closer around her chest.

"Well, yeah, but it's your first visit. You have to say you've been in the ocean your first time."

Riley smiled and nodded. Her hair flapped around her cheeks as they walked down the seawall stairs and crossed the thick sand leading to the water's edge.

Beth deftly removed her shoes and socks and rolled her jeans up to her knees. "Well? Coming?"

Riley stood for a moment, just taking in the view. They had come straight to the beach from their drive from Austin, and she was having trouble believing that only three hours ago she had been in her familiar room at UT and was now seeing the great expanse of the sea for the first time. Her eyes welled with the beauty and emotion of it.

Riley kicked off her shoes and rolled her jeans up the same way Beth had. She walked forward, her toes digging into the wet sand, and stopped beside her.

"Here it comes," Beth said as the tiny wave broke a few yards away from them.

The water rolled over their exposed feet, and Riley inhaled sharply at the cold. "Holy sh—"

"It'll pass!" Beth laughed. "And hey! You've now completed a first in your life." She beamed.

Riley smiled back and kicked the remaining water off her feet now that the wave had receded back into the ocean. "Do I get my trophy now or do I have to stand here longer?"

Beth pulled her back to the dry sand. "That'll do. I won't be so kind-hearted once the summer comes, though. I will require you to be fully submerged then."

Riley looked back out across the water. The thought of being even waist-deep in that great expanse terrified and exhilarated her.

"Come on," Beth said. "Back to the car. My parents have dinner all ready. We don't want to be late. An Earle family Thanksgiving is not to be missed."

Riley followed obediently, secretly nervous about meeting Beth's family. She had never been good around other peoples' parents. Having none of her own, she was always afraid that she would do or say something wrong. How did families behave with each other? How was she supposed to fit into their plans? She wanted desperately for Beth's parents to like her. Was it just because she wanted to be a gracious guest or was it something more?

She glanced at Beth from the corner of her eye as they walked and felt a stirring deep in her chest. She hadn't really cared about impressing many people before, other than with her playing ability, but she wanted desperately to impress Beth. Despite the novelty of these new feelings, Riley worried that they could only bring trouble. She knew herself too well. If she didn't put every ounce of effort and concentration into her goal of becoming a professional musician, she'd never achieve it. Some things came easy to people, and while she did have innate musical ability, it was her years of obsessive practicing that had set her apart from her peers. The constant fear of being overshadowed, now that she was in the midst of real talent, scared her to death. What if she couldn't do it? What if she was no

THE MELODY OF LIGHT

better than her aunt and uncle? What if she never learned to live free
from the torment of the memories of her abuse?

They had reached Beth's car, and as they hastily retreated into
it from the chilly shore wind, Riley collapsed back into herself.

See? See what distractions do?

She screamed inwardly. The brain storms were approaching.
If she didn't calm herself down, they would blow at a gale. Here
she was, with a girl she was growing to like more than any person
she had ever known, seeing the ocean for the first time, and being
welcomed into a family's home for Thanksgiving. What in the hell
was wrong with her? Why couldn't she just be happy in the moment?
Why did everything have to be tethered to her past or darkened by
the fears of her future?

Why couldn't she enjoy her life?

"What's wrong?"

Riley realized that she had been brooding in silence as they
drove from the beach to Beth's family home. Some road trip
companion she was turning out to be.

"Oh. Nothing. Just thinking," she replied.

Beth didn't press the matter, but continued to drive, occasionally
pointing out historic buildings and her previous schools.

Riley knew that Beth deserved someone better than her,
someone not quite so temperamental. But still, every time she looked
at her or heard her voice, she felt...trapped. Beth's personality, her
geeky, but captivating looks, the adorable way her eyes lit up when
she got excited about something...Riley was hooked. Her head was
continually trying to tear her away, but something, some kind of
gravitational pull, kept drawing her closer.

Riley was lost to it.

❖

There sat Beth's mom, excitedly scrolling through pictures
on her iPhone, showing Beth the new wing of the museum where
she worked as an archivist. There stood Beth's father scrubbing
clean the pots and pans that had been used to cook their sumptuous

Thanksgiving dinner, dancing almost imperceptibly to the music that was quietly drifting from the wireless speakers. The immensely old grandfather sat sleeping in his faded Longhorn jersey in the recliner in front of a TV that silently played a Texas football game. There was even a cat—of course there was a cat—curled up on the back of the couch, stuffed full of surreptitiously procured bites of turkey.

Riley still sat at the kitchen table, taking in the modern Rockwellian scene. Something stirred in her memory from long ago. Did she spend holidays like this with Aidan and her own parents? She couldn't remember for sure. Maybe she had only imagined times like this. Happy, simple times before her parents died, before she was placed in the protection of those who had only wanted to harm her, before she was abandoned to the system. Or maybe she really had been a part of this once.

Beth and her family painted such a sweet and domestic picture that it actually pained Riley to watch them. A deep-seated need for a real family of her own squeezed at her heart, and she found that she wanted to stay in this room, surrounded by this love, forever.

"Hey, Riley, come check out this picture." Beth motioned her over to the couch where she sat with her mother.

Riley obliged as Beth said, "This is one of the exhibits Mom is helping with in the new wing."

Beth's mother moved the iPhone so that Riley could see the screen and said, "Beth told me that you're a cellist, so I took these pictures for you. We can actually go by the museum tomorrow if you'd like to see it in person."

Riley looked at the screen and saw close-up pictures of whalebone flutes, hand-carved crude instruments that Riley assumed were supposed to be fiddles, and a rotting concertina that was full of holes.

"Cool! Where are they from?" Riley asked.

"There are a lot more. Most were donated by individual collectors, but they were all used aboard ships or in the many pubs by the docks around here," Mrs. Earle replied.

"Mom works at the Galveston Maritime Museum. The new wing is for their collection of day-in-the-life entertainment at sea stuff. Instruments, scrimshaw, French postcards, ships in bottles, stuff like that."

"Yeah, I'd love to see that."

"No problem," said Mrs. Earle. "The museum is closed tomorrow, so I'll give you girls a private tour."

"Thanks!" Riley was delighted. She hadn't really known what to expect from this trip, but so far, it was far exceeding her expectations. She looked to Beth. "Now I see where you get it."

"What?"

"Your love of the ocean and nautical stuff."

"Oh, I just started working at this museum a few years ago," Mrs. Earle said. "I worked in a library before that. Beth came into the subject matter on her own."

Beth nodded in agreement. "When I was ten, I was in this summer day camp and we'd go on little field trips. We did actually end up going to the maritime museum, though, so you got that part right. They had a special exhibit at the time about famous modern-day ocean explorers, and a name caught my eye. Sylvia Earle. I was so excited to find out that a female explorer had my last name that I became obsessed with learning more about her. Mom and Dad bought me book after book about her and the ocean, and that, as we say, was that. Since then I've gotten to hear her speak twice, and she's definitely my biggest influence. So yeah. That's why I'm studying ocean sciences and want to move into nautical archaeology."

"I didn't even know such a thing existed." Riley said.

"Well, if you stick with me I guarantee you'll become an expert."

Mrs. Earle smiled. "Why do you think I got the job at the museum in the first place? Beth knows everyone who works and volunteers there. When she heard they were looking for an archivist she told them about me, and"—she flourished her hands—"I got the job. Although I think she did it just to get free admission." She looked at Beth with suspicion.

Beth feigned innocence. "Hey, does it hurt that I just happen to benefit from the deal?"

Mr. Earle's voiced drifted in from the kitchen, "I sell car insurance and she uses my family discount too!"

Beth yelled back, "And you use my professors and TAs to have an excuse to get back out on the water. There's nothing wrong with having a symbiotic relationship!"

Riley could feel the love emanating from the Earle family in waves. She had never been around anything like it. Even when she was at her friends' houses in Whitehill, the girls and their parents never had any interaction. Now, seeing what having a family could be like, Riley never wanted to leave.

Later that night, after thanking Mr. and Mrs. Earle and saying good night, Riley sat on her bed in the guest room writing an email to her brother. She had tried calling him and they had gotten to speak for only a few minutes before he was called to duty. She let him know that she'd update him in an email.

Aidan,

Happy Thanksgiving! I hope they're not working you too hard today. Do you get a special meal at least? I don't want to make you jealous, but I just had the single best Thanksgiving dinner of my life. Beth's family is pretty much the coolest ever. I thought it might be awkward spending a major holiday with strangers, but they really welcomed me and made me feel comfortable right away. Her dad works in car insurance and her mom works at a museum. Her grandfather is an old fisherman who loves the Longhorns and the Cowboys. It's a little sad, though. When I leave here, I'll go back to being solitary me. I've never gotten to be a part of a family gathering like this or see how real families interact with each other. Even in high school, I mostly just saw my friends arguing with their parents, and I was obviously never invited to a holiday meal. This is different. I swear they're like a Hallmark commercial or something. They seem too good to be true.

Anyway, I envy what they have, but I'm still having

the best time. Beth took me to the beach today. I actually stood in the water! It probably seems silly to you after all of the time you spent in San Diego, but it was a nice thing to check off of my bucket list. Beth and her mom are even giving me a private tour of the maritime museum tomorrow. I swear, I could stay here forever. Does Galveston have a symphony? I'll have to ask.

My only problem, as per usual, is my head. Yes, you know what I mean. Being around Beth is making the anxiety and the depression come around more often. It feels like I'm fighting with myself and there really shouldn't be any reason to. This just makes me even madder, of course. I wish I could just have a baby roller coaster of emotions, not the scary-ass roller coaster of doom with loops and broken seat restraints.

Anyway, I know Beth likes me, she's pretty open about that, but she hasn't made a move and there's no way I'm going to. I'm too busy trying to not drown. I'm afraid that if I loosen my grip on why I'm here even a fraction, it will all get swept away. I'm so scared that school is too much for me to handle as it is. I almost feel like I don't deserve the good things that have happened to me lately. You and I have never gotten something good that lasted. It's almost like the universe wants to toy with us just to see how we'll handle getting knocked down.

And that's why I'm scared. It's stupid, it's fatalistic, and I'm pretty sure if I keep up my bitching and moaning, it will turn out to be self-actualizing, but that's why I have you. You have to slap me around (metaphorically or I'll kick your ass) and tell me to toughen up.

But anyway, that's what's going on here. Little sis is battling brain storms and doubt, but still having a great time.

If Beth decides to tell me how she feels, I don't know if I'll be strong enough to resist. If Beth never tells me how

*she feels, I don't know if I'll be strong enough to cope with
the disappointment.*

Happy Thanksgiving, Bro. Love you!
Riley

Just as she hit Send there was a knock at her door. She opened
it to find Beth standing with a plate of chocolate chip cookies and
milk.

"Good night snack?"

Riley actually laughed and groaned at the same time. "I feel
like I've eaten enough to send an entire army into a food-induced
coma! But sure, come on in. I'm not one to turn down snacks."

Beth smiled and placed the cookies and milk on the nightstand
before jumping onto the bed to lie on her stomach, feet kicking
playfully in the air. "It's an Earle tradition. On the evening of every
Thanksgiving, we have cookies and milk to usher in the Christmas
season. You know, bookend style. Cookies and milk for us tonight,
cookies and milk for Santa on Christmas Eve."

Riley smiled at this. Santa was one tradition the workers at the
Home tried their best to fulfill. Every year, the kids of the Home
were taken on a field trip to the mall to tell Santa their Christmas
wishes, and every Christmas Eve the kids got to make and decorate
fresh sugar cookies for themselves as well as for Santa's visit.

"Sometimes I miss him," Riley said wistfully. "I always wished
for sheet music or gift cards, and he always came through."

"Santa's still around. He just takes a different form when you
get older." Beth bit into a cookie and smiled.

Riley sat on the bed next to her and stayed silent.

Beth finished her bite and sat up to face her. "So. Are you
enjoying your stay so far?"

"Oh yeah. Your family is amazing. You're really lucky." She
couldn't help the hard swallow that followed. Beth must have
noticed because she sat up and put her hand on Riley's knee.

"Missing your brother?"

Riley nodded. "I always miss my brother, but…" She paused.

"I've never had what you guys have here. I mean, not that I really remember anyway. The only things I have left from my parents are a few everyday items in a shoebox. I think I'm a bit envious if I'm being totally honest."

Beth bit her lower lip then said, "I didn't really think about that. I hope we're not making you uncomfortable. I just really wanted you to have a good holiday. You seemed to need it."

Riley covered Beth's hand with her own. "This has been the best Thanksgiving I've ever had. Your parents are super cool and have been the only parental types that I've ever felt comfortable around, so nothing could've made this trip better."

Beth beamed. "I'm so glad to hear you say that. There is one thing, though." She looked down at their touching hands. "There's only one more thing that can make it perfect for me."

Riley's cheeks heated. She guessed what was coming next.

Beth took a deep breath. "This is so not like me, but I just have to come out and say it or I'm going to explode." She looked deeply into her eyes. "Riley."

"Yeah?"

"I don't think it's any big secret if I tell you that I've been mad crushing on you since I first saw you at Metro Haus." She said it hesitantly as if asking a subtle question.

Riley didn't know how to respond, so she made a noncommittal shrug, her face burning even more.

"Well, I have. And trust me, this is scary as crap for me right now." She laughed nervously. "But. Yeah. I just wanted you to know. Maybe it's stupid for me to tell you right now with you held captive in my house, hundreds of miles from campus, but…yeah. I just couldn't stand not saying something. So. Anyway. Yeah. I really like you. Like, a lot. Just so you know."

Riley opened her mouth, not sure of how she was going to respond, but Beth said, "I mean, you don't have to say anything now. I don't want to make it all weird. And it absolutely won't affect our friendship…on my side at least. I just needed to be honest with you. So take whatever time you need." Still, she looked expectant.

Now that it had been said out loud, Riley had a decision to make. Should she continue to be trapped by her fears or should she do what every nerve in her body was demanding she do?

She looked into Beth's beautiful green eyes behind those glasses and was lost. Beth's gravity had her. She was already pulled in. And she was fine with that.

Riley squeezed Beth's hand as it rested on hers and said, "I adore you, Beth Earle. The nights that I don't see you studying and trying to sneak glances at me at the coffee shop feel lonely, and the time since I've gotten to know you I feel like I don't want to be around anyone else."

Beth's eyes widened and the largest smile Riley had ever seen on her face formed. "No way."

Riley laughed out loud and Beth flushed saying, "Sorry. I…I don't know how to be romantic. I'm just…God, I'm so freakin' stoked."

Riley snorted with laughter and picked up Beth's hand, clasping it between her own. "So. What now?"

Beth sat forward with unbridled excitement. "Can I please kiss you? I've been fantasizing about kissing you for so damn long. I'm sorry. Forward much? Again, not good with flowery romantic stuff."

Riley laughed again. "Flowery romantic stuff not required with this girl. And yes, I wish you would."

Now that the time had come, Riley felt comfortable and eager. Not like when she kissed Tori. She had been surprised and nervous then. It had been her first real kiss, so she supposed that was normal, but with Beth she felt like there was nothing in the world more comforting while at the same time exhilarating and electrifying.

When Beth leaned in and pressed her lips to Riley's, she moved like she really meant it. The kiss was soft, but determined and excited at the same time. Riley felt a fire ignite in her stomach and surprised herself when she was overcome with a new and unexpected passion that caused her to roll Beth down onto the bed. She covered Beth's body with her own and kissed her passionately in a way she hadn't even realized she knew how to do.

Beth definitely didn't complain. If it hadn't been for Mr. Earle calling from downstairs for Beth to say good night to her grandfather, Riley was pretty sure she would have experienced another first in that very bed. As it was, they pulled away from each other, both out of breath and grinning stupidly.

"Holy crap," Riley said, still trying to fight down the growing tingling in her abdomen.

"We must...do that...again," Beth said, still smiling broadly.

"You don't have to ask me twice."

Beth ran her fingers down Riley's cheek. "I'm hoping this means what I think it means."

"That we're both amazing kissers?" Riley joked.

"Well, I would say that's obvious." She grinned. "Do you...I mean, are you my...are we..."

Riley leaned down and kissed Beth again, this time tenderly, then said, "Yes. If you can put up with me."

Beth's eyes crinkled. "I'll do anything for you."

Riley kissed her again and then rolled over, freeing Beth to get up from the bed.

As she reached the doorway to go downstairs she said, "'Night, Riley." The way she was looking at her made Riley's heart melt. No one had ever looked at her with such pure tenderness before.

"'Night." Riley smiled back, her entire body aching to feel Beth's touch again.

With a final glance, Beth left the room and closed the door behind her, leaving Riley trembling and exultant in her wake.

❖

The next morning, with the sensations of the night's dreams still fresh on her mind, Riley came downstairs to the smell of cooking eggs, veggie sausage, and toast. Beth stood cooking at the stove, and her mother sat checking email at the kitchen table.

"Morning," she said to them both.

Beth turned around happily and bounded over to her, pulling

her into a hug. Riley looked nervously at Mrs. Earle, who simply smiled and patted the chair next to her.

"Do you want to go see the museum after breakfast?" she asked as Riley sat down.

"Yeah. Sounds great."

Beth had returned to the stove and was shoveling the eggs and sausages onto three plates. The men were already out fishing for the day.

When she had set the plates down and joined her mother and Riley at the table, Mrs. Earle spoke again. "Beth tells me that you two are now an item."

Riley choked on a too large bite of toast. Beth kindly patted her on the back as she coughed and spluttered.

"Mom! Don't embarrass her!" To Riley she said, "We're kind of open and honest here. I'm sorry if you wanted me to wait to tell them. I was…excited." She squeezed Riley's shoulder.

She had stopped coughing so she replied, "No. I mean, that's fine. I just wasn't expecting it. Especially with the…" Riley didn't want to say "the gay thing," so she just let the sentence trail off.

"Oh, psh," said Mrs. Earle. "We've been wondering when our Beth would find the woman of her dreams. I'm just glad we've been able to meet you so soon!"

Woman of her dreams?

Riley looked at Beth inquisitively and Beth just shrugged and nodded. "I've been talking about you for months now."

"We couldn't get her to shut up about you, really. I'm just surprised it took her so long to say something to you."

"I'm *shy*, Mom!"

Now Riley's cheeks were really burning. Beth had been talking about how much she liked her to her *family*? Was this something she herself would have done if she had had a mother to talk to? She was at once embarrassed and delighted.

"Okay, we're done mortifying you," Mrs. Earle said with a melodious laugh much like Beth's. "You girls finish up and we'll get going."

When Beth's mother had left the kitchen, Riley looked incredulously at Beth, who simply said, "What? I had to tell her. She kept asking anyway. 'When are you going to tell her?' 'Do you think she likes you too?' I swear she talked about you more than I did."

"What if…what if I'm a disappointment?"

Beth's head tilted to the side. "How is that possible?"

Riley shrugged. "I dunno. I don't know how to impress parents. I'm not very good with families."

Beth leaned forward and planted a soft kiss on Riley's warm cheek. "You don't have to impress them. You're everything you need to be just being yourself."

Quietly, Riley said, "You don't know my whole self."

"No. But I'm looking forward to discovering every single part of you. Good, bad, beautiful, difficult, all of it. I want *you*, Riley Gordon. No concessions necessary."

"I hope so."

You may not like what you find.

❖

Riley and Beth were inseparable for the rest of their time in Galveston. Even parting to sleep in their separate bedrooms was torture. They knew their classes and jobs were sure to get in the way once they got back to school, but the allure of Beth's empty apartment was too delicious to ignore.

Soon after they arrived back in Austin and classes started up again, they fell into the closest thing to a rhythm they could achieve. They met for lunch when they could, had dinner together on Tuesday and Thursday nights, and spent the rest of their time rehearsing, working, and studying for their end-of-semester exams.

Despite her worries about passing her classes and doing well in the music program, Riley was excelling. Beth was a large part of that. As a sophomore, she had the experience to help Riley organize her schedule to get in the most efficient and useful study time. They spent quality time with each other too, of course, but Riley was finding that Beth was just as driven to succeed as she herself was, and she made sure they didn't let their blossoming relationship get in the way of what they had to do.

After almost a month of officially being together, Riley decided that all of their hard work and dedication to school, despite being a detriment to their budding relationship, deserved a real romantic night out. She had everything planned. She had bought tickets to the Austin Ballet and, this being the last night Riley and Beth had together before a slew of end-of-semester finals were to dominate their last week before the Christmas break, Riley was ecstatic.

Now, inside the darkened Bass Concert Hall, the music built to a crescendo and crashed down upon them in a wave of impassioned melody. The two dancers reacted in kind by flowing and leaping with immense strength and grace across the winter wonderland of the stage. Riley glanced over at Beth, who was wiping a small tear from the corner of her eye. Nothing in the world could have made Riley happier at that very moment. Her chest swelled with emotion and her own eyes became misty.

When the fervent timpani rolls accented by final insistent chords filled the room, Beth reached over and squeezed Riley's hand. Squeezing back, Riley knew that, in this one moment, by the shared experience and appreciation of something so beautiful, she and Beth had unlocked a more intimate level of their relationship.

Riley was desperate to welcome Beth deeper into the world of music she loved so dearly. Now they sat together with their fingers entwined, falling even more in love, listening to the final notes of Riley's favorite piece of all time, the "Pas de Deux" from Tchaikovsky's *The Nutcracker Suite*, and she felt truly happy for the first time in her life.

❖

Riley and Beth exited the Co-op on the Drag and crossed the street to the West Mall, backpacks, now lighter, slung over their shoulders.

"Okay, the whole textbook buyback thing is bullshit," Riley said as they walked toward the iconic UT tower.

"I know, right? 'Hey, pay us fifty bucks for a textbook you'll never actually need, and, at the end of the semester, we'll give you twenty-five cents for it. Beat that deal!'" Beth mocked.

"Thank God most things are going digital now, otherwise I'd never be able to afford it, scholarship or not!"

They walked past the Texas Union and the multitudes of student organization tables and made their way in silence down through the Six Pack on the South Mall toward the Littlefield Fountain. Beth seemed nervous about something.

They took a left on East Twenty-first Street and headed toward the stadium and Riley's dorm.

"So. I have a question for you," Beth said hesitantly.

"'Kay," Riley said simply.

"What are you doing tonight?"

"Deep question. I can see why you're so nervous about it." Riley winked.

"Don't be snarky. I'm asking you out." Beth slapped her backside.

"Oh! Well, then, I should tell you that I already have plans…"

Beth's face fell.

"To spend time," Riley continued, "with the nicest, most beautiful woman I've ever met."

"Oh. Em. Gee. That was *the* cheesiest thing I've ever heard anyone say in the entire history of ever."

"And you loved it."

"Yes. Yes, I did. But anyway, asking you out isn't quite right either. I mean do you want to come over to my place tonight? I want…I want you to stay…with me…tonight. We've been so busy with finals that I don't feel like we've really gotten to spend time together…alone."

Something tingled in Riley's stomach and she nodded in agreement. "Between-class snogs are the best part of my day, but I agree with you wholeheartedly."

❖

Riley had stayed at Beth's apartment before, but their workload had kept them from really getting to spend much time together even then. This night, however, Riley knew that she and Beth had nothing but each other on their minds.

Still, Riley was nervous. Not about being with Beth, but about her own self-consciousness. It wasn't every day that someone she had fallen in love with was going to see the extent of her prior abuse.

"There's something I need to talk about first," Riley said as she and Beth pulled apart from a long and passionate kiss as they sat on the couch.

"What's that?" Beth looked concerned.

"You haven't seen…all of me…yet."

Beth grinned with a mischievous twinkle in her eyes. "Well, no, but I'll admit it hasn't been the furthest thing from my mind." She ran her hand under Riley's shirt.

Riley kissed her on the cheek. "Naughty. But really, you're the first person that's going to really see all of the bad stuff."

"What bad stuff?"

"You know about these." Riley held up her arms to show the small red and white circles that dotted each.

Beth nodded and said, "Those in no way turn me off, Riley. You should know that."

Riley took a deep breath and removed her shirt and sports bra. As the fabric was lifted over her head, she heard Beth gasp.

"Oh my God."

Flushing with shame, Riley tried to hold herself in a vain attempt to cover the multitudes of cigarette burn and belt scars that covered her arms and chest.

Beth's mouth had fallen open. "I can't believe they did this to you. I mean…on your chest and stomach too? That's so messed up!" She gently twisted Riley around by the shoulders. "Back too? Riley, how did no one stop this?"

Riley shrugged. "Aidan tried."

"What about the authorities? CPS or the police?"

"They didn't know about it. Aunt Joan made me wear long sleeves everywhere and never took me to the doctor for anything. Aidan wanted to get help, but he was afraid they'd hurt me more if they found out. We were kids. We didn't know how to make the right decisions."

Beth was beside herself with outrage. "But I mean, what could you have done to make them want to do this to you?"

"It was like a game. If they didn't like something I did or if I didn't do something fast enough…" Riley made a hissing noise and mimed putting a cigarette out on her arm. "They even did it to get laughs from some of their drug addict friends. They weren't in their right minds most of the time…any of the time. Aidan has the burns too, but only because he tried to protect me."

"I swear to God, if they weren't already dead I'd kill them myself." Riley saw a frightening fury in Beth for the first time. "I promise you I won't let anyone hurt you ever again."

Riley's eyes watered.

"Do you trust me?" A fire had ignited in Beth's eyes.

"More than anyone."

"Will you believe what I tell you? No shame. No embarrassment."

Riley nodded halfheartedly. It was hard for her to take people's words at face value.

Beth took Riley's arms and pulled them down to her sides, exposing her body fully, burns and all. "You are so gorgeous. Nothing I see here"—she ran her fingers gently across Riley's chest—"changes how I feel about you. I want to see you. I want to feel you. I want to drink you in, body and soul. I love you."

She leaned forward and kissed the nape of Riley's neck. Riley gasped with pleasure.

"I love you."

She pushed Riley down onto the couch and kissed the old scars on her chest.

"I love you," Beth repeated. "I love you."

Her hands caressed her stomach, slowly working their way lower, while her lips met Riley's once again in a feverish and passionate kiss.

Riley quivered with ecstasy and euphoria. She felt like a new person. She had been so worried about exposing herself, her body, and her past to Beth, but this woman had proven to be nothing but loving and compassionate. She was in love and she was joyful in the knowledge that the feeling was requited just as fiercely.

Riley stood and took Beth's hand. They walked together to the bedroom, and Riley felt that she and Beth were both secure in the absolute understanding of each other and the comfort and bliss of unequivocal respect and love.

CHAPTER FOURTEEN

With the semester over, most students home for Christmas break, and Beth and her family on a holiday cruise to the Caribbean, Riley was alone. She had known she would be, and she tried to tell herself that she didn't mind. She was lonely, of course, knowing that she couldn't talk to the two people she cared about most in the world, but the happiness and hope that had been growing since she had met Beth sustained her. But still, there were only so many movies she could watch, websites she could browse, books she could read, or music she could practice before she just felt lifeless.

She had tried calling Aidan a few times, but he hadn't answered. It worried her, but she told herself to remain positive. It wasn't like he was overseas, after all. But now, on a gray and cold Christmas Eve, she wished more than anything that she could talk to him.

She rolled out of bed where she had been lying and looking up websites about famous shipwrecks to discuss with Beth when she got back. She shuffled over to the window and glared at Brooke's perfectly made bed. Her roommate had left for home a few days before, and Riley couldn't have been happier. They had barely spoken since the day that Riley had found Brooke's pendant. Not only that, but everyone on their floor seemed to have turned on her. They had been polite before, but now every time Riley appeared, conversation ceased and icy daggers were thrown her way. She just couldn't figure it out. Luckily, her coursework and Beth had taken up most of her time and energy, so she pushed the discomfort to the back of her mind.

Determined to stop brooding, she looked out her window to the football stadium across the street and concentrated on the recently made memories of Beth's soft fingers tracing loving patterns across her stomach and thighs. She shivered as pleasurable goose bumps pebbled on her skin.

There was a knock at the door, and she jumped in surprise. Who did she know that would be stopping by on Christmas Eve? Koji was back in New Mexico with his family and Tori was home in Dallas.

Still in her pajamas, she combed cold fingers through her tangled hair and opened the door.

"Hey, Nugget."

Riley's jaw dropped. "Holy hell!"

Aidan laughed his hearty and contagious laugh. "Merry Christmas to you too, ya little shit."

She flung herself into his waiting arms and whooped with happiness. "Why didn't you tell me?"

"I didn't know I could come until a week ago. And then I wanted to surprise you."

"Job well done. Come in!"

Riley led him inside the dorm room and he threw his backpack unceremoniously onto Brooke's bed.

"I was able to catch a ride Space-A on a C-130. It couldn't have worked out better. Am I interrupting anything?"

Riley glanced around the room. "Well, I was just about to start decorating for my annual Christmas Eve orphan's rave, but now that you're here…"

"Good. Get dressed. We're going out. We need to catch up. It's not the same over email or the phone. Where do you want to go for your Christmas Eve dinner?"

"Chuy's!"

Aidan looked at her incredulously. "Riley, I'm paying. Anywhere you want. It can be a special place. Fancy pants style."

Riley nodded. "Chuy's."

"Tex-Mex on Christmas Eve?"

"Is there ever a bad time for Tex-Mex?"

Aidan tilted his head, thinking. "Chuy's it is."

❖

During their meal, Riley hijacked most of the conversation because she just couldn't stop talking about Beth. Aidan didn't seem to mind, though.

"I can't tell you how glad I am to see you so happy. It suits you. You're like a different person," he said, beaming.

Riley shrugged. "I don't know about that. I just know that I love her. The stuff with Tori"—Aidan's smile grew at the mention of her name—"was definitely…fun. But there's so much more to how I feel about Beth."

Aidan nodded. "You're lucky to feel love like that. There are always women, but no one has ever taken my breath away or anything. Not like what you guys have. Full disclosure, I'm actually a little jealous." He took a large bite of his burrito.

"You? Jealous of me?" Riley couldn't fathom such a thing.

"Yep," he said, mouth full.

Riley's thoughts drifted back to Beth's loving face. She could see such adoration when she looked at her. "It's the best feeling in the world to know that I mean so much to someone. I've never felt like I was important or worthwhile before."

Aidan's brow furrowed.

"Except to you, of course."

Aidan sighed. "No, I get it. Neither of us had the easiest time growing up."

Riley scoffed. "You did fine! You were the popular one. Everyone loved you."

He shook his head and leaned back in his chair. A shadow passed over his eyes. "Everyone loved the facade I put up. Only you know the real me. And maybe my guys back at the base now. But all of that brashness and confidence was just to protect myself. I made myself bigger than life so that I could feel bigger *than* my life. Just like you protected yourself with music and introspection and quiet independence. Neither one of us wants to be hurt again."

Riley was shocked at the serious direction the conversation had taken. Aidan very rarely showed his true feelings or fears.

"And the amazing thing is that we've both made it. I mean, of course we can be hurt. Of course we *do* hurt. But the difference is that we're living our lives on our own terms now. No matter what happens, we will always know that we made it out and we did it for ourselves."

Riley sat pensively. After taking a few more bites of her enchilada, she said, "It's nice to think about it that way. I don't often think about my life as an accomplishment. I always see it as a battle. I feel like I'm in a constant fight to erase what happened to us and to prove that I'm worth it."

"That's what makes you so powerful, Riley. That's what Beth sees in you that you don't. She can see the fire that I've always seen. Not the anger or fear, but the determination and courage in the face of that fear. I know you struggle with it. You know I know better than anyone. But having that fear doesn't make you weak. You've never succumbed to it. You always face it head on and keep going. That's your fire. That's your strength."

Riley's eyes watered. She didn't know what to say. She had spent so many years terrified of her past and the future unknown that she didn't feel in the least bit brave or strong. Still, it was so comforting to hear him say it that she almost believed that it could be true…if only for the moment.

❖

The next morning, Riley woke to the sound of birds chirping resiliently in the frost-covered landscape outside her window. She was swaddled in the sheets of the most comfortable bed she had ever slept in. After their dinner at Chuy's the previous night, Aidan had surprised her with her Christmas present. He had been able to book them a suite in a four-star Hill Country resort just outside of town at the last minute. He figured that would allow them to spend

Christmas morning in style for once. He had gallantly taken the sofa bed in the adjacent living room while Riley had the master bedroom to herself. They had spent the evening making s'mores in the suite's gas fireplace, listening to Christmas carols on Internet radio, drinking champagne, and exchanging stories about their lives, girls, and some of the idiots they had to deal with on a daily basis.

Riley missed Beth, but she felt blessed with the opportunity to spend some quality time with her only remaining family again. Aidan hadn't changed much, of course. Women were always at the forefront of his thoughts, he still pretended to be non-judgmentally superior to many around him, and his laugh and his smile were still as infectious as ever. Riley didn't know why it continued to surprise her, but she still couldn't wrap her head around the fact that they were from the same stock. They were so different from each other, yet their bond was as strong as any family's could hope to be.

As Riley reveled in the feel of the 600-count sheets and listened to the birds outside, the familiar cello refrain that she used as her ringtone filled the room. Wiping the sleep from her eyes, she smiled as Beth's smiling face flashed on the screen.

"Merry Christmas, sweetie," she said when she answered.

Beth's voice was like music to her ears. She hadn't heard it for a week. "Merry Christmas, love."

"Aren't you still on your cruise?"

"Yeah. Just docked in Honduras, though. I'm actually going to have a white Christmas if you can believe it. It still counts if it's sand, right?"

"Wrong."

"Well, I'm sure I won't have an ounce of fun if that makes you feel better. I mean, a private cabana at Mahogany Bay with an endless supply of girly drinks and bar food? Who needs it?"

Riley could hear her smiling as she teased. "Yeah. Sounds awful. Too bad I'm not there to help you cope."

Beth's voice turned a shade somber. "Now, that would really make today amazing. I hate that I can't share this with you. You'd love it. And oh what I wouldn't do to get you into that hammock with me right now."

Riley blushed as her face broke into a pleased smile.

"But really," Beth continued, "How are you doing?" Riley could hear the worry in her voice. Beth had felt awful about leaving Riley alone for Christmas, but Riley had insisted that she not give her a second thought while she was off adventuring with her family.

"Well, you're not going to believe where I am right now. And who I'm with."

After Beth's squeals of delight at her news that Aidan was in town and about their weekend getaway, she could tell a weight had been lifted off Beth's shoulders, and that made her happy.

"I want you to meet him," Riley said.

"What? Now? On the phone?"

"Why not?"

Beth agreed and Riley took her phone in to the living room where Aidan was still sleeping.

"I have to wake him up."

"Riley, don't!"

Riley ignored her and poked Aidan on the shoulder. His leg hung off of the pull-out bed, and his mouth was open and drooling on his pillow. "Aidan, wake up. It's Christmas morning!"

He made a small groan as he closed his mouth and blinked his eyes open.

Riley simply smiled, put the phone on speaker, and held it out to him. "Meet Beth."

"Beth?" he asked groggily.

"Yes. Beth."

He sat up and rubbed the sleep out of his eyes. "Your Beth?"

Riley rolled her eyes, but smiled. "Yes. My Beth."

He looked confused.

"The love of my life?" Riley offered.

Aidan finally smiled. "I know. I'm just waking up." He turned to the outstretched iPhone. "Hey, Beth! Merry Christmas!"

Beth's voice sounded from the speaker. "Hi, Aidan. It's nice to get to talk to you finally!"

"You too. I've heard a lot of things about you."

"All good I hope."

"Horrible. Just the most horrendous things you can imagine."

"Aidan!" Riley protested as Beth laughed.

"All true, I assure you," she replied.

"But really, I wanted to thank you," Aidan continued.

"Thank me for what?" Beth asked.

"Thank you for showing my little sister how amazing she is. I've said it since she was born, but I think it means a lot more coming from you. I've never seen her this happy in my life. I mean it."

Riley grinned broadly as Beth said, "Thank *you* for helping to make her the amazing woman she is. She talks about you constantly. I'm glad she has you."

Aidan puffed up a little and winked at Riley. "You're welcome, Beth. Anything for a lovely young woman such as yourself."

Riley's eyes narrowed. "Aidan, don't hit on my girlfriend."

Both Aidan and Beth laughed. Aidan continued, "Beth, I feel that I have to do the standard big brother thing just once before I let you go enjoy your Christmas."

"Okay, what's that?" she asked.

"Don't break her heart, don't mistreat her, and love her with your entire soul, or I'll be super pissed and all that fun stuff."

"Aidan!" Riley objected.

Both Aidan and Beth laughed again. Beth said, "Riley, it's okay. He's absolutely right. He won't be nearly as upset with me as I'll be with myself if any of that happens. Aidan, it was amazing getting to meet you finally. You guys have a great Christmas, okay? I'm so glad you got to go to Texas to spend it with her. I felt awful that I had to leave her alone."

"You can't keep us apart. We've been through too much," Aidan said. "And it was great meeting you too. I can't wait to see you in person some time. Now go say your sweet nothings or whatever to Riley without her brother being a creeper in the background."

"Bye, Aidan!"

Riley took the phone off speaker and walked back to her bedroom.

"I hope that was okay," she said when she was alone.

"I'm really glad I got to talk to him. He sounds like a great guy.

I have to go now. International call, you know. Merry Christmas, love. I can't wait to see you again."

"Thanks for calling, sweet girl. I love you." Riley held the phone tight to her head, trying to keep Beth close.

"Love you!"

Riley hung up the phone and smiled. The two most important people in her life had finally met on Christmas Day. She couldn't think of anything better.

Riley shuffled, still smiling, into the kitchenette and made two mugs of instant hot chocolate and then flipped on the TV to see the Grinch beaming as his heart grew three sizes. Riley smiled. She, Aidan, and the other kids at the Home had loved watching that particular cartoon during the holidays.

She turned around and set the hot chocolate on the coffee table with a loud clink.

"Here," she said as she tapped the steaming mug, "start Christmas off right."

"Thanks, Nugget." He took the drink and began to sip carefully. "Beth really does sound wonderful. Thanks for letting me meet her."

"I'm glad you got to."

Aidan stretched. "I'm not used to getting to sleep in. What time is it?"

Riley checked her watch. "Ten thirty. I have your present here when you're ready." Riley smiled as she put the gift bag on the bed next to him.

"You didn't have to get me anything!"

Riley rolled her eyes. "You got me a mini-vacation at the nicest hotel I've ever seen. What I got you doesn't even come close. At least you get to open it in person. It's a good thing I'm a procrastinator or else it would already be in the mail to you."

"Well, if you insist." He sat up and gleefully pulled the tissue paper out of the bag. He smiled as his hand wrapped around a new wallet. He lifted it out of the bag and looked impressed. "You know, I actually need one of these. My leather one is trashed. Thanks!"

Riley smiled. "I got it at the military surplus store. It's brand new, though. They said it's made out of military-grade tactical woven something-something and it has a special panel for your military ID. I thought it might be useful. You've had that leather one since high school."

"Absolutely! I love it." He opened up the Velcro flap and his eyes widened as he saw several photos already placed in the provided sleeves.

Riley had never seen him cry. Not once. Not even when their parents had died. But he started crying now. He took one look at the pictures Riley had pre-inserted in the wallet and broke down. Riley didn't know what to do. He was always the one who consoled her. He was the strong one. But now, all of a sudden, he had tears running down his cheeks. Riley was scared and uneasy.

"Aidan?" she asked. "Are you okay?"

He nodded, sniffed, and then pulled her into the tightest hug she had ever received from him.

When he released her, she gasped for air.

"Sorry," he sniffed, once again flipping through the pictures.

Riley didn't know what to do, so she nervously scratched her arm and said, "I know it's super old-school to put photos in wallets, but I didn't know if you'd be able to take your iPhone with you overseas, and I thought it might be nice for you to have hard copies in case you get lonely...or sentimental...or whatever."

Aidan nodded and smiled, patting the edge of the sofa bed where he sat. "It's perfect. Sorry for the crying. I just...to see the people and things I love most in my life right here, all together...it just makes me so happy. And sad. But mostly happy." He turned to smile at her and then went back to the first picture, looking at them in order.

The first photo was of Aidan and Riley together as children. It was a posed photo their parents had gotten taken at the mall photography studio when Riley was only about three years old and Aidan was six. The second was of their parents together. They stood looking into each other's eyes with their arms wrapped around each other in a candid embrace on the dance floor of their wedding reception. The next picture was another professional photo of Riley seated with her cello. Every student in the orchestra had gotten to take one for the yearbook. The next photo was of the rest of the contents of the heirloom box that Riley currently kept in her dorm room.

"I wanted to make sure you had access to them, even if just in picture form," Riley explained. Aidan nodded appreciatively and pulled her into a short hug again. She knew what it meant to him.

The next picture was one that Beth's mom had taken of her and Riley at Thanksgiving. They stood huddled together at the end of a pier, the cold ocean breeze freezing their windswept hair forever in time. Beth beamed at the camera, her arm threaded through Riley's as if she never wanted to let her go. Riley, however, was gazing in blissful awe at her as if she couldn't quite believe that she was real.

"You two are sickeningly adorable, you know that?" Aidan said with a note of envy in his voice.

Riley smiled. "Yeah. We are."

The final picture was the most recent one she had taken with Aidan. He stood in full dress uniform, flashing his stellar smile, as handsome as the men and women in a recruitment poster, with his arm around Riley's shoulders. She had begged him to wear the "fancy" uniform just once before he had gone back to the School of Infantry back in August. He had obliged and they had gotten their picture taken on the veranda overlooking the lake when they had eaten a last dinner at The Oasis. The young and attractive waiter had been instantly smitten with Aidan, of course, and when he had found out that Riley was his sister and not his girlfriend the flirting had begun in earnest. Aidan had laughed it off like he always did. He did love the attention.

Standing by his side in the photo, Riley looked rather drab in her old gray Goodwill slacks from high school and white button-up shirt. Still, it was one of her favorite pictures. Her red hair was behaving itself for once, the Texas sky glowed orange in reflection on the lake below, and they both looked truly happy. The picture also represented new beginnings. It had been taken the weekend that she had moved into the dorm, and it forever captured in time Aidan's road to self-discovery as a newly minted Marine and Riley's first steps into adulthood as a first-year college student.

This time, her own eyes started to well up. Everything she loved was represented in that wallet. She was glad that Aidan would get to take it with him when he was deployed. She felt that she could be there with him, if even in just this small way.

Aidan turned to face her. "This means the absolute world to me."

Riley simply smiled and nodded, afraid of breaking down. Something new had appeared in his eyes, though. She could read his mood so well. She knew what was coming. Riley steeled herself and asked, "Where?"

Aidan sighed. "Jordan. On the border of Syria."

Riley felt her soul plummet through her feet. She swallowed a lump the size of a boulder in her throat. "When?"

"Two weeks."

"How long?"

"Five or six months."

She nodded dejectedly. Aidan must have sensed the panic rising in her because he took hold of her hands and said, "It'll fly by. You'll be busy with school, and I *know* Beth will keep you occupied." He winked slyly.

Riley rolled her eyes and sighed in sad resignation. "Neither of us can say anything that will make me not terrified, so let's just enjoy the day. How many Christmases do I get to spend at a luxury resort?" She smiled bravely and Aidan nodded appreciatively.

"Massage at the spa, Christmas lunch in the restaurant, and then a movie in Bee Cave?"

"Sounds perfect."

This was it. There would be no turning back now. The fear of Aidan going overseas had been a fear never truly realized while he was safely at home in the States, but now it was happening. Really happening.

I need you to be strong now, Riley.

CHAPTER FIFTEEN

Riley lazily traced her fingers across the soft skin of Beth's bare back as they lay together in the darkness of Beth's room. Since Beth lived alone in a small apartment by campus, Riley was happy to spend most of her time off there. Ever since classes had resumed a month ago, Riley had found being around her roommate intolerable. She had no idea what had happened to cause an even larger rift in their already icy relationship, but Brooke's behavior had shifted from disdainful two-facedness to unabashed hatred. Riley took a deep breath and reveled in the fresh smell of Beth's shampoo. She wouldn't think about Brooke now. Not with the delights of the beautiful young woman lying next to her.

Beth made a pleased noise and rolled onto her side, pulling Riley into her embrace. "It kills me that we don't have time to do this more often," she purred into Riley's neck.

"Hey, I'm game again if you are." Riley smiled and slowly moved her hand lower down Beth's back.

Beth groaned in what sounded like half desire and half frustration. "God, I wish we could, but you still have that gig with Tori tonight, right?"

Riley sighed. "Yeah. It'll pay well, though. Another wedding. Then I have to cover for Koji for a four-hour shift late tonight."

"And tomorrow?"

"School and rehearsal all day, and I need to start practicing for my end of the year solo performance."

"Starting early."

"Yeah. I want it to be perfect. I'm already terrified."

"When will I see you again?"

"I work Tuesday night, but I'm free after nine. You?"

Beth pulled her in tighter. "Yeah. And if you don't come over here and do precisely what you did to me tonight, I'm never speaking to you again."

Riley laughed. "Empty threats."

She shivered as Beth touched her delicately on her inner thigh. "You're not supposed to call my bluffs."

"You are not making his easy for me." Riley reluctantly tore herself away and got out of the bed.

"I sincerely hope not!" Beth smiled wickedly.

Riley got dressed and felt a blush cover her scarred body as Beth watched her dreamily, head propped comfortably on her hand.

"What are you doing for the next couple of days?" Riley asked to distract herself.

Beth sat up and slipped a faded blue T-shirt over her head. "Math assignments, full day of Bio and Chem, an essay, and more research on my Intro to Oceanography project."

"The biology of water protons thing?"

"Ecology of oceanic phytoplankton, but close."

"Nerd."

"You love it."

"God, I do."

Beth smiled.

They were quiet as they each dressed fully and then Beth asked, "How's he doing?"

Riley shrugged as she thought about the most recent phone call from her brother. "So far he's loving it over there. Sand, danger, and all. I feel like a bitch, but I really wanted him to hate it. Make him realize he did a stupid thing or something. But no, he feels like he's in a movie. He does love being a badass."

"You're just worried about him."

"Duh."

"I think it's so sweet that you guys care so much about each other. I can't imagine not having my family around. I'm glad you've always had each other."

Riley nodded. "I don't know how I would've survived otherwise. When Mom and Dad died...I mean I was really young, but I still remember the lights and noise of the police cars, ambulances, and fire trucks as they raced down the street. All of us kids at the daycare watched them speed past. We thought it was cool. There had been a deafening boom and we could see smoke in the sky, but we were too young to realize what it meant." She paused. "Half of the kids in that daycare lost a parent that day in the refinery explosion. We were all from the same area. Only Aidan and I lost both, though."

Riley didn't talk about her parents often. She had told Beth the longest version of the story she had told anyone, but it still pained her to think about them too much. She had felt abandoned when they died. She knew it hadn't been their fault, but to a scared and lonely five-year-old, it had seemed like her world had come crashing to an end. If Aidan hadn't been there to help her she would have disappeared into the system, and she was certain that she wouldn't have made it to where she was today.

Beth walked over and placed her hands on Riley's hips.

"God, who knows what else would've happened at Aunt Joan and Uncle Ted's if he hadn't been there." Riley felt a rising sense of panic as the memory of the punches, slaps, and burns brought back actual sensations of pain.

"Shhh." Beth pulled her into a tight hug. "You don't have to worry about that now. No one will hurt you again. I've got you."

Riley shuddered and let out a sob of torment.

It took a long while for her regain her composure, but Beth just held on, as solid and stoic as anyone Riley had ever known.

Riley's breathing finally slowed and she said, "I'm sorry."

"What do you possibly have to be sorry about?"

"I'm a damn mess. You shouldn't have to deal with this kind of bullshit. My baggage is a psychotic bitch." She sniffed into Beth's shoulder.

Beth ran her hand comfortingly down Riley's back. "You could start growing a purple horn out of your head and I would still be here for you."

Riley chuckled appreciatively as she wiped her face on Beth's shirt. "I have never once done anything in my life to deserve someone like you."

"Well, you can repay me later with more of what we did this afternoon. Would that make you feel better?"

Riley's knees grew weak, but she hugged Beth tighter and said seriously, "Thank you. For everything. For this. For being you. For loving the mess that is Riley Gordon."

Beth kissed her cheek. "Thank you for being *my* Riley Gordon. Mess and all."

Riley took a deep breath and stepped out of the embrace. "If I don't go now I'll miss the gig completely. Tori would kill me."

"Running off to be with the other woman again, I see. You're going to forget all about me, hanging around with that insanely attractive goddess of a violinist."

Riley knew she was joking. She had told Beth about her initial attraction to Tori and instead of being jealous Beth had been ecstatic that Riley had chosen her instead. "Yeah. Don't wait up." Riley gave a dramatic wink.

Beth pretended to pout so Riley picked up her cello, ready to leave, and leaned over to whisper in her ear, "When I see you again in two days I'm going to make you forget your own name." She then kissed her gently on the soft skin of her lower neck, eliciting a lovely shiver, and then turned and walked out of Beth's front door.

She heard, "Oh, you are just plain evil!" as she walked away.

She smiled, immensely pleased with herself.

❖

After playing in the quartet at the wedding, Tori joined Riley at Metro Haus to keep her company during her shift. It was fun hanging out with her now that her hormones were placated and well cared for by Beth. She didn't feel as nervous or awkward anymore. Of course, Tori's cool factor still intimidated her, but overall, she was just happy to have another good friend.

Tori sipped her coffee and then asked, "Is she everything you hoped she'd be? I don't see you nearly as often now that you two have gotten together, so I assume so."

Riley rested her elbows on the counter and gazed into the distance as she leaned her head onto her fists. "I'm crazy about her. I really have no idea what she sees in me, but I think she is perfection personified."

"Careful about pedestals, Riles."

Riley shook her head. "No, I mean, I know that she has flaws. Nobody knows about flaws like I do. I know she's not a supermodel. I know that when she gets really into her schoolwork she can seem a bit distant and cold. I see how stubborn she can be when she really sets her mind to something. But she is still perfect in her imperfectness. She's a beautiful human being and is made even more so by the way she works at bettering herself and the world around her even when she struggles. I love her geekiness. I love those nerdy glasses. I love her mousey brown hair. I love those freckles. Tori, I really love her. I never thought I could love someone this much or this quickly, but I've fallen and I've fallen hard."

"Tell me how you really feel!"

Riley blushed and stood upright. "Sorry. I'm always thinking about her."

"Well, now you're just making me jealous." Tori winked.

Riley snorted. "You're not allowed to be jealous with every lesbian in the music school throwing themselves at your feet and a soccer player girlfriend back east. And no matter what you say, I'm nowhere near any of their leagues. I have a hard enough time coming to terms with the fact that you or Beth finds me attractive at all. Especially with the crazy that I have to deal with on my own."

Tori wadded up her napkin and threw it at Riley's face. "One of these days you'll figure out how a mirror works and see what we all see. Riley, you're a geeky, but hot redhead. You look like you just jumped out of the pages of an Irish fairy tale. You're quiet, so that makes you mysterious. And your long face and blue eyes are incredibly interesting. I go for interesting over traditional beauty any day of the week. I mean, check out any gathering of sorority girls or look at any beauty magazine. I'll give you twenty bucks if you can distinguish one from the other. The amazing thing about you and Beth, and even me for that matter, is that we all look like ourselves. We look like real people, not like contestants in a lemming beauty pageant. We're unique and we...are...*hot*." She slammed her hand down on the counter for effect.

Riley laughed. "Thank you for the compliment, but the next lesson should be in humility, I think."

Tori winced. "Not a concept I'm very familiar with."

Riley feigned shock. "No? I would never have been able to tell!"

Running her fingers through her pixie cut, Tori shrugged. "Honesty is the best policy, and I'm happy with my ability to serve my community as eye candy. It's all for the greater good."

Riley rolled her eyes. "You're a goddamned saint, you are."

"Your words, not mine. And anyway, this saint has to head home. Big paper due tomorrow. See you at rehearsal!" Tori pushed her stool back and rose to leave.

"Yeah, see you tomorrow. Thanks for keeping me company." Riley waved as Tori left the coffee shop. Riley couldn't help the glance at her backside as she walked out.

❖

Two nights later, Riley was once again staying the night with Beth. Brooke had made staying in her dorm room all but impossible. When she was away at her boyfriend's it was fine, but when she was there, Brooke would only give her the silent treatment and put her things away as if she was afraid Riley was going to take them. She acted almost like she was afraid of *her*. Riley tried to make polite conversation, ask her about her classes, compliment her outfits, but nothing worked. It was just so much easier to grab a change of clothes and head over to Beth's.

She felt loved, safe, and truly happy with Beth, but the undercurrent of fear and anxiety was always there, just below the surface.

❖

Riley's sleeping mind betrayed her. In her dream she was crouched in the living room of the now burned down house and Aunt Joan was with her and laughing maniacally. She could feel the unbearable pain, smell the burning flesh, as the lit cigarette was pressed roughly to her arm. She hadn't washed the dishes like she was told to do. It didn't matter that she had just walked in the door from school. It didn't matter that she was unable to reach the sink unassisted. The cigarettes still burned her skin just the same. Aidan was powerless to stop it because Uncle Ted had locked him in the garage for some menial misdeed or another.

Her mouth opened wide in a scream and she sat bolt upright in the bed. Beth was sitting awake next to her within seconds.

"Shh. It was just a dream," Beth soothed her as she rubbed Riley's back. "You're safe. No one's going to hurt you."

The words made no sense to Riley's confused and terrified mind. She looked down at her arms in the dim light of the early morning. The scars looked livid and raw as if they had just been made. Crazy with fear and still struggling to wake from her horrific dream world, Riley threw off her covers and tumbled out of the bed.

She scrambled to her feet and looked wildly around the room, hoping to find escape.

"Riley, it's…it's okay." Beth sounded scared now. A part of Riley's frantic mind could hear and understand the worry in her voice, but the dream held her too tightly. She crashed back against the dresser, knocking many framed photos onto the floor, and then dropped down into a tightly curled ball, shivering and whimpering for her aunt to stop.

Beth rushed to her side and grasped her shoulders. Still caught in the memories of her aunt's clutches, Riley lashed out. She shoved Beth as hard as she could, sending her reeling back into the bed frame. Riley only stared, trying to make sense of what she was seeing with her eyes in contrast with what she still saw in her mind.

Slowly, realization hit her and she clasped her hand to her mouth in shock.

Beth winced as she slowly pushed herself to her knees, but was already saying, "It's okay. It wasn't your fault." Her eyes watered with pain, but she smiled hesitantly and stood slowly as if afraid of scaring a wounded animal. Offering Riley her hand, she said, "Come back to bed. I'll do whatever I can to make you feel safe. I'm here to listen if you want to talk about it. Or I can just hold you. Whatever you need."

Riley could tell that every word was genuine. Still, she was so embarrassed and horrified by what she had done that she only felt the need to run. It was one thing to have Aidan and the staff at the Home have to deal with her night terrors, but to attack the woman she loved was quite another.

She stood, shaking from head toe and said simply, "I'm so sorry." She then grabbed her keys off the nightstand and ran out the door, still in her pajamas and wanting only to get back to her dorm room where she could ride out her humiliation in solitude. She prayed that Brooke would be at her boyfriend's.

As she drove the short distance back to campus, her phone rang and Beth's face popped up on the screen, smiling and looking adorable with her glasses on a bit crooked. Riley didn't answer. She knew she'd overreacted, and ignoring Beth's calls was inconsiderate at best, but her shame overrode everything else. How could she have hit her? It wasn't a little shove either. It was a full-armed defensive lashing out that had really hurt her. She had only ever done that to Aidan during one of her nightmares, and he had been big enough to shake it off.

Riley could still see the pain on Beth's face and she began to cry. Why did she have to ruin everything? Why couldn't she be normal for once? This was what came of falling in love and dragging someone down with her. It wasn't fair. Again, she knew that she was wallowing in self-pity and should probably pull over and at least talk to Beth, but fear held her back. She still felt like a coward after all.

Eventually the phone stopped ringing, but Riley never checked the five voicemails that Beth left for her. Soon she pulled back into the parking garage near her dorm and slowly made her way back to her room. The campus was still fairly dark and empty as students still had a couple of hours of sleep left before morning classes. Riley was thankful for the quiet.

When she arrived back in her room, she was relieved to see that Brooke was indeed gone so she could brood in peace. She sat on her bed slowly, trying to dissect her rampaging emotions for the millionth time.

A knock at the door startled her out of her planned isolation. Riley got up to answer it, puffy-eyed and feeling confused and depressed. When she opened the door Beth stood there, furious and deeply hurt.

"May I come in?" Beth asked with calm intensity.

Riley hung her head and nodded.

"Sit down," Beth commanded.

Riley sat on the edge of her bed and Beth knelt in front of her, placing her hands on Riley's thighs and squeezing. She had never seen Beth so angry or serious before.

"Riley, I want you to listen to me and I don't want you to say anything until I'm finished, okay?"

Riley continued looking at the piece of carpet she could see between them, but nodded again.

"Okay. What happened was *not* your fault. Do you think I don't know about your dreams? Do you think that I've never had to watch you toss and turn as you run from whatever monster you see in your head? It kills me to see you so scared in your sleep. I'd wake you up to help you, but you'd never get any rest at all."

Riley was shocked. She hadn't realized that her bad dreams

were so prevalent. Luckily, she didn't remember having most of them in the morning. It was only the really terrifying ones that woke her in a panic. No wonder Brooke wanted to stay away so much.

"What happened tonight was nothing that you could help. I know you didn't know it was me there. I know that you'd never hurt me."

"But…I *did* hurt you." Riley's lip trembled.

"It hurt, yes, but *you* could never hurt me. Not unless you pull another stunt like this."

"That's why I—"

"No, not the striking out. The leaving. Do *not* run away from me again. I'm not your enemy."

"No, you aren't. I am."

Beth sighed and got up to sit next to Riley on the bed. She put her arm around her shoulders and then moved Riley's head to rest against her breast. She held her face in her other hand. "When will you learn?"

"Learn what?" Riley asked, voice muffled.

"Just how incredible you are."

Riley snorted. "Yeah. I'm Wonder Woman, Xena, Merida, and Hermione Granger in one magnificent ginger package."

Beth leaned her head onto Riley's. "Make fun all you want, but if you could see what I see, you'd fall in love with yourself too."

Riley's heart surged. Hearing those words was exhilarating, even in her state of self-pity.

"Now. Other than having an amazing girlfriend who's here to stroke your ego, what else can we do to help you through this? What do you fall back on when you have these dreams?"

Riley thought about it for a moment and said, "My music, of course, and Aidan, and sometimes I just look at my heirlooms."

"Heirlooms?"

Riley lifted her head from Beth's chest and nodded. "Pretty much my only valuable possessions on this earth. Valuable to me and Aidan anyway."

Beth looked interested. "What are they?"

Riley wiped the remaining tears from her eyes. "Let me show you." No one had ever cared enough to see her little shoebox of memories before.

Riley knelt and pulled out the drawer under her bed where she kept the ragged box. Her brows creased as she rummaged around only to come up empty. Fighting a rising sense of panic, she opened the next drawer. Again, nothing.

Beth could tell there was something wrong because she asked, "Is everything okay?"

There was a tremor in Riley's voice as she answered, "It's not here."

"Your heirlooms are missing?"

Riley nodded, now frantically tearing through every drawer in the room.

"When did you last see them? What do they look like?"

Riley swallowed hard. "They're in an old Adidas shoe box. I took them down to the office to scan in some pictures for Aidan's Christmas present, but I *know* I brought them back up here. I *know* I did."

"Well," Beth said, standing and rummaging through Riley's closet, "where else do you think you could have put them?"

"I don't know!" Riley was seconds away from losing it all over again. How could she misplace the single most precious collection of family memories she had?

Beth attempted to calm her. "Don't worry. I'm sure they're around here somewhere. Maybe Brooke has seen them. You can ask her when she comes back."

"Brooke couldn't give two shits about my stuff."

Beth signed. "Riley, c'mere."

Riley continued to throw her meager possessions across the room in an attempt to find the box. "Beth…" Tears sprang from her eyes. "That stupid collection is the only thing in the world I can't lose. It's my family when they're not here. It's my parents. It's Aidan."

Beth bent down and kissed the top of her head. "I know. I'll help you find it, okay? I'm sure it's around here somewhere. Just come to bed for a little while. You need sleep. You have class and work in a few hours."

Riley sniffed and followed Beth under the covers of her bed. She was sniffling and worried sick, but Beth's warm body and steady breathing soon calmed her. Still, she wouldn't be able to get any more sleep.

CHAPTER SIXTEEN

S everal days passed and there was still no sign of the box of heirlooms. She and Beth had checked the downstairs office where the scanner was, the lost and found, and every inch of the bedroom. Even putting up flyers in the hallways hadn't led to any clues. Riley was distraught and terrified of having to tell her brother that she had lost the only physical connection they had left to their parents.

Despite Beth's best efforts to placate her, Riley couldn't help but worry and fall into a depressed funk. Even Tori noticed.

One day after rehearsal, Tori approached her as Riley packed her cello back into her case.

"What are you and Beth doing this weekend?" she asked as they walked out of the music building and toward Riley's dorm.

"Oh, you know, wild orgies, heroin parties…the usual."

Tori wasn't amused. "Gettin' a little old, Riles."

"What is?"

"The pouty thing. Either you're going to find the shoebox or you're not. Don't let it ruin your life."

Riley's temper flared. "Goddamnit, Tori. You have *no* idea how much that stupid box means to me. Don't you dare belittle it!"

"Whoa. Sorry. I didn't mean to piss you off." Tori held up her hands in surrender. "I just meant that I hate seeing you so upset over this."

"I have every right to be upset!" Riley spat.

"I know. I know. But I'm just saying that you still have those memories and the connections without the baubles and knickknacks. It's a horrible tragedy, yes, but you still have Aidan and you still have your friends. We want to help you. That's all."

Riley's anger waned as self-consciousness washed over her. "I just…God, I don't know what I'm going to tell Aidan. He'll be so disappointed in me."

"He'll get over it. You told me that you gave him pictures of everything that was in there. That's something. That's still memories."

"It's not the same."

"I know. But listen, I'm heading over to Bookwoman on Saturday to pick up some new lesbish books. Wanna join? I guarantee it will make you feel better."

"Lesbish?" Riley actually cracked a smile.

"Who *wouldn't* feel better with a new armful of queer literature from our favorite feminist bookstore?"

"Can I bring Beth?"

"Duh. Pick you guys up at noon?" She turned to leave, still looking at Riley over her shoulder.

"Tori?"

"Yeah?"

"Thanks. I need a good kick in the ass sometimes."

Tori winked and turned to walk up the street toward the Drag.

Aidan,

I'm sorry I'm not telling you this over the phone, but I'm just too embarrassed and too pissed off at myself. So I'm just going to say it.

I lost the heirloom box. Don't ask me how. I have no frackin' clue. I saw it at Christmas when I took pictures of everything in it for you to have, put it back in the drawers under my bed, and then…poof…gone. I've put up signs in the hallway, talked to the people at the front desk, looked in every study and game room, but nothing. It's like it just completely disappeared. I even asked Brooke and that bitch just all but ignored me. I just don't know what's up with her. You'd think I murdered her puppy or something.

Anyway. I hate writing to give you bad news, but there it is.

Now I'm going to change subjects to make you forget about what I just told you.

How are things over there? Tired of the heat and bad military food yet? Are you staying safe? Keep your head down and don't do anything stupid or I'll kill you myself.

Just so you don't worry too much about me and my unreliable ways I'll also say that I don't know how I could have made it through this year without Tori and Beth. Especially Beth. I'm falling more and more in love with her every day. She's the first person to ever make me feel like I can let my guard down. I don't very often, of course. You know how I am. But she has seen more of the demons than anyone else but you. And she loves me in spite of them. Sometimes I want to scream at her to go. Save herself. But the selfish part of me wants to latch on and never let her go.

When she holds me in her arms…

God, I feel the most profound sense of comfort. It's unreal sometimes.

She draws me in even when I think I should run.

I am just so madly, insanely, in love with that girl. It's the most horrible, terrifying, ecstatic, and wonderful feeling in the world.

I don't know why I'm gushing about all of this to you. You don't need to know about your sister's mushy love life. I just thought that maybe you could forgive me for what I've done if you also knew about something that's going well for me. For the first time in my life…I. Am. Happy.

Stay safe, Aidan. I love you.

Riley

Saturday afternoon, after an enjoyable lunch at Texadelphia and an hour at the feminist bookstore, Tori dropped Beth and Riley off at the dorm. Each carried a bag full of new books they knew they wouldn't have time to read until the summer and Riley found that she did actually feel a lot better.

After a kiss good-bye, Beth walked to her car to go home and work on a project while Riley went up to her dorm room. As she passed the notice boards in the hallway, she saw that her lost heirloom flyers had all been taken down. Her brows creased as she stormed down the hallway. Who in the hell would do that? She knew that the answer to that question already.

She unlocked the door to her room and saw Brooke standing with her back to her, packing clothes into a suitcase. As she set her bag of books on the bed, her heart leapt into her throat. There was the box. It was sitting in the center of the bed as if it had been there the entire time. She quickly took the top off and tears of joy sprang from her eyes she inventoried its contents. Everything was there. She grasped Aidan's dog tags tightly in her fist and held her mom's glasses and her dad's hat to her chest.

She turned around, cheeks gleaming and asked, "Where did you find it?" Despite their past, she wanted to hug her.

"I didn't find it." Brooke continued packing and sounded vicious. "I took it."

It took a moment for Riley to register what she had said. "What do you mean you took it?"

Brooke whirled around, hands on her hips, and looking livid. "You disgust me, Riley Gordon."

Riley stared, wide-eyed and slack-jawed.

"You are a liar and a thief and I wanted to teach you a lesson."

"W-what?"

"I know you took my pendant. I know you stole it and only gave it back because I made you feel guilty when I told you how important it was to me."

Riley's brain was reeling, still trying to figure out what she was saying.

"Y-your necklace pendant? You lost that. I found it in the rug by the wall. I left it on your desk for you!" She pointed to the small bowl on Brooke's desk.

"Liar! I know your background. You thought you could help yourself. You thought you'd get a few extra bucks if you took it. Thought I'd never notice because I have other jewelry. It's too bad you just happened to take the most important piece."

Riley's confusion turned into defiant anger. "I did not! Brooke, you lost that pendant and I found it when I was plugging my computer in. I thought you'd be happy! I'd never steal anything from you, you judgmental freak!"

Brooke rolled her eyes and turned around to continue packing. "You're just lucky I didn't call the campus police on you. And the funny thing is I'd never have had proof that you did it if you had never returned it. So after that I made sure that everyone in this dorm knew what a sneak and bitch you are. And I took that stupid box from under your bed. I've seen you pawing through that crap. I could tell that it meant something to you and I wanted you to know how it felt. I don't even know why I gave it back. I should've thrown that shit in the Dumpster just to revel in the joy of watching you suffer."

The unfairness of what was happening made Riley's blood boil. She was someone who had dealt with anger her entire life, but she had never been as furious as she was now in the face of this grievous accusation.

"Brooke, I did *not* steal that goddamned pendant." Riley balled up her fists and pressed them to her temples in frustration. "You know what? I have been trying to ignore the way you treat me and excuse your rude and selfish behavior all damn year, but now I see that you really are nothing more than the abusive, horrendous bitch I first thought you to be."

"Please." Brooke slammed the suitcase shut. "You can try to defend yourself all you want, but I am so not staying here anymore. You can have this cell to yourself. I'm moving in with Chad."

"Thank God."

With that, Brooke took her suitcase and walked out of the room, slamming the door behind her.

Riley was livid. She couldn't believe that someone could think such awful things of her. And not only that, but to also spread vile gossip about her to everyone in the residence hall? She was surprised that it had never gotten around to the administrators. She could have been kicked out if people believed it to be true.

Riley whipped out her iPhone, intent on venting to Beth. It was then that she realized…Brooke was gone. Brooke was *gone!*

Glory frickin' hallelujah!

❖

Nugget,

I'm so glad to hear you got the box back. I don't know what to say about Brooke, though. The whole thing is so overdramatic. I can't believe that something so stupid and offensive actually happened. I swear, Riley, your life is like a weird soap opera sometimes.

I will say that I'm kind of happy it happened too. I'm glad you don't have to live with her anymore. And say what you want about our lack of parental units, she actually has parents and they raised her to behave like that. I'd say we still got the better end of the deal, wouldn't you?

I'm also glad to hear that you've finally found some happiness. Beth is a good influence on you and it's time you found someone who can bring out that joy in you. It's been way too long.

Anyway, I have to go now. We're going on a pretty long string of missions this week and I may not be able to write you back or call for a bit so just know these four things:

1) You are an amazing person and worth every ounce of air that you breathe.

2) Beth and your friends are there for you. Lean on them if times get tough. Talk to them. Let them love you.

3) Mom and Dad are looking down on you and they are so proud of who you've become and what you've accomplished.

4) I will always, ALWAYS, love you and be there for you. Even if I'm a million miles away. You're my little sister and family is everything.

Also, here's another pic of me and the guys on our LAV. The answer is yes. It's just as hot and dusty as it looks out here and there are some scary bits and politics that I don't understand, but we've been trained well and damn if we don't look good. ;)

Love ya, Nugget,
Aidan

Chapter Seventeen

The following weeks passed fairly normally considering how strange the weekend had been. Riley did tell Beth everything that had happened with Brooke, and it had taken hours to persuade Beth to not physically harm her. Beth might appear meek and frail, but when she was angry, Riley knew that she was a force to be reckoned with. Her defensiveness filled Riley with pride.

She and Beth had settled back into their routine of seeing each other for lunch between classes, spending the night together when they could, and continuing to work on their own projects and assignments. With spring break and midterms steadily approaching, they both knew that they would have to support each other in their scholarly efforts. Of course, that didn't mean that their evenings were *always* occupied by studying and practicing. Their willpower wasn't strong enough to keep them from enjoying each other every chance they got.

During one such evening, after a particularly pleasurable experience, Beth curled herself around Riley's warm body and purred, "That was just the reward I needed. My project for Oceanography is done."

"Congrats!"

"Yeah. It's basically my midterm, so now I just have Bio and Chem to worry about. I'm kinda over it at this point to be honest."

"Well, you're luckier than me. We're working on new music for a big concert in March, I still sound like ass on my solo recital material, and don't even get me started on the regular courses. I have two weeks to figure all of this out for the tests, and it's just not happening."

Beth hugged her tighter and kissed the back of her neck. "You're exaggerating."

"I dunno. I just feel like I can't stay ahead. If it wasn't for this"—she reached back and clasped Beth's thigh—"I think I would've had a nervous breakdown by now."

Riley could feel Beth's lips form a smile. "Again, overreacting. You're too high-strung for your own good. But don't get me wrong. I'm glad to help with that." She moved her hips in even closer.

Riley felt flushed all over again, but said, "I really need to stay focused these next two weeks. Do you mind if I just stay at my dorm full-time until midterms are over? Just for the sake of convenience and study time? You can sleep in Brooke's old bed if you want. It's so much easier with her gone."

"Whatever you need. Also, I wanted to ask if you'd be interested in heading over to New Orleans with me for spring break. It's not the best time to go with all the crazy parties and drunk people, but the D-Day museum is hosting a special seminar about sunken WWII ships. A few of the world's most prominent maritime archaeologists will be there!"

Riley could hear the excitement building in Beth's voice. "But spring break is only two weeks away! Isn't that kind of short notice for such a big trip?"

"I just found out about it today. My professor and her grad students are going, and they thought I'd like it too. She's taking a whole group. Discounts on the hotel rooms and everything. They had someone drop out, so there's a room free."

"Nerdy grad students."

"Hey, not every college student would prefer to spend spring break sleeping in a puddle of their own mai-tai-flavored puke in the French Quarter."

Riley squeezed her eyes shut. "Beth? Gross."

"And anyway," Beth continued, "the idea of having you all to myself for a whole week makes me…"

"Yes?" Riley opened her eyes, rolled over to face her and smiled.

Blushing, Beth said, "Just come with me? Please?"

Riley leaned in and kissed Beth softly on the lips. "Say that again."

"What?"

Riley kissed her again, harder this time, and Beth gasped when they parted.

"Say it," Riley commanded again.

Beth voice shook as she implored, "*Please*."

Riley smiled as she positioned herself over Beth's trembling form. "Yes, ma'am."

❖

Two weeks later Riley walked in to her dorm room and slammed her backpack down on the bed.

"What now?" Beth asked with sleepy irritation in her voice. She had been taking a nap after having just finished her last midterm before spring break.

"I'm pretty sure I just nailed my English exam." Riley danced around the room, unable to settle down.

"I bet you did. Come here and give me a hug." Beth opened her arms wide.

Riley did a little twirl in between the beds and yelled, "Screw you, midterms! You're *done*!"

Beth jumped up and wrapped her arms around Riley to stop her from pacing. Laughing, she said, "Settle down. You're going to break something."

Riley hugged Beth back fiercely and took a long, deep breath. "You're my beacon, you know that?"

"What do you mean?"

"Whenever I get lost you always find me and lead me back. You're my beacon of light when things get dark in my head. It's cheeseball, but true. And that's why I'm so happy. Thank you."

Beth smiled and kissed her cheek. "And you're the fire that

keeps me entranced. Every day since I've met you has been the best day of my life."

Riley pulled away. "Even with the messed-up baggage?"

"What's an adventure without a little baggage? Besides, I love being the one who brings you back. The one who will always be here to love you, no matter what happens."

Riley hugged her again and breathed in the clean smell of Beth's skin. It soothed her.

"Now," Beth said, "midterms are over and we have nothing but time to spend together. We leave for New Orleans tomorrow afternoon, so go ahead and get packed."

Riley pulled away and said, "Yeah. I'm so ready for this trip. I need the break."

She went to her closet and pulled out a ratty duffel bag. "I'd say we don't need *too* many clothes, but I guess we have to do *some* things in public, huh? Sightseeing and the like."

Beth answered with a well-connected slap to Riley's butt. "You're so bad…I love it."

Riley smiled as she shoved some shorts and socks into the bag as her cell phone rang.

"Hello?" She didn't recognize the number.

"Riley Gordon?"

"Yep."

"Hey. This is Rebecca from the San Jac desk downstairs. You have some visitors waiting for you in the first-floor lounge. Are you nearby?"

"Yeah, I'm upstairs. I'll be right down."

"Who was that?" Beth asked as she laid herself down on Riley's bed and opened her tattered copy of Dr. Robert Ballard's *The Eternal Darkness*.

"Desk downstairs. Apparently, someone's here to see me."

"Who?"

Riley shrugged. "Probably Koji and his new boyfriend. He said he wanted to introduce me before they left for South Padre Island for spring break. God knows if they'll even make it back from the debauchery they have planned, so I'd better go."

Beth had started to read, but murmured, "Mmm," in agreement. "Be right back."

Without looking up, Beth waved like a royal with closed, cupped hand and said, "I'll miss you ever so much whilst you're away!"

Speaking loudly over her shoulder Riley said, "Once again... NERD!"

Riley walked downstairs and smiled at Rebecca at the front desk. The young woman smiled back nervously. God, those damn lies Brooke had spread about her. Everyone thought she was a thief and probably psycho on top of it. She was so ready for this year to end. She wondered if Beth would let her move in to her apartment. It was within walking distance to campus, and she already knew she would like her roommate. Plus, there were just so many perks.

As she was pondering the pleasures of getting to spend every night with Beth, she turned the corner into the lounge expecting to see Koji. It was empty except for two people.

Her heart jolted painfully and then felt as if it had turned to molten lead. She could hear the thunderous crack as she realized that her life had just changed. Every ounce of her soul crashed through the floor with excruciating abruptness.

Standing in front of her with looks of professional sympathy were two Marines in green Alpha uniforms.

She stuttered to a stop and felt her body vibrate in revolt of what was about to happen.

"No." The words escaped her mouth in a whisper of desperate finality. It wasn't going to be true. This wasn't happening. There was no way that this could possibly be happening. Not to her.

The sergeant spoke, "Are you Miss Riley Gordon?"

Riley stared blankly.

"Ma'am, I'm Master Sergeant Estrada and this is Staff Sergeant Singer," he said gesturing to the somber Marine next to him. "Ma'am, are you Riley Gordon, sister of Private First Class Aidan Gordon?"

This wasn't right.

Riley nodded almost imperceptibly.

"Would you like to sit down, ma'am?" Master Sergeant Estrada gestured to one of the lounge's couches.

She shook her head almost as imperceptibly.

He hesitated, but continued, "Ma'am, the Commodore of the Marine Corps has asked me to express his deep regret that your brother, Private First Class Aidan Gordon, has died in action in Jordan."

A disconcerting buzzing noise filled Riley's ears and she felt all of the blood leave her head. She swayed.

The Marine shifted his weight forward as if to catch her and said, "Ma'am, please come sit down."

Riley did as she was told. She didn't want to think.

The Marines sat in the chairs opposite her. "Ma'am, your brother was on a routine patrol when his LAV hit an IED. A roadside explosive. He was positively identified by his fellow Marines and commanding officer." He paused, apparently waiting for a question.

Riley couldn't feel anything. It was like she was watching a horrible movie through someone else's eyes. What a terrible scene. It didn't belong. It wasn't right.

"Ma'am, is there someone you could call to help you? A family member?"

Riley nodded, but she didn't really know why. She had nothing.

Someone else's mouth asked a few questions. Someone else with her voice struggled to understand, to figure out if there was any kind of doubt that may give her hope. Someone else's ears listened while the Marines in their perfect uniforms with their perfect looks of detached sympathy explained the next steps, the paperwork, the burial arrangements, the benefits she would receive as Aidan's only living relative. Someone gave them her Social Security number, told them a national cemetery burial would be fine, said thank you to the young staff sergeant who would be her casualty assistance officer there to take care of everything and offer support.

They had spoken for a long time, apparently. The light in the room had changed. The bright daylight had turned dusky. The darkness was slowly descending.

The Marines rose to leave, told her they would contact her again in a few days to work out more arrangements, and again expressed their condolences.

"This must be hard...for you," said the someone speaking through Riley's mouth. "You have a difficult job."

The Marines nodded solemnly and left the room.

Riley stood alone in the room for a few minutes, willing her brain to shut off. As if struggling through black tar, she turned and staggered to the ladies' bathroom, where she threw up what felt like every meal she had ever eaten. Her body, her mind, her heart, her whole being was protesting this absurd, this horrific turn of events. She couldn't wrap her head around it. She didn't want to. If she did she would disintegrate into a billion torturous shards. She could already feel them piercing their way out from her heart, forcing their way through her skin. The pain would only get worse. She couldn't breathe. She tried to take a breath and the bitter, stale, traitorous air refused to enter her lungs. The pressure on her chest was too great.

Abject panic descended upon her in a roiling wave. She cowered in the bathroom stall, trying in vain to breath, trying to move, trying to do anything to wake up.

Her thoughts flew to her brother. He always helped her when she descended into this madness.

Her brother.

Aidan.

She needed him and he was gone.

It didn't make sense.

She looked around wildly.

The world shouldn't exist.

The world without Aidan *couldn't* exist.

She had no frame of reference for this. Yes, her parents had died when she was a little girl and her world had been shattered, but Aidan had been there to pick up the pieces. He had been her light in the darkness during their time with their aunt and uncle. He was her light at the Home when she had no one else. Now that light had been snuffed out by the violent machinations of some other mother's son a world away.

Lost in her maddening thoughts, Riley heard the bathroom door open and a voice that she recognized as Rebecca's say, "Are you okay? Do you need any help?"

Riley shut down. It was her very last coping mechanism. When all else failed, her body disconnected from her mind and she simply existed purely on automated instinct.

She rose from the floor and exited the stall saying in an even voice, "No. Thank you."

Rebecca moved aside to let her pass, looking sympathetic and nervous.

Riley looked down at the keys she had taken out of her pocket. She should go tell Beth what had happened. She should let Beth hold her. She should let Beth take the pain away. But Beth would never be able to do that. Riley loved her so much. So, so damn much. But she had been worried about Beth having to deal with her problems before. Now the thought of what she would have to put Beth through for the rest of their lives together was unthinkable. She couldn't do that to her. She wouldn't.

Instead of going back upstairs to her room, she turned and walked out the front door. She didn't have a jacket. Now that the night had descended, the wind had a biting cold and she shivered yet felt nothing. She walked to her car, sat stiffly in the seat, and started driving.

She didn't think about where she was going. She just drove. The memories of every moment she had shared with Aidan in their short lives replayed in her head. She saw his football games. She saw him sitting next to her on the couch at the Home playing Xbox. She saw the ashen look on his face as the ambulances raced past their daycare to the refinery explosion that had killed their parents. She saw his wolfish grin and flirtatious winks at the girls in high school. She saw him getting slapped hard across the face and then kicked as he tried to protect her from Aunt Joan's fury. She saw him rub the salve on her arms and legs where the cigarette burns had made angry red blisters. She saw him step off the bus in full uniform, fresh from basic training. She saw him holding her tight against his chest as she kicked and flailed after waking from night terrors.

She saw him dead, his body battered and bloodied, thrown far from the LAV and the team he had grown to love.

Unbearable.

Agonizing.

Searing.

Unendurable.

❖

She pulled the car to the side of the road and got out, shaking again when the wind pieced through her shirt. She had been driving for hours. She hadn't woken up. Her world hadn't resolved itself. Her world would never be the same again. Her world had ended.

She walked to the railing and trembled as she climbed to the other side.

It didn't look that far. Maybe it was because the darkness of the night obscured most of her view of the frigid water below. Still, she wondered if it would hurt much. Would it be over quickly, her body immediately succumbing to the bone-crushing force, or would she simply be painfully bent and twisted, only to sink slowly beneath the gentle waves, her body spasming violently as water replaced the life-giving oxygen in her lungs?

She shook her head to clear her thoughts. None of this was helping. What was the use in dwelling on it? She should just jump and be done with it. The more she thought about it, the more she hesitated, and hesitation wasn't high on the list of things she wanted right now. She had gone over the events that had led her here over and over again in her head. How much more torture could she stand?

No. This world was too hard. Every day as she was growing up she had tried to hold on to the belief that things would change for the better, that she would be rescued from the hell that was her life. After all, surely it was impossible to be kept so low forever. Even the most tragic lives had some rays of sunshine, right? Some glimmer of light in the darkness?

That was what she had thought, but the rays of light in the life of Riley Gordon had been few and far between. And now that the unthinkable had happened, she just couldn't bear the pain. It needed to end, once and for all. She was useless and she refused to drag the one person in the world who cared down with her. So what was the point in continuing?

The well-known cloud of despair descended upon her the more she thought about it. She was making the only decision that made sense to her confused and anguished mind, yet she was still afraid of it. This had all made so much sense as she walked to the bridge, alone and shivering in the biting wind, in the middle of the vast expanse of Texas Hill Country, but now that she was here, standing on the outer ledge of the deserted Bluebonnet Highway Bridge at three o'clock in the morning, she was having doubts.

She took a deep breath, possibly her last, and leaned forward slowly, the wind stinging her numbed face, and willed herself to gain the courage to loosen her grip on the railing. She could barely hear the fast-moving river below, but she knew that it was there, waiting for her, ready to welcome her into its eternal embrace.

Now was the time.

The headlights approaching from down the road didn't even enter her consciousness.

As she slowly relaxed her fingers, the memories poured forth once again in a flood of abuse, sadness, and fire. Now, with the river rushing beneath her, she felt that it was finally time to put that fire out.

Images of Aidan and Beth swirled in her head as she closed her eyes and leaned forward. She was going to die with the thoughts of the two people she loved most in the world playing on repeat in her head.

A cold hand grabbed onto her arm and jerked her back.

"Riley?" A voice she knew as well as her own trembled in abject fear behind her. "Please come back."

She opened her eyes slowly and carefully turned around to see Beth shaking and crying in front of her. Her vise-like grip hadn't loosened a bit.

"Beth." Riley's voice was steady.

"Riley, please. Come back to me."

The terrified look in Beth's eyes caused a stirring deep in Riley's chest. Without saying a word, she climbed back over the railing and stood stooped and broken in front of the woman who had just saved her life.

"For God's sake, Riley!" Beth sobbed and pulled her into an inescapable hug. "Don't you ever fucking do something like that again!" Her voice cracked as another sob caught in her throat. *"Goddamn it!"*

The last ounce of strength Riley had evaporated and her defenses ruptured. She crumbled to the pavement and let out a howl of anguish as horrendous as any ever heard. Every hurt she had ever received, every injustice, every terror, tore through her soul and ripped apart her universe in one screaming wail of unimaginable agony.

Beth cried with her and held her tightly as she rocked in wretched misery and lost herself in the malignant ruination of her loss.

❖

Riley opened her eyes and blinked drowsily. A faint light illuminated Beth sitting next to her in bed. A slow trickle of memories replaced the fitful dreams she had been having. Riley remembered what had happened that night. Her world crumbled all over again. How was she going to be able to live with this agony? It still didn't seem real, but the anguish tore at her. Beth quickly put her computer on the bedside table and wrapped herself around Riley's shaking body.

When the worst of the trembling had passed, Riley gratefully accepted a tissue from Beth and blew her nose. Her face was puffy and her head felt like an axe had split it clean in two.

Speaking quietly and in hiccups of air, Riley said, "Thank you." She could feel Beth's wet cheek resting on her shoulder.

Beth said quietly, "I've never been so scared in my whole life. I don't know..." her voice cracked. "I don't know what I would've done if I hadn't found you." She shivered.

"How did you?"

"You didn't come back, so I checked downstairs and the girl said that you seemed really upset after talking to some Marines. I didn't know what else to do so I tracked your iPhone. I know your password, remember?" Beth pulled Riley into a sitting position. "I followed you all night. Riley, I could murder you for doing what you did. What in the hell were you thinking?" She shook Riley a little and then realized what she was doing. "I'm sorry. I'm so so sorry. This isn't your fault. I can't even," she gulped, "begin to imagine how you feel. Just...oh my God, Riley." She began crying again. "Just don't ever do that to me again."

Riley was silent for a while, disintegrating both in sorrow and shame. Finally, she managed to mumble, "Thanks for the sleeping pill."

Beth shrugged and sniffed. "You needed it."

Riley blew her nose again and hung her head. "I am sorry. For everything. For me. For this."

Beth kissed her forehead. "My heart is breaking for you. For Aidan." She swallowed hard. "But don't try to face this alone. I'm not much, but you have me. And you also have Koji and Tori and even my parents. Just let me know what you need and I'll...we'll do it."

Riley sighed shakily as tears ran down her cheeks. "I'm sorry. It's just...God...it hurts so much." She broke down again and Beth pulled her in to her embrace let her sob in her arms.

"I want you to know one thing, and no matter what, you have to remember it. I will *always* be here for you. You are never going to try to protect me from yourself or your pain. Understand? You are my world. I'm going to be by your side through all of this. I love you *so* goddamned much." She kissed her on top of her head and held her even tighter.

Riley could barely breathe. Nothing was ever going to stop this horrendous pain. "I can't believe he's gone." She wailed again and it seemed like she'd never be able to stop.

Chapter Eighteen

The funeral had been unbearable. It was lonely, inconceivable, and the absolute worst experience of Riley's life. She had been inconsolable and even wondered how she had been able to survive it at all. Surely the human heart could only take so much. It just didn't make sense that her brother, her Aidan, was shut into that dark box, never to speak to her again. It wasn't right. It wasn't possible. Yet there she sat, in the midst of thousands of other indistinct grave markers, being told by someone who didn't know him that he was in a better place. There she sat, watching the honor guard fold the flag and hand it to her on bended knee as if it were some sort of solace to her. There she sat, with Beth doing her best to support her, as her brother's lifeless body was lowered forever into the cold, impersonal ground. She hadn't wanted to live at all. She had wanted to follow him down into that hole, never to feel that kind of misery again.

Beth's parents had come up for the funeral and then took both her and Beth down to Galveston for the remainder of spring break and the following week. Riley stayed in bed the entire time despite the kind and anxious coaxing of the Earles. She couldn't seem to gather the energy or the courage to face the world. What world was there to face anyway? She had experienced pain and loss, fear and depression, but nothing could compare to what she was feeling now. She still had moments where she couldn't catch her breath, couldn't think, couldn't move, and couldn't stop crying, yet Beth was always there. Always waiting to bring her back from the brink.

Mr. and Mrs. Earle spent time with her as well. They told her repeatedly that she would never again be alone and without someone to talk to. Riley appreciated the sentiment and tried her best to appear grateful, but she knew she was failing miserably. Nothing could break through the clouds that had descended upon her.

One evening, a week after classes had started back, Beth brought her news from school. All her professors had agreed to send her homework via email and discussion board until she was able to return. Even Beth's professors had done the same so that she could stay in Galveston with her.

"Tori said that all your music professors have given you a pass for the next few weeks. You don't have to go to rehearsal or anything," Beth said softly, running her fingers through Riley's tangled hair.

Riley lay on the bed with her back to Beth. "What's the point anyway? I'm never playing again."

She didn't know why she said it, but once it was out of her mouth she knew that the feeling was true. Playing her cello reminded her too much of her childhood, of her mother, of Aidan. He had pushed her to excel when he heard her raw talent and saw her love of the instrument she had chosen. When she had started playing, it was also like their mother had come back to them in some small way. Now everything was lost and the thought of playing again was too painful.

"Riley," Beth implored.

"No!" She wouldn't discuss it. Her heart shattered all over again. The only thing that ever granted her true escape was now tainted and she was too weak to fight it.

Beth sighed, kissed Riley's cheek, and left the room, closing the door behind her. Riley could hear the whispered conversation in the hallway.

"I don't know what to do, Mom. I don't know how to help her."

Beth was crying. Riley had caused this. Everything she had been afraid of had come true. She had been selfish and had let herself be drawn in by Beth; this beautiful, warm, and loving young woman, knowing that her troubles were too much to put on anyone, and look what had happened. She was ruining her life too.

Mrs. Earle whispered back, "Give her time, sweetheart. Remember how you felt when Grammy died? That was bad enough, but at least she had a good, full life and a family that loved her. Riley just lost the only person she's ever had in this world."

"She has *me*," Beth protested a little too loudly.

"Shh. I know, sweetie, but as much as she loves you, and I can see that she loves you more than I suspect she'll ever be able to say, she just lost her entire family. You told me about her parents. You told me about her childhood. Can you imagine the bond she and her brother had?" Riley heard Mrs. Earle choke back tears too. "The pain she must feel is infinite. Nothing is ever going to change this loss for her. She will never get over it. *But*," she said, obviously stopping Beth's unsaid comment, "you have to give her time to find her new normal. Most importantly, if you really love her—"

"God, I love her so much, Mom." Beth sobbed. Riley heard the shuffling and muffled sounds of a desperate embrace.

"If you love her like I know you do, you're going to have to be strong for her. It won't be easy, especially with the stress you're under in school, but if she's worth it to you, you're going to have to do anything and everything you can to be there for her."

"I know, Mom. That's not even a question. I just…I hurt so much *for* her. I don't think she knows how much I care, even when I tell her. I'll do anything in the world for her. Anything. *Anything*."

Riley heard rustling as the pair walked down the hall and downstairs. She felt a confusing mixture of appreciation, grief, guilt, love, and depression as they left. Her burdens were now the burdens of the entire Earle family. It wasn't fair to any of them.

Footsteps ran back up the stairs and the door opened quickly as if someone had heard her thoughts. Riley rolled over to look. Beth was staring at her, tears running down her face, hand still on the doorknob.

"Nothing I can say can change this or make it better. But you

are *never* going to be alone again. My family is your family now."
Beth stood straighter. "No matter what happens from this point on,
we face everything together. You have a family that loves you and
you have a home." She paused as Riley stared through tears. "I don't
know if that makes a difference to you, but I…I just needed you to
know that."

Riley's chest expanded with the most profound sense of love
she had ever felt. She got out of the bed and threw herself into Beth's
welcoming and strong arms.

"Together. For better or worse. You will never be without a
home again. You are ours and we are yours."

Riley bawled into Beth's chest as she held her even tighter.
Beth and her family had saved her life, in more ways than one.
She would never be able to repay their kindness and support and
she knew that she would never be expected to. In this time of
devastating sadness and loss, she had found the one thing that she
and Aidan had desired and dreamed of their entire lives. If only he
could be there to share it with her.

❖

A few days later, Riley and Beth left the Earle home in
Galveston to head back to school. Mrs. Earle had already set up
weekly therapy sessions for her with the university's counseling
services and Beth had promised to help her with her transition back
to student life. Riley continued to stay in the dorm and Beth all but
officially moved in with her there. She didn't want her to be alone
for a second.

Tori, Koji, and several other music students stopped by to
bring her flowers, give their condolences, and even bring her food.
Riley still didn't feel like herself and would randomly burst out
crying in between classes, but she was determined to finish out her
first year to the best of her abilities. Aidan would expect nothing
less and she would be damned if she was going to disappoint him
after all of this.

However, she still outright refused to pick up her cello.

"Riley, do you honestly think this is what your brother would want?" Tori pleaded with her as they walked through the halls of the music building.

"I know it's not," Riley said sullenly.

"Well, then?"

"Tori," Riley said with heartbroken exasperation, "it *hurts*. I can't play because the music *hurts* me. It hurts so much that I want to set fire to my own skin just to feel something else!" Her eyes welled with tears.

"Shh," Tori whispered, pulling her into a hug. "I know it does. But it also heals. Trust me. Sometimes you have to rip off the bandage to heal the wound."

"Don't wanna," Riley said, resorting to despondency and standing limply in Tori's arms.

"Music was something that linked you two together. You told me about your mother playing her favorite classical songs for you both when you were children. You told me about him listening to you practice, going to your concerts, and pushing you to succeed. Music is in your soul, Riley, and music will help you keep your family close. Music is what's going to help you mend."

Riley took a shuddering breath. "Help me."

"Of course I'll help you. So will Beth. We're here for you no matter what."

"I don't deserve either of you."

Tori laughed and released her from the hug, holding her at arm's length. "Damn right you don't." She winked coyly and Riley smiled. It was the first time she had done so in two weeks.

❖

Riley left her job at the coffee shop. She didn't have the energy to work there anymore. Not with the way she felt. Koji and her other coworkers had gotten her an entire box of apple fritters and a card for free coffee for a month as a going-away present. She couldn't really bring herself to miss the job, though. She would miss working with Koji, but she knew she had made a friend for life and didn't worry too much that she might never see him again—she knew she would.

Now that she wasn't expected to play with the symphony for the rest of the semester, she had only her regular classes and her potential recital to think about.

"You don't have to do the solo recital, you know." Tori said as she and Beth sat with Riley in the cramped practice room. It was rare that one or both of them wasn't by her side since she had received the news.

"Yes, I do. You told me so." Riley glared at the sheet music on the stand in front of her. It was the first time she had picked up her cello since Aidan's death. It had been difficult since she practically screamed if she heard any music at all lately. It tore at her as if actual knives were ripping through her flesh. Music was light and life to her, and the light had been snuffed out in the most violent and ruthless of ways.

Tori shook her head. "I already talked to Professor Cryder. She said that you're exempted from it this year. She knows how well you can play. You don't have to prove anything. I mean I don't want you to give up playing, but doing a full recital is stressful and I don't want you to overdo it."

Riley lashed out, grabbing her music stand and throwing it violently into the corner of the room. "There's nothing else I *can* do!" she screamed. It was all she could do to not smash her cello on the ground. "I never want to play again, but...but that's not what... he would want!"

Beth reached over and placed her warm palm on Riley's thigh. "Honey, we're going to support you, whatever you decide."

"I'm just so...so...*so fucking angry!*"

A man with a nervous expression peered in the practice room window and then walked away. Apparently, the rooms weren't soundproof enough.

"These pieces are crap!" Riley kicked the bottom of the music stand as it lay on its side, the sheet music spread across the carpet. "This is all bullshit!"

"Okay. Calm down." Tori stood and picked the stand up from the floor.

Riley started crying again and buried her face in her hands. It was mortifying to not be able to keep it together for even one day. The anger that constantly boiled inside her was poisonous and exhausting, not only for her, but for her friends. She knew that. She was constantly afraid of it.

"I'm taking her home," she heard Beth say. "Come on, sweetie. You don't have to play. I'll make you some chicken and dumplings while you do your homework tonight. Take your mind off it."

She really, really, didn't deserve friends like these.

Riley sniffed, put her cello back in its case, barely able to even look at it, and let Beth lead her out of the room and back to the car.

❖

That evening, after Riley's papers had been written and she had studied for her finals, she sat staring at her recital sheet music and said dejectedly, "Beth, I can't fail. I have to do the recital. I have to do it. For him. I feel sick, but I dunno. I don't want to disappoint him." As much as she did not want to play, it was as if the recital had come to represent the ultimate proof to her brother that she had successfully made it through the first year of her adult life. It was confirmation that she would be able to make it on her own. If he was somewhere in the ether watching over her, she wanted to show him that his faith in her had been validated. Now more than ever she wanted to make him proud, no matter the pain it cost her.

Beth put their leftover dinner in the refrigerator and sat next to Riley on the couch. Laying her head on her shoulder she said, "You don't have to do this for anyone but yourself. I won't think less of you if you don't, and Aidan won't either."

The panic flared again, unbidden, and Riley shot up off the couch. "I don't know what else to do! I don't want to do it, but I *need* to do it! I can't do it, but I *have* to do it!" She grabbed the already crumpled music from the coffee table and balled it up even smaller. This music is *shit*! *Everything is shit!*"

Beth surprised her by standing up from the coach, ripping the paper from her hands and saying, "Okay. Fuck it."

This was enough to snap Riley back to her senses. "What?"

"Fuck it. Fuck. It."

"You…you don't usually say—"

"Yeah, I don't usually do this either." Beth stormed over to the kitchen, lit the pilot light on the gas stove, and threw the sheet music onto it.

"What in the hell?"

Flames engulfed the paper, and a wave of heat rushed into Riley's shocked face.

"You're going to burn the apartment down!"

Beth turned toward her, the reflection from the fire in her eyes, and pointed at the impromptu blaze. "This is not what you need. Your professor chose that music for you a lifetime ago. That's what she wanted to hear. This recital isn't about school anymore. She excused you from having to do it already. Like you said, it's about you. It's about Aidan. It's about keeping that connection and starting to heal. Play what *you* want to play. Play what you would play for him. Tell him good-bye in the language you know best."

The word "good-bye" plunged into her heart like a sword, yet Riley felt the first spark of hope ignite in her chest since Aidan's death. Beth was right. This was far beyond a grade or a performance. This was the way she was going to keep their connection alive. This was how she was going to speak to him again, even if it was as a farewell.

Tears ran down her cheek as the final sparks and glowing embers faded. "This. This is why I love you."

The intensity left Beth's body and she sighed with relief. "You're going to be amazing no matter what you play, and I know he'll be so proud of you."

Riley gazed past Beth. "I know exactly what I'm going to play." Her voice caught as the repressed melodies once again played in her head. They were her all-time favorites. They were the songs that nearly brought Aidan to tears when he listened, imperfect as she played them. They were the songs her mother had played when she was a baby.

"He'll hear these and know—" She swallowed hard. "He'll know that I'm going to be okay."

Saying these words, she finally believed it. Aidan wouldn't want her missing out on life because he had been taken away from her. He loved life. He lived it to its fullest, and it was now her responsibility to make sure that all of his love and all of his sacrifices weren't in vain. She felt the beginnings of a new and reenergized spirit begin to surface. The pain would always be there, of course. It hurt so much she could barely cope, but now the light was reemerging. She was starting to hear the music again.

Aidan,

I don't know why I'm doing this. I know you're not on the other end of this email. I know you're in the ground at the VA cemetery in Austin. But I also know that you're not there. Something is there, but it isn't you. I know you. I see you. It doesn't make sense for you to be gone. You're still here...somehow. Maybe it's just my memories. Maybe it's just wishful thinking. Maybe the sorrow has driven me bat-shit crazy. I dunno. All I know is that I still have things to tell you, and the thought of you not being there to listen is unimaginable.

This wasn't supposed to happen. This doesn't happen to us. It can't. Not when we've lost so much already. The universe has got to be playing some sadistic joke. I keep thinking I'll wake up from another of my nightmares, but this one appears to be real. I'm stuck in an endless horror from which I'll never wake. What the hell is that all about? The universe has a sick goddamned sense of humor. There are so many things I want to tell you. Every day I think of something that I should ask. How am I supposed to deal with that? How am I supposed to continue on knowing that you're not going to be there for me?

I want you to know that, even if I never said it out loud, you are my hero. Always have been and always will be. You took care of me when Mom and Dad died. You protected me as best as you could from Aunt Joan and Uncle Ted. You gave me good advice, gave me a shoulder to cry on, and kicked me in the ass when I needed it. I want you to know that I will miss and love you until my last moment on this earth. I want you to know that, despite the pain I'm in, I'm going to continue with my music and I'm going to live the best life I can.

But mostly, I want you to know that, wherever you are, you don't have to worry about me. You were always so protective and my biggest supporter. Nothing in my life will ever be the same without you in it, but I know you wanted nothing but love and success for me. I have found a part of my soul in Beth that I didn't even know I was missing. Her family has even stepped in to be a family for me as well. So, Aidan, please don't worry. My broken heart is in good hands, and they will help me through this.

It's also amazing that my first year of college is done and I made it through. My end of year recital is this weekend. I thought you'd want to know that I made it this far. At first I wasn't going to do it because it hurts too badly to play. But I'm sure you can guess the two people who made me change my mind.

Aidan, I'll be playing Mom's songs. For you. Now they're our songs. Our family's. I only wish you could be here to hear them. I honestly don't even know how I'm going to get through it. I can't get five measures in to any of them without breaking down.

But anyway, I needed to let you know. I need you to know how I'm feeling and how I'm doing.

But most of all, I need my big brother.

CHAPTER NINETEEN

Riley gathered up her music and stood from the chair in the practice room.

"Ready?" Beth asked. She straightened Riley's suit jacket and lovingly cupped her cheek in her hand.

Riley simply nodded, sorrow and nerves fighting for supremacy in her chest.

"You're going to be wonderful, sweetie."

Riley nodded again, less sure.

Beth then took a step back, taking Riley's cello with her to the hallway. "There's someone else here who wants to wish you luck." She looked to her left and nodded.

Confused, Riley looked to the door to see who wanted to see her before the recital.

A handsome and extremely tall man with dark hair and sorrowful brown eyes stepped into the door frame, white hat under his arm. Tears sprang into Riley's eyes as she took in the full dress blue Marine uniform. She recognized this man from pictures Aidan had sent from his training and deployment. It was his best friend, Craig.

"Hello, Riley." He had a soothing voice and he held out his hand for her to shake.

Riley had never met or spoken with him, but she felt a connection with him already. She rushed into his arms as if she'd known him for years, and he held her tightly as she sobbed. With her head on his chest, she could hear his breath catching as well. She wasn't the only person who had loved and lost her brother.

When she had calmed down, she pulled away and said, "Sorry. I got tears on your uniform."

Craig, eyes misty, said, "Don't be." He took a steadying breath. "Riley, Aidan asked me to get in touch with you if anything ever happened to him. He didn't want it to be just by letter. He asked me to come in person. I made the same deal with him for my family. I just…I never thought I'd have to do it." His voice cracked.

Riley looked at the ground and tried not to lose her self-control again.

"He gave me your and Beth's contact info so…here I am…with Beth's help. I wanted to check with her first before just showing up." He turned and smiled at her thankfully. "Our unit just got home." His eyes looked mournful. "I know it's not the same as him being here, but I wanted to keep my promise to him. I'm here for you and I want you to know"—he wiped a tear from his eye—"I miss him too. We all do. You should know that Aidan was the greatest guy any of us have ever met. And he was so…*so* proud of you. Talked about you all the time. Told us about your music. He was like a proud brother and father all in one."

Riley smiled weakly. "Thanks, Craig. That really…" She wanted to tell him how much it meant, but the words wouldn't come out.

Craig was silent for a while, but finally said. "Beth told me about your recital today and how you're honoring Aidan with your performance. I thought this would be the perfect time to offer my support."

Riley bowed her head. It still didn't seem like a simple recital was nearly enough to honor her brother. Hardly anyone ever came to the year-end recitals anyway. It was usually just a few friends and the professor in a small rehearsal room like the one where she initially auditioned. What was so special about playing a few meaningful songs in contrast to the depth of her loss?

Beth cleared her throat and said, "I don't mean to rush you, but everyone's waiting, Riles."

Everyone who?

Riley was surprised when Craig offered his arm to her to escort her from the practice room to the rehearsal room where she was to play. She took it gratefully as it helped to steady her as she walked in weak and heartbroken silence. Beth quietly followed with Riley's now priceless cello. Aidan had bought it for her, and although it wasn't the nicest one around, she wouldn't trade it for the world now that he was gone.

They walked in silence down the stairs to the first floor of the music building and as they entered the room, Riley gasped as she saw every single chair filled and a line of six fully uniformed Marines standing against the wall, waiting to welcome her in.

She looked at them in bewilderment. She knew these faces. They were all in Aidan's unit. Rafael smiled at her sympathetically with pain in his own eyes.

Craig turned her to face him. "Riley, we all want you to know that, even though it's not the same, you will *never* be without brothers." He gestured to the Marines standing at attention along the wall and then took her hand in his. "We will always be here for you. He was our brother, and now we are yours. Forever."

Tears spilled down Riley's face once again. This time, however, she heard other sniffs from the audience and looked to see many wiping their own eyes. Beth, in particular, seemed to have lost her composure.

"Thank you." Riley hiccupped quietly in between great gasps of air. "Thank you." They were the only words she could think of that meant enough.

Beth, still sniffling herself, brought over a box of tissues for Riley to use and then said, "Ready?" in a wavering voice.

Riley nodded and sat on the lone chair facing the stepped seating in front of her. She was awestruck by the show of support in the room. There was Beth, now sitting between Koji and Tori on the front row. Koji's boyfriend sat next to him and on the other side of

Tori sat Professor Cryder, beaming with pride. Completing the first row were Mr. and Mrs. Earle, also wiping their eyes and smiling as if she were their own daughter. The rest of the chairs were filled her fellow music school students and symphony orchestra members.

Riley's heart was immeasurably sore and weary, yet she had never felt so much love in her life. Her soul was positively bursting with it. She realized for the first time that, although she had never had the family she had wanted growing up, a true family was one whom she chose and who chose her. Looking from the audience to the Marines standing against the wall, she saw the love and support of that new family. Aidan, a forever-missing piece of her heart, was gone, but she would never be alone again.

Trembling, she picked up her cello and placed it snuggly between her knees. She glanced back at her accompanist and nodded. The room silenced. She closed her eyes, took a deep breath, and readied her bow above the cello's taut strings.

The pianist started playing the first notes of Dvorak's fittingly titled "Songs My Mother Taught Me." When Riley pressed her bow down and felt the familiar vibrations of sound, she experienced a true sense of peace for the first time since that terrible day. She saw her mother, eyes closed and smiling, as she played the song on repeat while Riley and Aidan played with Legos on the living room carpet. She saw herself sitting in the Home's activity room struggling to move her bow in time with her fingers, Aidan teasing her playfully. She saw Aidan glowing with pride from the audience of her first youth symphony concert.

When the piece was finished, she moved on to her mother's favorite song, "Traumerei" by Robert Schumann. This was the one piece of music that Riley felt captured her desire for happiness and healing in the face of this tragedy. To her it conveyed a feeling of gentle hope, even in the midst of sometimes fiery doubt and fear.

Finally, to end the recital, she played a song that she had only recently discovered. It wasn't her mother's and it wasn't something that Aidan knew. It was a piece she had fallen in love with that she had wanted to share with her brother when he returned from overseas. It was the music she had chosen to thank him for his unwavering love and support. She would share it with him now, in front of his brothers, her colleagues, and her friends.

She looked around the room again, smiling gratefully to those who were there to share the moment with her. Beth and Tori were both weeping openly. Beth mouthed, "I love you."

Riley swallowed hard, but mouthed the words back, looked to the vast sky beyond the ceiling, and then closed her eyes once more.

The passionate notes of "Gabriel's Oboe" by Ennio Morricone flowed from her instrument. She swayed, lost in the insistent emotions of the melody. For just a little while, she was part of the music again. She and Aidan were together once more.

As the song neared its end, Riley felt as if she really was saying good-bye. She had fought the knowledge of her brother's death. She had succumbed to despondency even to the point of wanting to take her own life. And she had known pain beyond anything she had thought she could possibly endure. The pain was still there. It still stabbed. It still seared. But there was also love, a love that would always remain with her. A love that was now being offered and strengthened by so many others.

The finals notes of the piece faded into the air like mist, and she could hear his words once more.

I need you to be strong now, Riley.

She didn't hear the audience applauding her performance. She didn't see them wiping their eyes. But she did feel Beth's warm hand close around her own. She felt Tori take her cello from her, and she automatically rose from the chair and bowed to her friends.

When she straightened, she managed to choke out, "Words… will never be able to convey my appreciation. For all of you. For this. Thank you."

Loving faces radiated back at her.

Beth stepped in front of her, cheeks stained with a flow of tears, and said, "You are the most amazing woman in the world, Riley Gordon. I love you. I will always love you."

Riley smiled, wrapped her arms around the woman she knew she would love for the rest of her life, and buried her face in her neck. They stood in their embrace for a long while. The audience filed out quietly until Riley and Beth were left alone in the room. Beth finally pulled away enough to place the softest of kisses on Riley's lips. They were salty from the mixture of both their tears.

Everything had changed. Nothing in her life would ever be the same. She knew she would never be able to get over her loss, but at the same time she realized that the world would continue to spin on and on. But now, with her soul mate at her side and Aidan in her heart, she would hang on for dear life.

"Are you ready?"

Riley took a deep breath and nodded.

Hand in hand, they walked out together. With Beth leading the way, Riley left the darkness behind and reemerged into the light.

About the Author

M.L. Rice was born and raised in the plains of Texas. She graduated with a degree in radio/TV/film from the University of Texas at Austin, where she was a proud member of the Longhorn Marching and Basketball Bands. After college she moved to sunny Los Angeles, where she currently lives with her wife and three cats. She enjoys scuba diving, hiking, kayaking, swimming, spending too much time on video games, going to the theater, and playing in Disneyland. She volunteers for various nonprofit organizations, travels whenever she can, collects and plays multiple instruments including the trumpet, cello, and great highland bagpipes, and is also a member of the U.S. Coast Guard Auxiliary.

Soliloquy Titles From Bold Strokes Books

The Melody of Light by M.L. Rice. After surviving abuse and loss, will Riley Gordon be able to navigate her first year of college and accept true love and family? (78-1-62639-219-9)

Maxine Wore Black by Nora Olsen. Jayla will do anything for Maxine, the girl of her dreams, but after becoming ensnared in Maxine's dark secrets, she'll have to choose between love and her own life. (978-1-62639-208-3)

Bottled Up Secret by Brian McNamara. When Brendan Madden befriends his gorgeous, athletic classmate, Mark, it doesn't take long for Brendan to fall head over heels for him—but will Mark reciprocate the feelings? (978-1-62639-209-0)

Searching for Grace by Juliann Rich. First it's a rumor. Then it's a fact. And then it's on. (978-1-62639-196-3)

Dark Tide by Greg Herren. A summer working as a lifeguard at a hotel on the Gulf Coast seems like a dream job…until Ricky Hackworth realizes the town is shielding some very dark—and deadly—secrets. (978-1-62639-197-0)

Everything Changes by Samantha Hale. Raven Walker's world is turned upside down the moment Morgan O'Shea walks into her life. (978-1-62639-303-5)

Fifty Yards and Holding by David Matthew-Barnes. The discovery of a secret relationship between Riley Brewer, the star of the high school baseball team, and Victor Alvarez, the leader of a violent street gang, escalates into a preventable tragedy. (978-1-62639-081-2)

Tristant and Elijah by Jennifer Lavoie. After Elijah finds a scandalous letter belonging to Tristant's great-uncle, the boys set out to discover the secret Uncle Glenn kept hidden his entire life and end up discovering who they are in the process. (978-1-62639-075-1)

Caught in the Crossfire by Juliann Rich. Two boys at Bible camp; one forbidden love. (978-1-62639-070-6)

Frenemy of the People by Nora Olsen. Clarissa and Lexie have despised each other for as long as they can remember, but when they both find themselves helping an unlikely contender for homecoming queen, they are catapulted into an unexpected romance. (978-1-62639-063-8)

The Balance by Neal Wooten. Love and survival come together in the distant future as Piri and Niko face off against the worst factions of mankind's evolution. (978-1-62639-055-3)

The Unwanted by Jeffrey Ricker. Jamie Thomas is plunged into danger when he discovers his mother is an Amazon who needs his help to save the tribe from a vengeful god. (978-1-62639-048-5)

Because of Her by KE Payne. When Tabby Morton is forced to move to London, she's convinced her life will never be the same again. But the beautiful and intriguing Eden Palmer is about to show her that this time, change is most definitely for the better. (978-1-62639-049-2)

The Seventh Pleiade by Andrew J. Peters. When Atlantis is besieged by violent storms, tremors, and a barbarian army, it will be up to a young gay prince to find a way for the kingdom's survival. (978-1-60282-960-2)

Asher's Fault by Elizabeth Wheeler. Fourteen-year-old Asher Price sees the world in black and white, much like the photos he takes, but when his little brother drowns at the same moment Asher experiences his first same-sex kiss, he can no longer hide behind the lens of his camera and eventually discovers he isn't the only one with a secret. (978-1-60282-982-4)

Meeting Chance by Jennifer Lavoie. When man's best friend turns on Aaron Cassidy, the teen keeps his distance until fate puts Chance in his hands. (978-1-60282-952-7)

Lake Thirteen by Greg Herren. A visit to an old cemetery seems like fun to a group of five teenagers, who soon learn that sometimes it's best to leave old ghosts alone. (978-1-60282-894-0)

The Road to Her by KE Payne. Sparks fly when actress Holly Croft, star of UK soap *Portobello Road*, meets her new on-screen love interest, the enigmatic and sexy Elise Manford. (978-1-60282-887-2)

Swans and Clons by Nora Olsen. In a future world where there are no males, sixteen-year-old Rubric and her girlfriend Salmon Jo must fight to survive when everything they believed in turns out to be a lie. (978-1-60282-874-2)

Kings of Ruin by Sam Cameron. High school student Danny Kelly and loner Kevin Clark must team up to defeat a top-secret alien intelligence that likes to wreak havoc with fiery car, truck, and train accidents. (978-1-60282-864-3)

Wonderland by David-Matthew Barnes. After her mother's sudden death, Destiny Moore is sent to live with her two gay uncles on Avalon Cove, a mysterious island on which she uncovers a secret place called Wonderland, where love and magic prove to be real. (978-1-60282-788-2)

Another 365 Days by KE Payne. Clemmie Atkins is back, and her life is more complicated than ever! Still madly in love with her girlfriend, Clemmie suddenly finds her life turned upside down with distractions, confessions, and the return of a familiar face… (978-1-60282-775-2)

The Secret of Othello by Sam Cameron. Florida teen detectives Steven and Denny risk their lives to search for a sunken NASA satellite—but under the waves, no one can hear you scream… (978-1-60282-742-4)

Andy Squared by Jennifer Lavoie. Andrew never thought anyone could come between him and his twin sister, Andrea…until Ryder rode into town. (978-1-60282-743-1)

431 West Cen...
Whitewater, WI 53190

Sara by Greg Herren. A mysterious and beautiful new student at Southern Heights High School stirs things up when students start dying. (978-1-60282-674-8)

Boys of Summer, edited by Steve Berman. Stories of young love and adventure, when the sky's ceiling is a bright blue marvel, when another boy's laughter at the beach can distract from dull summer jobs. (978-1-60282-663-2)

Street Dreams by Tama Wise. Tyson Rua has more than his fair share of problems growing up in New Zealand—he's gay, he's falling in love, and he's run afoul of the local hip-hop crew leader just as he's trying to make it as a graffiti artist. (978-1-60282-650-2)

me@you.com by KE Payne. Is it possible to fall in love with someone you've never met? Imogen Summers thinks so because it's happened to her. (978-1-60282-592-5)

Swimming to Chicago by David-Matthew Barnes. As the lives of the adults around them unravel, high school students Alex and Robby form an unbreakable bond, vowing to do anything to stay together—even if it means leaving everything behind. (978-1-60282-572-7)

365 Days by KE Payne. Life sucks when you're seventeen years old and confused about your sexuality, and the girl of your dreams doesn't even know you exist. Then in walks sexy new emo girl, Hannah Harrison. Clemmie Atkins has exactly 365 days to discover herself, and she's going to have a blast doing it! (978-1-60282-540-6)

Timothy by Greg Herren. *Timothy* is a romantic suspense thriller from award-winning mystery writer Greg Herren set in the fabulous Hamptons. (978-1-60282-760-8)

Irvin L. Young Memorial Library
431 West Center Street
Whitewater, WI 53190